Two's Company

Sue Haasler was happily childless until she met and married her husband with whom she has a three-year-old daughter. She lives in London, and now writes full-time. *Two's Company* is her first novel and has been optioned for film by Warner Bros.

Two's Company

SUE HAASLER

ORION

First published in Great Britain in 2001 by Orion,
an imprint of the Orion Publishing Group Ltd.

Typeset by Deltatype Ltd, Birkenhead, Merseyside

Printed in Great Britain by
Clays Ltd, St Ives plc

The Orion Publishing Group Ltd
Orion House
5 Upper Saint Martin's Lane
London, WC2H 9EA

Acknowledgements

Love and thanks to: my family; Heiko for love and the laptop; Mika for being a little inspiration and for sleeping sometimes; Karen for pies, pints and putting up with my wittering; Emma the e-mail queen; Gisela and Keith generally; and, in order of appearance, Hilary Johnson, my agent Sarah Molloy and my editors Jane Wood and Rachel Leyshon for their support, enthusiasm and hand-holding skills.

For Heiko and Mika

Saturday afternoon in Selfridge's cosmetics hall: the smell of the face-paint, the roar of the crowd. Very heaven.

If shopping is the new religion, its cathedrals are those beautiful department stores, lush with everything from the most expensive designer items to egg whisks and reels of cotton. To me, shopping is department stores. And, it goes without saying, bookshops. I'm not really a fan of those huge shopping centre/mall things because I do take a perverse enjoyment in the experience of negotiating a busy street, dodging the umbrellas and pickpockets, and trying not to breathe near anyone selling hot dogs (apparently they all have tuberculosis).

Though I have to make something clear right now: this is not going to be one of those sex-and-shopping bonkbuster things. I wish it was, but although sex and shopping are probably my two most favourite things, I'm in the wrong income bracket for Gucci and Prada, and I'm more Dolcis than Dolce e Gabbana. I've never even been to Harrods, if you can believe that. This may seem strange for someone who has just been extolling the virtues of department stores. Surely many people would claim Harrods as the pinnacle of the genre?

The fact is, I'm a North London girl, by habitat if not by birth, and Knightsbridge is a bit off my beaten track. I would have made the effort, normally, but I've just got this grudge against Harrods, like my granny had a grudge against Julie Andrews in *The Sound of Music*. First, the tourists put me off, sitting smugly on the tube clutching their moss-green and gold Harrods carrier-bags, probably containing a small box of toffees or 'English' mustard, something cheap just so they can prove to the folks back home in Hoboken or Hartlepool that they've been there. Then I was deterred because they wouldn't let in the then-popular Australian soap star Jason Donovan wearing shorts. Well, what chance do my legs have of getting in, then?

Harrods aside, I do love shopping – finding a gorgeous pair of shoes or earrings, indeed clothes generally, smellies or even some decent chocolate when cash is short – but what I love most is coming home with a bag full of new, clean-smelling paperbacks.

I've got this sort of fetish thing about books. I don't really like hardbacks. They're like certain types of men: inflexible, unwieldy and absolutely no use in bed. I would go for paperbacks every time: to continue the man analogy, they're soft, yielding and, above all, portable. However, I'm a fanatic about keeping them clean and pristine (books, not men). When I'm in a bookshop, it's normal for me to look at every single copy of my chosen title to find one free of creases, smudgy marks and what-have-you: basically, one that doesn't look like someone has touched it. And that's how they stay. I know people who break the spines of books so they can hold them in one hand while doing something else with the other (no, not that – at least, I hadn't thought of that until I wrote that last sentence, I actually had in mind things like eating or holding a ciggie). I know people, and it pains me to have to say it, who turn back the edges of the page like little ears to mark their place. I even knew someone once who, although perfectly lovely generally, had a disturbing tendency to write notes in the margins of her books; in pencil, admittedly, but I shudder even to contemplate it. None of my friends dares borrow any of my books: they can't trust themselves to return them in a satisfactory state and they don't want to ruin a good friendship. When I was a kid, and most of the others my age wanted to be astronauts or pop stars, I wanted to be a librarian, and catalogued all my books, stamping them with a classification number using my John Bull Printing Outfit. But I didn't lend any of them: they might have come back blemished, and I just couldn't take the risk.

So ... shopping. One particular early October Saturday I was in one of those wonderful department stores that smells of perfume and leather as soon as you walk in at the door. Part of the loveliness of these retail nirvanas (is there a plural of 'nirvana'?) is that they have all the facilities you could wish for: you can spend your heart out, get a bracing cup of mid-shopping coffee, and then 'freshen up' afterwards. You can even have a relaxing pedicure 'while you wait', as if there was any other way to have a pedicure. My friend Laura tried that once and, according to her, the pedicurist spent the whole time having an argument with one of the other staff, and it was alarmingly obvious that her mind wasn't on the job, which isn't what you want from a person who's wielding an emery board at your foot. Laura got out as fast as possible, and it took about ten minutes to unglue her ruby red toenails from her sock.

Anyway, I was *en route* to the ladies', deep in thought about a small black satin handbag I'd seen on the way in – could I possibly justify the purchase of yet another bag? – so I almost collided with a large, denim-covered posterior. Actually, at second and third glance, the posterior proved to be not so much large as ... well, pert. But there was a horrible smell around it that put me off a bit. And then there were the piercing shrieks.

The owner of the posterior straightened up, swung round towards me, and the smell and the screeching got louder. I involuntarily stepped back a couple of paces, clasping a hand to my nose, before my odour- and sound-assailed brain could register that standing in front of me was a jaw-droppingly good-looking bloke clutching a bright red, screaming child. Which had obviously filled its nappy.

'Oh, God, Lily, why now, eh? Couldn't you have waited for half an hour? Come on, shush,' and he continued making soothing sounds. Or I think he did – he continued making soothing faces anyway – all further sounds being blocked out by the child's 100-decibel roar. Cute Bloke then noticed I was there. 'She needs changing,' he explained. No shit. Or rather – shit. 'But the problem is, the baby-changing room is in the women's toilets. I tried going in, but I nearly gave an old lady heart-failure – I should imagine she's on her way to the police even now.' He paused for long enough to give me an impossibly gorgeous smile, considering he was trying to hold a screaming miniature kick-boxer, and said, 'I know it's cheeky of me to ask, but it is an emergency. I don't suppose you could . . . ?'

Could what? Oh, no, mate. Oh, no no no. I don't do babies, and I definitely don't do pooey babies. 'Maybe you could come in there with me while I change her?' he suggested. 'Then if anyone comes in, they'll just assume we're together and they won't be so alarmed.' I calmed down: this was a plan I could accommodate.

'Okay,' I said, with what I hoped was a can-do yet seductive smile. 'Lead the way.'

'I think you should lead the way,' he said. 'Just in case there are any more old ladies in there.' I pushed open the door and went in, holding it back for him, as his arms were full of writhing child and assorted nappy-changing articles.

The baby-changing cubicle was directly opposite the door, and consisted of a little pull-down tray thing on which to place the baby. Mercifully, the child stopped her awful shrieking as soon as she realised relief was at hand. I stationed myself by the door, as far away from the smell as I could get without actually throwing myself out of the window, and found the perfect angle to observe the nappy-changer without having to look at the nappy being changed. He was tall, well over six feet, with a body that was slim but

4

hinted at a nice bit of muscular definition, and he had really strokable-looking hair, cut short but not severely, and curling slightly on what seemed to be a very kissable neck. Very nice indeed.

The door swung open, disturbing my reverie and forcing me to sidestep quickly so that I was practically behind it. A sturdy, middle-aged town-and-country-looking woman appeared, lugging her own bodyweight in John Lewis carrier-bags.

'Hello!' she said, staring hard at the alien male presence in this all-female sanctum. 'Either I'm in the wrong place,' she said, 'or you are. And I'm not, because I'm as regular as clockwork in this establishment. I shall call the manager.' As he opened his mouth to protest, she dropped her carrier-bags and whipped a mobile phone out of a shoplifter-size pocket.

I stepped forward. 'He's with me,' I said breezily. 'He's changing the baby.'

'Goodness!' she said, pressing the cancel button on her phone. 'Whatever next? Well, I must say you've got him well trained, dear.' She picked up all her bags and proceeded with some difficulty into a cubicle. He resumed his disgusting task, which seemed to be in the final stages: what builders call 'making good', and I resumed my position by the door and watched him working. He did it so quickly and efficiently that there was no doubt it was a job he was used to. He *is* well trained, I thought, and wondered who had trained him. She was a lucky woman, whoever she was.

'There,' he was saying. 'That's you sorted out.' He turned towards me, the child snuggled in his arms. She looked at me rather smugly, as she had every right to do from such a vantage-point. 'Say thank you to the nice lady,' he suggested to her. She responded by burying her face in his chest. I was beginning to seriously envy this girl. He smiled gorgeously at me again, and I wondered whether being a 'nice lady' was a good thing or not. 'Thank you ever so much, you're a lifesaver. I hate it when they just assume everyone who might need to change a baby is a woman, don't you?'

'Oh, yes, absolutely. Hate it. Very discriminatory,' I managed.

'It is, isn't it? I should write them a letter. I bet I won't, though. Anyway, thanks again.' He opened the door to leave, and I just stood there as it swung shut behind him.

2

'But you hate babies! I bet you nearly died! I wish I'd seen that!'

My best friend Laura. She was shrieking with laughter at my description of the nappy-changing episode, which of course I'd embellished slightly for comic effect, implying heavily that my role had been a more active one.

'And then what happened?' she demanded, after she'd finished wiping her eyes.

'Nothing,' I said.

'Nothing? You let him escape?'

'Well, I had to go to the loo then, didn't I?, and when I came out he'd gone. I had a quick look round the toy department, and Children's Clothes, but he'd vanished.'

'That's a shame. He sounded most promising,' Laura said, pouring more wine, 'But it's just as well. For one thing, he's most probably married or, at least, in a relationship if he's got a kid. And for another thing, he's most likely a prat, if your judgement is as spot-on as usual.'

Now that was a bit harsh. 'Meaning?'

'Well, just look at Nic the Pric,' she said.

Ah. The ex-boyfriend. As in my ex-boyfriend.

'That was just an aberration.'

'It's him who's the aberration!' she shrieked. 'Do you want any afters?' Stupid question. We flagged down a passing waiter and ordered something in which ice-cream and chocolate – the two major food groups – were the predominant features.

There was a bit of a lull in the conversation while we ate. This gave me a few minutes to ponder Nic.

It had started so well. I was recovering from a seriously broken heart, my erstwhile true love having decided to go and work on a trout farm in Scotland ('Amongst his own kind,' Laura had said). After a suitable period of mourning I took the advice of agony aunts the world over and enrolled in a couple of evening classes. Laura, cunningly reasoning that I should go for something that would be most likely to attract men, suggested car maintenance, but I was paranoid that I'd be publicly humiliated when they found out I can't drive. Nor can I be doing with anything involving power tools (so noisy! so likely to drill, saw or sand their way through a limb or put an eye out!), which meant woodworking and so on wasn't an option either. I didn't fancy languages, because all my French teachers at school were fascists. So I decided on film studies. My reasoning was that women go and see films and either enjoy them or don't, but men, in my experience, go to see films so they can show off to other people about how many obscure arty films they've seen and how knowledgeable they are about Cinema with a capital C. Therefore a film studies course must be more a bloke thing than a girl thing.

While I was pondering the adult education prospectus, I also decided to enrol on a sort of hippy drippy learning-to-love-yourself type course, as my self-esteem was a bit low, and it dovetailed nicely with the film studies, timetable-wise.

As it turned out, the film studies course was quite useless in terms of men. There were only six of us on it, and while it's true I was the only female, the other five were not exactly living advertisements for testosterone. Plus the course was so absolutely boring and banal that I almost cried with relief when the first session was over. We had spent an hour and a half pondering the significance of Rock Hudson, without even getting to the bit about him being gay, and the tutor didn't seem at all amused when I mentioned Rock's splendid work on *Macmillan and Wife*. I never went back for the second session, and I suspect I wouldn't have been welcome anyway. Leave the boys to ponder German expressionism on their own.

Luckily (I thought at the time), the learning-to-love-your-self yielded much better results, in that I learned, fairly quickly, to love the tutor. He introduced himself at the first session as 'Nic – N-I-C.' I must've misheard, because for several weeks I laboured under the impression that his name was Nick Aniseed. He was an irresistible combination of intense and dog-eared: big on eye-contact, with huge grey eyes that went right through you and out the other side, but dressed in that kind of thrown-together way that strongly suggests he's single. It also tells you, with almost 100 per cent accuracy, that he's heterosexual. None of the gay men I know would be seen outside the house in an unironed shirt.

If I'm being honest, Nic's course was the biggest pile of hippy nonsense this side of the Atlantic, which Laura had no hesitation in pointing out when I recounted the first session, in which we had to get into pairs and introduce our 'partner' to the rest of the group using only colour adjectives of their choice. As in: 'This is Jane, and she describes herself as basically a mauve person with the occasional puce moment.' I told Jane that I'd like to be described as 'burnt umber,' which I remembered from my childhood paintboxes, but we couldn't decide what colour that was, and Jane accused me of having a negative attitude (she was having a puce moment, no doubt), so I settled on green.

'Ah, sap!' Nic had exclaimed. 'Living things, growth, life. That's a very positive colour to choose. Excellent.' I felt quite pleased, then very sad for feeling pleased.

The second session sounded better.

'Today's session will focus on touch,' Nic told us. Cool. We were asked to get into pairs (again, learning to love yourself was clearly not a solo activity), and one of the pair was going to be blindfolded, while the other person led them around the building finding interesting things for them to touch. There were a couple of blokes on the course I wouldn't have minded a bit of blindfolded touching with, but after Nic had finished his introduction there was a total scrum for them. As a result, I found myself paired with a man who was quite possibly a serial killer in his day job. I tried to remember what colour he'd described himself as the previous week, and had a nasty feeling it was black. Half an hour of being led sightless around a deserted, echoing university building on a winter's night, having my hand grabbed and dragged across Artex every few minutes, and I thought my number was up. I was very relieved when Mr Black's watch beeped, indicating that it was time to return to the classroom.

It was at the third session, which I almost missed because it was raining and I'd had a pig of a day at work, when things got really interesting. Nic had brought in a bag of apples, and the idea was for each person to eat their apple very slowly, 'savouring' all the sensations and experiences that you normally don't notice because you're also watching *East-Enders* or cutting your toenails or whatever. Unfortunately, they were rather nasty little sour apples, so I didn't enjoy mine at all. I had to pretend it was a Terry's Chocolate Orange just to get through it. However, I couldn't help noticing when Nic bit into his apple that he had the most beautiful teeth. I've always been a sucker for teeth, if you see what I mean.

During the mid-session break we went to the bar for a pint and a bag of dry-roasted peanuts to take away the taste of the apples. Nic spent the entire half-hour talking to one of the other students, a female who was all long-hair-and-legs, and I found myself feeling a bit jealous. My emotions so often signal themselves in negative ways, I find.

Anyway, the second half of the session involved, for reasons I no longer remember, getting into pairs yet again and spending ten minutes staring deeply into the eyes of the other person without speaking. By careful manoeuvring I managed to avoid being paired with the serial killer again, and as we were an odd number that day I found myself with Nic.

Ten minutes of staring into those eyes and I was gone.

'What are you thinking about? You've got ice-cream running down your chin,' said Laura, licking the last traces off the back of her spoon.

'I was thinking about when I first met Nic,' I said.

She groaned. 'Oh please, let's not go through that saga again. You're better off without him, you know you are.'

'I know,' I admitted, 'but I can't help feeling sad about it sometimes. It was so nice to begin with. And he is bloody gorgeous, visually speaking.'

'Anna! The man is a prick! He's Nic the Pric!'

'He's not that bad . . .'

'Where do you want me to start? He's miserable and moody—'

'Sensitive,' I countered.

She snorted unattractively. 'He's moody, is what he is. He's a domestic disaster – did he ever do his own washing once while you were together?' I shook my head. 'Plus, he's off his face half the time, and off the planet the other half.'

'I get the picture,' I said. 'I know you've never had much of an opinion of him.' In fact, I had occasionally wondered whether Laura was jealous in some way of Nic. 'But you don't know him like I do. He can be really lovely.'

'You mean the singing in bed?'

'Well, not just that.' This sounds a bit mad, but Nic had a beautiful voice and would sometimes sing old Pink Floyd and Bob Dylan songs to me in this husky half-whisper when we were in bed; it was dead sexy.

'So how come you finished with him if he has all these star qualities?'

'I don't know,' I said. 'He's just so high-maintenance. It's like he's not really equipped for modern life, and I had to take all the responsibility for everything. It was more like being a parent than a partner.'

'That's men in general, though, isn't it?' Laura commented, signalling to the waiter that she was ready for coffee.

'Nice arse,' I muttered, as the waiter departed in the direction of his milk-frothing machine.

Laura gave me a look. 'Did you see that interview with Germaine Greer on TV the other night?' she asked me. I hadn't. 'She was talking about her new book. And she said that the best thing about being the age she is now—'

'How old is she?'

'Oh, sixtyish, I think, I don't know – but the best thing about being whatever age she is is that she can see an attractive young man, and admire his beauty, but she doesn't have to have him.'

'Laura! What are you saying? Are you saying I pop my cork for every man I see?'

'No, I'm just telling you what Germaine said. She can appreciate men as *objets d'art*, without the lust factor.'

'How depressing. Still, I expect she has hobbies.'

'Either that or she's married. I don't lust after other men either since I married Dan.'

'Oh, please, don't start the smug-married routine. Anyway, I'm happy as I am, thank you. I think thirty is a bit young to give up on the lusting, but from now on I'm going to do it from afar. I've had it with all that relationship stuff, what with Trout Man and then Nic. I plan to enjoy my freedom for the foreseeable.' I ignored Laura's 'Yeah, right' look. That's the problem with married people: they think the rest of the world can't be happy unless they're in a relationship too. Either that or they want everyone else to suffer like they're suffering.

The waiter reappeared with the coffee. What would Germaine Greer have made of him, I wondered. A bit skinny, maybe. A bit too full of himself. Those silly little shaved lines across his eyebrow. Nah.

'Anyway,' Laura said, stirring her espresso, 'before I forget, it's Dan's work's Christmas party next Friday.'

'In October?'

'That's what I thought, but apparently they all sat down with their diaries, like they do, and it's the last weekend before New Year that they'll all be in London. You know what they're like. So, anyway, what about coming? It's usually a good do.'

Dan works in the social services department of the local council, in a large, open-plan office with a floating population of about fifteen other social workers who, apart from Dan and a woman called Sheila, the other token 'married', all seem to live lives of various degrees of hecticness (hectitude? hecticity?). Their parties usually end up with them all roaring drunk, and engaging in furtive and/or embarrassing incidents, which, by some secret consensus, are not spoken of in the harsh fluorescent light of the office the following Monday but make great gossip at the pub later.

'I suppose I could always set the video for *Coronation Street* . . .' I conceded.

3

When I got home, my answering-machine was flashing.

'Anna, it's me. Are you there? Pick up . . . You're not there? You must be! Go on, pick up. Oh, fuck it, then, never mind. It's me, Nic. Ring me.' Of course it's him Nic, he can't believe I might actually leave the house for any reason, let alone have a social life. He probably pictures me lurking by the answering-machine, deliberately not picking up the phone because it's him. Which, of course, I would never do.

Since Nic and I split up, he occasionally gets a bit whingey and needy and gives me a call. I realise now that this is no different from when we were together.

Shortly after we became a couple, I stopped attending his course, partly because I didn't need to learn to love myself any more (you automatically love yourself when you fall in love and it's reciprocated, don't you?) and partly because the course was total bollocks.

I didn't know whether I was relieved or not to find out that Nic didn't normally teach that course: the usual tutor had gone away to India to 'find himself' (or more likely to 'find' cheaper and/or better drugs), without giving enough notice for the college to cancel the course. In desperation, and facing the sack, he'd asked his friend Nic, who did some teaching at the same college, to take over for a term. After a spell of voluntary work in the Himalayas, Nic had rather fancied himself in this role, so he threw himself into his new job, using the other guy's teaching plan and a couple of those dreadful American self-help guides to base his lessons on.

Unfortunately it was a while before he divulged this piece of information, during which time he was happy to leave me under the impression that he was some kind of psychologist or counsellor or therapist; someone who was really in touch with his feelings. He managed this by using a lot of hippy phrases and was stoned out of his tree for much of the time.

When he was feeling 'centred' (as he described it, though centred in relation to what I have no idea), he gave every appearance of being the somewhat dishevelled sex god for whom I had mistaken him on that long-ago apple-eating day. He could be charming, kind, funny and incredibly sexy, and he was also a talented musician: if I hadn't already fallen for him, hearing him play the cello would have clinched the deal.

But when he was in that mood men get instead of being pre-menstrual, he just hung about all the time, metaphorically and sometimes literally tugging at my sleeve for attention. At first I thought this was quite endearing, but after a few months and several late night pasta-and-plonk girlie chats with Laura, I reached the conclusion that Nic was an emotion drain, and I didn't have the energy to keep up with his dramas as well as my own. So I dumped him, which I think is the first time I've ever been a dump*er* rather than a dump*ee*. I must say that having now experienced life on both sides of heartbreak fence, I did feel a tad more sympathy for Trout Man. Only a tad, mind. I could still throttle him with barely a qualm if he walked in here today.

After breaking up with Nic, it was the wheedling that got me down. I've never met anyone who could wheedle quite as comprehensively, and the fact that he often did it with a great measure of charm only made it worse.

All this had happened several months ago, and Nic had seemed to be over it, in fact had appeared to be moving on with his life rather well in that he had been seen stepping out with another woman – no prizes for guessing, she was another learn-to-love-yourself student. Now, I was surprised to hear from him, but not sufficiently intrigued to be bothered to ring him back. I watched *EastEnders*, which I'd taped, then went to bed.

4

I didn't ring him the next morning either. I slept in a bit, and woke up groggy after drinking too much wine with Laura, so it was all I could do to get to work. I did think of hanging a sicky, but with Christmas coming I'd be needing a couple of sick days to get my shopping done.

Laura and I work for an employment agency, recruiting and placing relief nurses and care staff. Our clients are hospitals, nursing-homes, day-centres and so on. They call us requesting someone to do a piece of work, and we ring up anyone on our books who matches their requirements and try to persuade them to supply it. When that fails, which it usually does, we ring up anyone on our books who doesn't meet the requirements but who is desperate for the work and will go anywhere and do anything. Then we ring the client back and assure them we've found exactly the right person for the job.

It can be quite stressful, when a client keeps ringing every ten minutes to check if you've found anyone. It's normally the matrons, or whatever they call themselves, of care homes – I think they're terrified that they might have to wipe a geriatric bottom themselves if we can't find someone else who will. Of course, we don't use the term 'geriatric' in our office. They're 'elders'. As in elderflower. We do a lot of work for social services departments, hence the need to be on top of the politically correct terminology – and, in fact, that's how Laura met Dan.

He'd phoned up asking us to find a home carer for a 'frail elder' with a sexual fetish for bicycle wheels (trust me, you really don't want to know); he stressed to Laura that she should make sure that the carer, whether male or female, turned up by any mode of transport other than a bike.

You can understand why Laura remembered Dan next time he called, and fairly soon they were getting all flirty with each other on the phone, until they finally met face-to-face at a seminar on New Horizons in Continence Management and romance blossomed.

When I got in that morning, Laura wasn't at her desk, which was rare as Dan normally dropped her off on his way to work and she was usually in before me. I asked Po-faced Vo, the receptionist and general dogsbody (and I'm not being metaphorical there), if Laura had called in sick. Po-faced Vo didn't have a desk, but rather a little conning-tower arrangement in the outer office from which only her head and shoulders were visible to visitors. It was hard to know whether that was more frightening than being able to see her whole body.

'There's a note in the diary to say she'll be in late,' she said, smacking her lips together to spread out the blob of Chapstick she'd just applied to them.

'That's funny. She didn't mention anything to me,' I said.

'Well, who are you? Her mother?' This was Po-faced Vo's idea of humour, and her doughy cheeks scrunched into her version of a smile.

'That's hilarious, Veronica,' I said, leaving her prodding at her switchboard as if it was a dead and/or slightly smelly animal.

By the time I'd hung up my coat and brolly, made some coffee, switched on the computer and changed the screensaver to a pattern that didn't hurt my dehydrated eyeballs so much, been out to Reception again to have a furtive glance at the staff holiday wall-planner (Veronica's idea) to see when would be a good time to plan my Christmas shopping sick days, and finally sat down at my desk, Laura was coming through the front door.

'Your mother's in there,' I heard Po-faced Vo saying, reluctant to let such an entertaining joke go. As a result, the look on Laura's face when she came into the office was a beautiful mixture of horror, bewilderment and fake cheeriness.

'Anna! What's the Po on about? Is my mother here? Where is she?'

'Calm down,' I soothed. 'It's Po's idea of a joke. She means me because I wondered why you were late.'

'Oh, thank God for that. One of the good things about my parents living in Canada is that they don't tend to make unexpected visits, but you never know with my mother.'

'So where've you been?' I asked.

She looked a bit shifty. 'Oh, didn't I tell you? Smear test, you know, just the usual. Anyway, I'd best get on, loads to do.'

This wasn't like Laura. Normally we find as many excuses as we can not to do any work before eleven (coffee break), though of course we have to look like we're working in case Po-faced Vo or the Saintly Clare, our boss, should happen to look in. However, Laura is an Aquarius, and as I had learned from Nic (Aries, but that's another story), one thing you mustn't do with Aquarians is nag at them if they've gone all introspective – it just makes them ten times worse – I concentrated on sorting through the database so that the computer mailing list didn't send Christmas cards to dead clients again this year.

At midday, the Saintly Clare, who had been out schmoozing potential clients all morning dashed in with a bag of goodies for all of us from Prêt à Manger. She isn't called Saintly for nothing.

'A desk lunch today, I'm afraid, girls,' she said. She reminds me of the oh-so-sensible headgirl character in those Enid Blyton boarding school stories who seem invariably to be called Hilary, full of jolly good common sense and awfully decent; frightfully good at lacrosse, too – whatever that is. 'We're going to be a bit busy this afternoon,' she continued. 'An Inland Revenue chap is coming over on Monday to go over the books.'

'Inland' and 'Revenue' are words to strike horror into the heart of most tax-paying citizens. Laura asked, 'Should we be nervous?'

'Goodness, no!' laughed Clare, flicking a crumb from her sensible Shetland wool cardigan. 'You know me, girls, I'm an absolute stickler for my financial records.' I have to admit that: She is a stickler for her financial records. It's me who gets stickled about it, generally. 'No, it's just routine, apparently. They pick out companies at random and pounce, just to keep us on our toes. But it means that I'm going to be closeted in my office sorting things out for the wretched man, making sure I've got all my P46s and P38-brackets-Ss and what-have-you. My diary's full for the rest of the week, so this is absolutely the last day I can do it. I'm going to have to leave you two to cope with everything else on your own. And, Veronica, I don't want to take any calls – unless it's Tubby, of course.'

'I thought Tubby was in Australia?' Veronica said.

'He is! And that's why you have to put him through. We've spoken to each other every day since we were married, and I'm not making an exception for any tax inspector chappie.'

As it turned out, the afternoon was fairly quiet – obviously the majority of care workers were also saving their sick leave until nearer Christmas. We hardly had any calls, except inevitably, from Tubby, and, unusually, Nic, whom Po-faced Vo announced as 'Mick'. I thought it was the bloke from a stationery company we no longer used, who had been ringing up almost daily to try to persuade me that I needed some fax rolls.

'No, we do not need any fax rolls, or photocopier paper, A4 ring-binders, lever-arch files, envelopes large or small, paper clips, staples, personalised Christmas cards or glue guns. Or glue-gun refills. Ever. Thank you.'

'Anna? Are you still taking that evening primrose oil? It does help to even out those hormonal fluctuations, you know?'

I know quite a few people who tack that irritating 'you know?' on to the end of sentences, but no one does it more irritatingly than Nic.

'Nic?' I said, trying to ignore Laura, who was making gagging faces.

'Yes, who did you think it was – W.H. Smith? I tried to call you last night, but apparently you were out.' There was a strategic pause, designed to allow me time to reveal to him where I'd been, which I didn't. He persisted.

'You weren't in.' Another pause. He gave up. 'Anyway . . . I really need to talk to you. I've got, like, a major life-change thing going on, you know? And I really would like to talk it through with someone.'

'What about talking to your girlfriend about it, then?' I tried not to laugh, as Laura held up a Blu-Tack effigy, presumably of my ex, and impaled it on a paper clip.

'It's something I really can't tell Betty-Ann about.' *Betty-Ann*? What kind of a name is that?

Suddenly I had a horrible thought. 'Nic, you're not trying to tell me you've got some nasty disease or anything, are you?' Oh, my God! The phone call from the ex that everyone dreads! Laura looked suitably horrified.

Nic made a funny little snorting noise (another endearing trait) and said, 'Oh, please, Anna, chill out and try to stop thinking of yourself just for one moment. This is about me.'

'For a change.'

'Alright, then, Anna, if that's the attitude you're going to take,' his voice took on a slightly metallic note, 'I won't tell you. I'll deal with this alone.' He hung up.

And the awful thing was, now I was really curious to know what he'd been going to say.

5

By the time Friday night arrived, I was in the mood for a party. The week had been dull and routine, and now that the evenings were dark, returning to an empty house was depressing. Every other house I walked past looked lit-up and cosy; people were rushing home to find someone waiting for them, maybe with a meal ready, or at least a cup of tea and a digestive. Most of the time I found living on my own infinitely preferable to living with Nic, or even, going further back, with Trout Man, who at least knew his way around a kitchen but never got the hang of turning off taps. I was suffering the early stages of that alarming syndrome, Single Before Christmas. No one to snog under the mistletoe, no one to argue with about whose parents we should visit this year, no one to help finish the After Eights. Okay, so there were compensations, but potentially a very miserable time of the year for the unloved.

I'm certainly not one of these sad women who doesn't feel complete without a man but at certain times (Christmas, Easter, bank holidays generally, birthdays, weddings, holidays, parties, Sundays, days when you've got some IKEA furniture to assemble, mealtimes, etc.) things seem more fun when there are two of you.

To amuse myself during the gap between *Neighbours* and *Coronation Street* I even tried to call Nic but only got his answering-machine and didn't leave a message because I didn't want him to think I was still in any way interested. Which I wasn't, of course, in the sense of being *interested* in him: I'd put that phase of my life behind me. I was just slightly curious and, if he *was* having some kind of problem, a bit sorry for him. However, as Nic tended to blow up the most trivial thing into a catastrophe, I wasn't seriously concerned.

I aimed to turn up about half an hour after the designated meeting time for the 'party', which was more of a semi-organised get-together in a pub. I hate to be early for these things, and particularly that night as I was going as a friend-of-Dan-and-Laura, although I know most of Dan's work-mates. It was freezing – almost Christmassy, fittingly enough – and the pavements were hideously slippery. Unfortunately so were the soles of my shoes, which were the sort that shops don't let you change if they break while you're walking in them because 'they're not meant for walking in'. They were the most gorgeous little ankle boots, made of the softest leather imaginable: they hugged my feet in a way that was almost indecent, so I just had to wear them, even though it meant I had to walk from the bus stop to the pub in a kind of exaggerated mince. I was watching where I placed my feet, avoiding drain covers, sudden gradients and the iciest patches, so I didn't notice that someone had come up beside me.

'Had a few already, Anna?'

I skidded and almost fell over, grabbing the arm of the person next to me. Unfortunately it was George-Preston-from-Accounts (Dan always describes his colleagues in terms that make them sound like *Under Milk Wood: The Next Generation*). Now, I have nothing against George Preston, but he is the type of person who monopolises you totally at a social gathering until you can hand him on to someone else. And as almost everyone else at this party knew George, it might be hard to pass him on at all. The fact that I was forced to hang on to his arm to avoid skidding down the street would only make things worse: George might interpret it as 'bonding'.

He held open the door for me to go into the pub. A wave of beery, smoky, noisy warmth engulfed me. From the icy October street I'd stepped into Christmas. The landlord had risen to the challenge of catering for a Christmas party in autumn. Tinsel and balloons hung from every nineteenth-century hunting scene (and there were a lot of nineteenth-century hunting scenes in that pub) and the bar was festooned with flashing green and pink fairy-lights. There was even a Christmas tree and the jukebox was playing 'Merry Xmas Everybody' by Slade. Hearing that song invariably makes me feel like a kid again: at that particular moment, combined with the smell of booze, it made me feel like an under-age drinker.

I could see some people I knew, in party hats and 'novelty' earrings; they seemed torn between saying hello to me and trying to pretend they hadn't seen me. This manifested itself in little bobbing movements: party hats appeared briefly then bobbed back down. I hoped this was because they were trying to avoid George Preston rather than me. Oblivious, George offered to buy me a drink, and as he made his way to the bar I looked around for an empty seat. I spotted Laura and Dan squashed in a corner with married Sheila, her husband and a couple of others I didn't know. They seemed deep in conversation and hadn't seen me.

I glanced around and was relieved to see one of Dan's friends, a woman called Sadie, with an empty seat next to her. I was guiltily glad that there was no room for George, who would have to sit next to someone else.

'Merry Christmas!' Sadie stood up to give me a hug. She towered over me, even though I'm not exactly what you'd call petite, and I noticed she was wearing stilettos that would give a shoe-fetishist palpitations. Then I was hugged by everyone else at the table, even though most of them didn't know who I was: it was the season of goodwill to all men, after all. A couple of empty glasses got knocked over in the process, which everybody seemed to find hilarious. 'Most of us have been here all afternoon,' Sadie explained. 'We're metaphorically almost on to the Queen's speech.'

'No chance of that,' someone else said. 'I'm a republican and, anyway, everybody always falls asleep for the Queen's speech, and I'm certainly not going to do that and waste valuable drinking time.' The rest of the table cheered.

Then George appeared with the drinks, and took quite a while to apologise to everyone else for not getting them one. 'Don't you worry, George,' Sadie assured him. 'There's a kitty but when it runs out we know who to come to for a top-up. Anyway, how are you, Anna?' she said, turning pointedly to me. George looked flustered, found himself a seat and hovered on the edge of someone else's conversation. Sadie and I chatted for a while about work. I kept waiting for Laura and Dan to realise I was there, but they seemed engrossed in their conversation with Sheila.

Sadie must have noticed me glance at them. 'Don't go over there,' she advised, rolling her heavily made-up eyes heaven-wards. 'That's the broody corner.'

'The what?'

'Sheila's showing off snaps of her brats – again – which, frankly, would be enough to make me doze off into the figgy pudding, were we fortunate enough to be served with one, which apparently we aren't, because somebody decided we'd be better off with finger food and bar nibbles, which frankly isn't my idea of a festive spread but what can you do? Dan and Laura, though, seem only too eager to hear the latest about little Ryan and little Giggsy, or whatever they're called.' She offered me a cigarette, which I declined, so she lit one herself and blew smoke out of the side of her mouth like a gangster. 'I feel so guilty smoking in front of most of these people,' she said. 'Workplaces are full of anti-smoking fascists these days. Those of us who still indulge are forced on to the back step of the building to conduct our vice away from the public gaze. My God, I'm twenty-six and I have to act like I'm thirteen, smoking behind the bike shed. The broody ones are the worst,' she added. 'Have you noticed that Dan hardly smokes at all now? It's bad for the sperm count, allegedly.'

'But Dan isn't broody,' I said confidently.

'Darling girl! Where have you been? I thought you and Laura were big pals.'

'We are.'

'It's practically all Dan goes on about these days. He's the United Nations Special Envoy for Folic Acid. "Sorry, Sadie, can't come to the pub because Laura's ovulating." That kind of thing. I'm more familiar with that woman's cycle than I am with my own! It's disgusting.' She shivered dramatically.

23

I felt like I'd stepped off a bus to find myself at the wrong stop. I couldn't believe what I'd just heard. Laura was my best and oldest friend, the nearest thing I had to a sister. We talked to each other practically every day about everything. We had no secrets . . . or I'd thought we hadn't.

I know it's not unheard-of for married people to want to have children, but whenever the subject had come up, Laura and I had always agreed that babies were something other people did. The already overpopulated planet could get on happily without further contributions from our corner of the gene pool, and we could do without the stress of stretch-marks, labour pains and screaming infants. We had entered our thirties confident that we were sufficiently evolved to resist any amount of ticking from so-called biological clocks. Now I found that Laura not only had a biological clock but apparently the alarm had started ringing.

Eventually Dan disentangled himself from the broody corner and went to the loo. On the way back he saw me, came over and gave me a hug. Dan is rather like a bear: tall, verging on chubby – you'd call him cuddly if you had to describe him in one word.

'You look edible,' he said. 'You're wearing your kinky sexy boots, too.' I was sitting with my legs crossed. He took hold of the foot on top and kissed it with a great show of slightly inebriated gallantry, then spoiled it by saying, 'I bet they were a bastard to walk in on that ice, eh?' Then he must have noticed I was looking a bit odd. 'Anything up, Anna?'

'Is it true that you and Laura are, I think the phrase is, trying for a baby?'

He looked a bit surprised. 'Oh. Yes. Hasn't Laura said anything?' I shook my head. 'Well, you can't blame her. You can be a bit sarcastic about certain things.'

'I thought Laura and I felt the same about having kids.'

'People can change their minds. Laura and I have got to that stage of our relationship where we want to have children. It's fairly common, you know.' Pompous sod.

'But why didn't she say anything to me?'

'Look, Anna, only the other day she was telling me about your little adventure helping a bloke change his baby's nappy in Debenham's.'

'It wasn't Debenham's, it was—'

'Wherever. She said you made it sound like the seventh circle of hell.'

'I did not!' I protested.

'She had been going to tell you then, but you were in full-on baby-hating mode, so she just kept stum. It's a sensitive subject.'

'But when did this change of heart occur? Was it your idea?'

'Look, you'd better talk to Laura about it, really, but don't let it spoil the party. You look like you lost a fiver and found a pound!'

Unfortunately, for me it *had* spoiled the party. In a way that Dan would probably never understand, the friendship between Laura and me might be about to change for ever. Since we had met in our first term at university, Laura and I had shared everything, and had everything in common, including a vestigial fondness for the work of Duran Duran. Even Laura's marriage hadn't changed our friendship, which had sustained me during my Trout-induced heartbreak, the fallow period afterwards and the tragi-comedy that was Nic. If Laura had a baby, her life would move into areas I didn't understand, where I had no experience – and, worse, no interest.

The fact was, I was jealous of a baby who hadn't even been conceived.

'Are you feeling okay, Anna?' George was at my elbow again. 'Only you look a bit grim. I thought you'd had a few before we arrived.'

'I had *not* had a few!' I said. 'And it's none of your business anyway!' George looked like a raccoon that had been kicked. 'I'm sorry, George. I'm just not in a party mood. I'd probably be better off at home.'

'I'll walk you,' George said, rising to the occasion. I was about to say no thanks, but then I remembered the ice, and my lethal yet oh so sexy boots, so I agreed that I could do with some help getting to the bus stop.

Which is how I ended the evening snogging with George-Preston-from-Accounts.

6

The next morning I woke up (alone! I'm not that stupid!) feeling about as bad as I could remember feeling since Nic and I broke up. I felt bad about Laura: bad that she couldn't trust me with something so important, and sad that our friendship had already altered and presumably now would alter beyond all recognition.

And I can't describe how low I felt about snogging George. Normally I would have phoned Laura straight away, and we'd have put the situation into perspective with a good shot of girlie sarcasm, but for the first time in my friendship with her, I didn't feel like ringing her.

I had a shower, trying to put George out of my mind as firmly as I'd put him out of the front door when he got a bit too frisky. At least my post-Nic virginity was still intact (I like to think that virginity is a renewable commodity). Nevertheless, I was overcome by waves of embarrassment, which had me making little eeking noises at unexpected moments. It's not that George is unattractive, it's just that he's *George*. How desperate did I seem?

I felt like a sad old cow.

7

On Monday morning I arrived at the office still feeling pathetic. As I arrived, Dan was just dropping off Laura. He pipped and waved as he pulled away, and Laura waited for me to catch up.

'Where did you disappear to on Friday night?' was her first and inevitable question. 'I didn't speak to you at all. One minute you were talking to Dan, and the next you weren't there.'

'Oh, I was a bit queasy. I just felt like going home,' I said, making a big deal of rummaging in my bag for the front-door key.

'Oh, here, I've got mine,' she said, and unlocked the door. She glanced sideways at me. 'Sadie said you left with George-Preston-from-Accounts.'

'He just walked me home, that's all,' I said, striding ahead of her up the stairs so I could keep my shamed face hidden.

'Oh, and the rest! Come on! Dish – what's he like?'

'What's who like?' asked Po-faced Vo, who was at her sentry position.

'Anna pulled on Friday at Dan's office party,' Laura said. Veronica gave a look that indicated she intended to rise above such base topics of conversation. More likely she had nothing to contribute: we were convinced she was a virgin by vocation as much as from lack of personal charm.

'I did not pull, as you so nicely express it,' I insisted. 'Nothing happened. End of story.'

'Don't worry, Anna,' Laura said sweetly. 'Dan will be getting all the dirt from Gorgeous George even as we speak. I'll know all about it by tonight.'

'There's nothing to know!' I protested.

Luckily, Clare appeared in the doorway of her office, which was directly behind Veronica's sentry booth. 'Can I have a word, Laura? And, Anna, can you look after Mr Taylor, please?'

She disappeared again, followed by Laura, who muttered to me, 'I'll talk to you later, young woman.'

'Who's Mr Taylor?' I asked Veronica, but the phone rang before she could reply.

She held her finger in the air like a schoolteacher demanding silence, and clicked at her switchboard. 'Caring Concern, Veronica speaking, how may I help you? . . . O-*kay*, I'll just put you through to Anna.' She prodded the switchboard again. 'It's Mrs Gurton from the Dwindlings. Do you want to take it in your office? I'll put it through to Laura's desk – Clare put Mr Taylor at yours.'

'Who *is* Mr Taylor?'

'The chap from the Inland Revenue, you know, the tax inspector.'

I went through to the office, somewhat relieved: the presence of Her Majesty's Inspector of Taxes would stop Laura from going on at me all day about George Preston.

The man sitting at my desk looked up and smiled in a friendly-but-preoccupied way. I stopped abruptly. It was the man from John Lewis's: the one with the baby. And the bum. And the smile. He was smiling it now: the very same one.

'I'm sorry, am I sitting at your desk?' he said. He hadn't recognised me. 'Clare said there was more space in here, I think she's got somebody coming for an interview in her room or something. I can move if you like,' and he started to gather up piles of paperwork.

'No, no,' I said. 'Please don't move everything. It's fine, really.'

The tax inspector? Tax inspectors don't look like that. Surely tax inspectors are little grey dandruffy people. The man who was currently sitting at my desk looked like a casting director's idea of a surgeon, or a pilot. Or an angel.

I sat down at Laura's desk and took the call. It was fairly straightforward, thank goodness: the Dwindlings was a relatively pleasant residential home for elders and we never had any trouble finding people prepared to work there. I rang Mrs Gurton back to confirm everything, then put the phone down.

Mr Taylor from the Inland Revenue was looking at me. 'I'm sorry,' he said again. 'I just realised that we've met before. You helped me change Lily's nappy in Selfridge's.'

'It wasn't Selfridge's, it was—' I started to say, then felt like a total idiot.

He smiled. 'I'm Michael Taylor, by the way.' He stood up to shake my hand. His hand was cool, and he smiled that enchanting smile again. He had the bluest eyes. I'm in love, I thought.

'I'm Anna Anderson,' I said.

'That's a nice name. It sounds Scandinavian.'

'Nothing so glamorous,' I said. 'I just get people making jokes about me having the same initials as Alcoholics Anonymous.'

'Or the Automobile Association?'

'Exactly.'

The phone rang again, and Michael Taylor sat down and carried on with his work while I took the call. While I was talking Laura came in. Clare must have warned her that the tax inspector was in our office, because she was clearly expecting someone to be there (thank God, otherwise she would probably have entered in full flow about Friday night and George Preston). Equally clearly, she'd had the same preconceived idea about tax inspectors as I had, and Clare hadn't put her straight about that. Which wasn't surprising, as Clare only has eyes for Tubby (there are many reasons why she is the Saintly Clare – although she did once confess to a

29

weakness for Dickie Davies in his 'World of Sport' days). The tax inspector introduced himself to Laura, and I felt a little jealous twinge as he held out his hand to shake hers. There I go again with that old possessiveness thing! She made a bit of small talk with him, then busied herself rummaging in the filing cabinet.

Clare had asked Laura to visit some clients who hadn't used Caring Concern recently, just to keep up our profile and make sure no other agency was undercutting us, so she was out for the rest of the morning. Clare was interviewing in her office. Michael Taylor carried on working, pausing only to accept a cup of coffee, or to ask me a couple of questions about the tax records. Clare keeps me more or less up to date with the payroll, 'in case I'm ever incapacitated', so I didn't have to disturb her to answer him. All morning I stole little glances at him. He had a kind of grace that you don't expect to see in a tax inspector; totally comfortable in his own body. He made shuffling through a pile of P11s look like an art form.

I wondered if I dared ask him out for lunch. It would be quite natural, after all, to offer to pop out for a sandwich with him; he wouldn't see it necessarily as coming on to him, would he? Though if he'd been ancient and dandruffy, or female and in any way like Po-faced Vo, I'd have snuck out on my own. I spent most of the morning trying to gather up courage to ask him. It would have been just too upsetting if he'd said no, but such a waste of an opportunity if he might have said yes and I didn't ask him.

Then at one o'clock he looked up from his work and said, 'Do you know anywhere nearby where can I get some lunch around here?'

'Well, there's a Sainsbury's fairly near if you want sandwiches. Or there's a nice pub down the road,' I said, trying to project a charm wave that would sweep him straight out of the office and on to one of the cosy sofas in the Flag. It worked.

'What about you?' he asked. 'Have you got time for a break?' I said I had. 'Maybe we could try that pub, then,' he said, which sounded like the best plan I'd ever heard, and all the better coming from him rather than me.

Veronica gawped at us as we left, but she was occupied with the latest Maeve Binchy and a low-fat yoghurt, so I didn't feel bad about not asking her to join us.

8

The pub was literally just round the corner and Laura and I went there quite often. It's one of those fake Victorian gin palaces, with books bought by the yard lining the walls. The food is okay, they have a good selection of wine, there's no loud music, and there are a couple of huge comfy sofas, in which Laura and I have spent many an hour putting the world to rights.

We ordered some food, and stood by the bar waiting to buy drinks.

'I feel like it's red-wine weather. What about you?' he asked.

'Feels more like cocoa-in-bed weather, if you ask me.' Oh, God, Freudian slip.

He pretended he hadn't noticed – or maybe, worse, he hadn't noticed. He led the way to one of the sofas, but once we were settled with our drinks, I felt suddenly awkward. However, he chatted with what I assumed to be professional ease about Caring Concern, how long I'd worked there and what I'd done before. 'My granny wanted me to be an air hostess,' I said, starting to relax a bit, probably thanks to the wine.

'Why?'

'Three reasons – travel, languages and international men.'
He laughed.

'No, seriously, those were her three main ambitions for me. She was very disappointed at how I turned out. I went to university, didn't do all that brilliantly, and left with no idea what to do next.'

'You didn't fancy life at thirty-three thousand feet, then?'

'I get terrible earache on planes, with the pressure, and I'm always deaf for a day afterwards. I can cope with it for holidays, but I couldn't stand it as a week-in week-out thing. Plus there's the non-stop smiling.'

'I can see the drawbacks. So what was plan B?'

'I did a secretarial course, and got a job with the health authority in Nottingham – that's where I did my degree. It was soul-destroyingly boring, so when a job came up where my friend Laura worked, at Caring Concern, I thought, Why not? At least I'd be in London.'

'Do you like it here?'

'Yes, I do. At least you can see the results of your work, meet the people who use the service face to face. And I love living in London.'

'And what about the travel, the languages and the men?'

Well, now he was getting a bit personal. I liked it. 'I get to travel all round the entire borough, which is dreadfully exciting, of course. Some days it's so hectic I even have to get a two-zone bus pass. Languages, no, because all my French teachers at school were fascists. And men . . . Well, all the people in the office are women, if you count Veronica. So, on the whole, Granny is probably turning in her grave.'

Actually, I sensed Granny revolving in her little urn even as I was saying the words. My granny had been a bit of a man-eater in her day, very glam and flirtatious. When I was young, she entered several Glamorous Granny contests and won easily, and her legacy to her only grandchild had been an age-defying complexion (she had hardly a line on her face until well into her seventies) and a set of Cardinal Rules, one of which was that if you want to impress a man you've just met, don't talk about yourself all the time. Therefore, 'How did you come to be a tax inspector?' I asked brightly, as if inspecting taxes was my favourite subject in the whole world.

He looked up at the ceiling and made a delicious little pout. That sounds a bit girly, I know, but if you'd seen it you'd have wanted to snog the face off him, too. I sincerely hoped he'd do it again. 'The six-million dollar question, eh? Just how does one get into such a riveting profession? Actually, it probably sounds sad but I like being a tax inspector. I get to work in different places, and meet different people. It's also nice to subvert people's expectations. They're usually expecting a hideous ordeal, and they're quite surprised when we're not as horrible as they're anticipating.'

Our food had arrived, so there was a bit of a pause while we began to eat. I suppose it should be awfully significant and I should remember what the food was, but I have absolutely no idea what we had – I'm not even sure I could taste it at the time. After a while he said, 'The main reason I joined the Inland Revenue was that it was the first decent job that came up, once Lily was on the way. Kids are expensive.'

Oh dear. He was about to spoil it all now. This was the point at which he would open his wallet and whip out his photos of the wife and kids. I didn't really want to know; I'd been enjoying the fantasy of sitting in a cosy pub drinking red wine with this beautiful man.

However, he didn't, but rather seemed to be waiting for me to say something. The spectre of Granny insisted that I show him some encouragement. 'Lily's your daughter?' I managed.

When I had thought earlier that he might look like an angel, I hadn't been far off. Now he almost literally glowed. 'Yes, bless her. She's ten months old, and absolutely wonderful. I can't believe how she changes every day. I go home each evening and she can do something she couldn't do the day before. She's incredible.'

Despite Granny, I couldn't find it in myself to be interested in a baby. As far as I could tell, there was nothing to differentiate one from another. And I didn't really want to know anything else about Lily because to know about her would be to know about her mother: his wife or partner, or whatever he called her. While I didn't know, I still had him to myself. But then, I thought, it's best to know now before you make a fool of yourself, so I asked, 'Who looks after her while you're at work?'

'My mother, mainly,' he said. 'She adores Lily. I worry sometimes that it might get a bit much for her, but she seems okay with it.'

'What about your wife? What does she do?' Oh, well done, Anna. There's nothing like the direct approach.

'I don't have a wife,' he said.

'Well, partner, whatever ... Lily's mum.' He frowned slightly, just a brief puckering of his eyebrows, but enough to show I'd strayed into a conversational no-fly zone. 'I'm sorry,' I said, 'it's none of my business.'

'No, it's okay. It's just strange to be having this conversation with someone I've only just met.'

I felt put in my place and embarrassed, and tried to lighten the mood. 'But we go back a long way,' I said. 'All the way back to last week in Oxford Street, remember?'

He smiled – already I loved the way the smile started with his eyes, then moved to the corners of his mouth, then involved his whole face. It was luscious.

'You're right, we're practically old friends. But I'd rather talk about something else.' There was a long silence. I couldn't think how to re-start the conversation. Each sentence that came to me I rejected because the only thing I could have said that would have made sense would have been to tell him I loved him. And of course I could never say that. Granny would have been mortified, had she not been already *mort*.

Instead, in a very short time, we would have to go back to

my office. Laura would be there, and I'd have to sit at my desk all afternoon, while this man I'd just fallen in love with finished his tax inspection then went home to his life with . . . whoever. I pictured someone tall and blonde; she must have a career because she wasn't at home with the baby, but she would be the sort who would rush back home, via the gym, and make something frightfully clever for supper with sun-dried tomatoes. I had to make a deliberate effort to stop this train of thought at the point where the dishwasher was being loaded because I couldn't bear to watch them progress to the bedroom.

Michael had finished his lunch. He pushed away his plate, picked up his glass and sat back. 'Aren't you hungry?' he asked.

I realised I'd just been pushing my food around the plate, and that I couldn't eat because there was something in my throat that felt perilously like tears. 'No, not really,' I said.

'I suppose we'd better be getting back to work, then,' he said. 'I'd really like another glass of wine, but if I have one all those columns of figures will end up as just one big blur.'

We walked back to the office, making small-talk again, although conversation was difficult because a face-numbingly icy wind was blowing.

Po-faced Vo glanced up as we came through the door.

'Nice lunch?' she asked, somewhat pointedly I thought.

'Fine thanks,' I said, following Michael into my office. Laura still wasn't back; she must have met Dan for lunch. Veronica handed me a pile of post, and a note about a couple of calls I needed to return. By the time I'd worked through them, Michael was gathering up his papers.

'Are you finished?' I asked, wretchedly.

'Well, for today, anyway,' he said. 'I'm going to have to come back tomorrow just to finish up.' Oh, happy day! 'I just need to have a quick word with your boss, then I'll be off.'

35

He held out his hand, and I clasped it, not wanting to let go. 'It was nice meeting you again,' he said. 'And thanks for lunch, I enjoyed it. 'Bye, then.'

And he'd gone. After I heard him leave the outer office, I went to the window and watched him walk away down the street, his black raincoat tugged by the wind. I thought he looked like a windswept angel, but you have to forgive me for that: my emotions were running high. I've never before felt such a sense of loss. As he turned the corner of the street I wanted to run after him and stop him – but then what would I do? What could I say to him? That after a morning of working next to him and an hour in the pub I couldn't live without him? How stupid did that sound?

Laura didn't get back till almost five o'clock, when I was about to leave. She asked me if I wanted to go for a drink. I said no, I just wanted to go home and have a bath. I was tired, it had been a long day.

'Livened up by that tasty taxman, I bet!' she said. 'Vo said you went out to lunch with him, you fast woman.'

'Oh, why is everybody so bothered about what I do all of a sudden?' I snapped.

'Hey! Come on, what's up?'

'I told you, I'm tired. I just want to go home.' Now, while Aquarians don't like being nagged at to reveal how they're feeling, they have no qualms about doing it to other people. She kept on at me until I cracked and agreed to go for a drink. We went to the same pub I'd had lunch in with Michael.

Laura sat me down and brought me a drink, then I told her all about it.

'I think I'm in love,' I said.

'Who with? Not the taxman?' I nodded.

'But I thought you were off men?'

'This one's different,' I said. 'He's adorable.'

'He did look a bit tasty.'

'He's wonderful. I can't really explain it, I'm just crazy about him. But it's no good. He's attached. Just my luck.'

Laura gave me a sympathetic look. 'Did he tell you he was attached?'

I explained that he was the same man I'd met in the department store, the one with the baby.

Laura listened as only a best friend can. 'Oh, Anna, what are you going to do?'

'There's nothing I *can* do,' I said, hopelessly. 'I'm just being stupid.' I tried a smile. 'It's this Christmas business. A girl mustn't be left on the shelf at Christmas party time. That's why I'm throwing myself pathetically at any man who passes by. I was even reminiscing fondly about Nic the other night, remember?'

Laura laughed, and tried to reassure me that I wasn't pathetic. To her eternal credit, she didn't refer to George Preston at all.

At home later that evening I made a large mug of cocoa, and sat in my old tartan pyjamas watching the exquisite Audrey Hepburn wasting herself on gnarly old Rex Harrison in *My Fair Lady*. Audrey as Eliza Doolittle was singing 'Wouldn't It Be Loverly?' and, bless her, all she needed to make life 'loverly' was a room heated by a coal fire and furnished with a large chair, upon which she would sit with someone's head on her knee. Presumably the head would be attached to a body, otherwise the song would assume some very sinister overtones.

I used to think Audrey could do so much better for herself than a big chair and Rex Harrison's old, brilliantined head on her lap (though to be fair to the woman, she does mention chocolate elsewhere in the song). Today, though, I thought: swap Michael Taylor for Henry Higgins, and it does indeed sound loverly. I knew exactly where Audrey was coming from.

A big tear plopped into my cocoa.

9

The next day I was up at the crack of dawn. In fact, dawn hadn't actually cracked when I jumped out of bed: it was still dark outside and, as I turned on the kitchen light, I noticed raindrops twinkling on the window-panes. Normally that would have been enough to send me back to bed with a mug of tea and a good book, but this morning there was work to be done.

I had a bath, washed my hair, shaved my legs, took ages with my makeup and even ironed my skirt. This was a bit of a challenge, as ironing is not part of my normal repertoire – I'm a firm believer in today's easy-care modern fabrics and miracle washing additives. Eventually I discovered the iron under my bed, behind several boxes of shoes and a woefully underused dismantled Abdominiser. I dragged it out and tore off the dusty faded wrapping, which bore the legend 'Happy 18th Birthday from Auntie Irene and Uncle Jack'. Bless Auntie Irene and Uncle Jack for knowing what a girl about to embark on womanhood really needs in her life, though they perhaps hadn't anticipated that it would take over a decade before I gave their gift its maiden outing.

By eight o'clock I was flagging. That's the problem with getting up early: you start full of energy but as the morning drags on you need ever-stronger cups of coffee to keep you going. But the prospect of spending all day in close proximity to that lovely man perked me up, and I sailed forth into the cold, damp autumn morning with a song in my heart and my metaphorical hat on the side of my head.

'Gosh, you're an early bird today,' Clare greeted me. 'And looking very smart, too. Which is just as well, because Laura

38

phoned to say she has an upset tummy so she'll be in late.' (For 'upset tummy' read 'hangover', I thought). 'I need you to pop over to Social Services. She was supposed to go to this care providers' meeting, but obviously she won't be able to now and we should have a presence there.'

Oh, no! Tragedy! 'I can't!' I said, trying not to sound as anguished as I felt.

'Why not?'

'Well, you need me here to deal with the tax inspector.'

Clare laughed and patted my arm. 'Don't fret about that, Anna. I've dealt with worse things than tax inspectors in my time. He seemed quite human, anyway. I'm sure I can cope. Best you get off now – the meeting's at Markham House, and you know what the traffic can be like down the high road.' She shoved a fistful of Caring Concern publicity material at me and propelled me to the door.

I trudged down the stairs cursing Laura for being ill, cursing Clare for being Clare, and cursing life in general. The morning's sprucing-up efforts had been in vain, and now I would never see him again.

But when I opened the front door, there he was, one hand poised by the doorbell, looking as bright and beautiful as a sunny seaside morning.

'Good morning,' he said. 'Are you on your way out?' I nodded, fighting a strong temptation to grab his arm and drag him out with me, I didn't care where to.

'I've got to go to a meeting,' I said.

'Oh. That's a shame.' He stepped into the small space inside the door out of the drizzle, so close to me that I could see a mist of raindrops on his hair and smell the fresh air on his skin and clothes.

'It is?' I said.

'Well, it's not the kind of weather you'd choose to go out in,' he said. I was thinking how easy it would be to kiss him, and then, for a mad couple of seconds, I wondered if he could read my mind: he was looking at me curiously, as if he could see right through me or might even be thinking the same thing. Good grief, Anna Anderson, get a grip on yourself, woman! Then he said, 'Well. . . have a good meeting. I might see you later.' He started to climb the stairs.

I went off to the bus stop, weak-kneed with lust, pondering what Laura had said about Germaine Greer. I couldn't imagine that any woman, no matter how old they were or how many hobbies they had, could look at Michael Taylor and not want to have him. I longed for Germaine's wisdom or restraint, or whatever it was, so that I could forget about him and get on with enjoying being young, free and single. That had been my plan, after all.

I'm just not built for networking. That's why Clare usually sends Laura to these dos: she can do that polite chit-chat thing as if born to it, while I have a real problem pretending that boring people and topics are interesting. If I'm being honest I'm actually quite shy, which sometimes masks itself as laziness. When I know I should be circulating, exchanging business cards and all the rest of it, the idea scares me rigid so I tell myself that it's not worth the effort and these people are too boring to exist. Though these Social Services meetings do attract their fair share of the terminally tedious.

The meeting I had to go to that morning would have been dull enough even if I hadn't been sulking, but I spent most of the time in a daydream, picturing Michael at my desk. In my mind's eye Laura, Clare and Veronica were all sitting on the floor at his feet, gazing adoringly at him like an ill-assorted harem.

I paid little attention to the formal part of the meeting, which was a presentation by the assistant director of Social Services, a small African man with steel-grey hair and a wonderfully soothing voice that bore my daydreams along like a barge on the Nile. The actual content of what he was saying escaped me, though. Many of the people sitting nearest to me were scribbling copious amounts of notes as if the pearls of wisdom he was producing were too profound to be allowed to escape. After what seemed like hours, during which his voice faded away into the background like the humming of a very pleasant bee, I became aware of chairs scraping and movement generally: everyone seemed to be heading for the back of the room, where glasses of white wine and nibbles had been arranged on a long table.

I decided that now was the moment to get back to the office, but before I could escape my elbow was seized by a jittery little blonde woman in a Laura Ashley dress. 'Caring Concern!' she chirped. 'Noticed your badge. I haven't seen you before, have I?' Well how do I know what you've seen before? I thought irritably. She stuck out a bony little hand. 'Penny Lambretta, commissioning manager for Respite Services.' I thought I'd misheard her name, but a glance at her badge confirmed that she really was called Penny Lambretta, just like those dinky little Italian scooters: rock and roll! Unfortunately, it was soon evident that her name was the only interesting thing about her – but as a commissioning manager she was one of the people who held the purse-strings at Social Services, Caring Concern's biggest customer, so I tried to be as professional as Laura would have been. This proved tricky: Penny Lambretta was into jargon.

'What do you think of the council's new best-value initiative?' she asked breathlessly, as if this was a topic of erotic fascination.

I had absolutely no idea what she was talking about. 'It's marvellous,' I said. She looked at me, waiting for more. 'A marvellous initiative,' I added.

'Particularly when you factor in the QAMs that came in last January,' she said. Maybe Dan would have had some idea what she was going on about, but it sounded like Ancient Hebrew to me. 'Quality Assurance Measures,' she prompted.

I nodded wisely. 'Oh, yes,' I said. 'Particularly when you factor those in.' I made a mental note that I really ought to read the newsy little council bulletins that came in to our office.

To my intense relief, we were joined by a tall man in a blazer who had hair sprouting from the end of his nose – not his nostrils, his nose. 'Can I interrupt, ladies?' he said.

Penny Lambretta fixed him with eyes that must have had the power to scare holy Jesus out of her underlings.

'*Women*, Councillor Penrose,' she corrected him, in a voice that could ladder tights. 'Not ladies, *women*.'

Councillor Penrose was about to be given a crash course in feminism: I grabbed my chance. 'Ooh, look!' I said. 'Someone I simply have to speak to is just about to leave. Please excuse me. Lovely talking to you.'

I returned to the office with all possible speed, but the traffic on the high road was as bad as Clare had predicted, and the bus crawled along.

It was already after twelve when I got back. Once again Veronica was immersed in Maeve Binchy and hardly bothered to look up. I did a nifty detour to the loo to run a comb through my hair and check my lipstick, then went through to my office trying to look as cool, poised and downright sexy as Audrey Hepburn in *Breakfast at Tiffany's*.

My chair was empty. There was no little black briefcase next to it, no black raincoat hanging up. He'd gone.

Laura looked up from her desk. 'Hi,' she said. She certainly looked hung-over: pale verging on greenish. No wonder she'd been late in that morning. I felt like strangling her. 'He's gone,' she said, waving her hand in the general direction of my desk, 'if that's what you were wondering.'

'For lunch?'

'Well, yes.' Hope sprang eternal. 'But he isn't coming back,' she added. 'He's finished.'

Oh, massive pool of gloom! I plonked down into my seat, which had only lately been occupied by the sexiest backside in the south-east, and allowed myself to be consumed by misery. In this task I was aided considerably by Laura, who seemed determined to make a bad situation worse.

'He got a call from a woman,' she said, and delved into a packet of McVitie's ginger snaps, produced a biscuit and started nibbling it. 'I answered the phone. She sounded quite posh. He arranged to meet her in some restaurant at the Angel for lunch.' The gloom deepened. I sat in silence for a few minutes, broken only by Laura gnawing rhythmically at her biscuit in a manner that was becoming seriously irritating.

'I don't care,' I said, making an attempt to sound breezy. 'Who needs men, anyhow?'

'Specially attached ones,' Laura mumbled. She reached for another ginger snap.

'Oh, good grief, Laura! Do you have to make so much noise with those bloody biscuits? You can't usually eat anything when you've got a hangover.'

'I haven't got a hangover,' she said, and looked a bit shifty, like she had the day before. She got up and shut our office door so we couldn't be overheard by Veronica. She was clearly bursting to give me some news, which kind of stole my thunder as I, suffering broken-hearted disappointment, was supposed to be at the centre of attention.

'I wasn't going to tell anyone yet, but I can't wait,' she said excitedly. 'Promise you won't say anything sarcastic, or get cross?' I promised, and felt my heart sink: I had a nasty suspicion of what was coming, and just couldn't deal with it on top of everything else.

Laura paused for a moment of added drama. 'It's not a hangover, it's morning sickness. I'm pregnant!' she announced, grinning almost as much as she had during her wedding. She and Dan had delivered their vows almost through clenched teeth, they had been smiling so hard. 'Dan and I are going to be parents!' she added rather unnecessarily, as if I was one of Dan's dementia cases who needed things repeating many times in many ways.

I should have been pleased for her. I should have been happy that she was so happy, I know that. But my first thought was completely selfish: Where does that leave me? We won't be able to get pissed together for at least nine months – maybe not ever again! She'll go all clucky, and start knitting things, and she and Dan will start referring to me, on the rare occasions I see them, as Auntie Anna.

Bloody kids, I thought gloomily, they're everywhere. First there's the lovely taxman, and now Laura. My best friend Laura. Laura the traitor.

One good thing about watching far too many soaps is that you get to know the correct response for any given situation, even if it's the last thing you feel like producing. I congratulated her in the proper manner; I even mustered up a fairly authentic girlie shriek and a hug and, from an arcane well of womanly information I didn't even know I'd stored up, I found myself asking the 'right' questions. From this I learned that the pregnancy had only just been confirmed and Laura was probably only about six weeks 'gone', as she aptly expressed it. The baby was due in June.

Inside, I was feeling that sense of separation I'd felt when Dan had told me they were trying to have a child. It hadn't taken them long, I thought, then realised that when Dan and I had had that conversation at the party Laura must already have been pregnant; that idea didn't make me feel too brilliant.

'We'd been trying for ages,' she confided. 'I'm sorry I didn't tell you, but you know what we've always been like about kids. So when Dan and I realised we really did want to have children, I got superstitious about it, like, now I wanted it to happen it wouldn't because of my attitude in the past.'

'That's silly,' I said.

'I know it is, but it's the way I felt. I thought, Well, I'm not going to say anything because chances are I'm infertile anyway. I mean, I've never been pregnant, never even had a scare, not like everyone else.'

'I've never had a scare, either,' I reminded her, a bit sullenly. Look at me! I've got the contraception thing sussed! Unlike some people . . .

'But you know what I mean,' she said. I didn't. All I knew was that this was turning out to be a very bad day indeed.

'I must say, though,' Laura ploughed on regardless, 'that Michael is just so sympathetic. I absolutely know what you saw in him. I told him I was having morning sickness, and he said that when Fiona had morning sickness—'

'Who?'

'Fiona, his girlfriend. When she had morning sickness she found eating ginger was really helpful, so I got Veronica to get me some ginger biscuits when she went out to the bank. Didn't tell her why, though. It's still under wraps to her.'

Oh, fine. Could this day get any worse? It was bad enough finding out that my best friend was in the process of having her life taken over by some child without having her indulging in parental chitty-chat with the erstwhile man of my dreams. Whose girlfriend was called Fiona.

Finally Laura noticed I wasn't looking too happy.

'Look,' she said, 'I know you really liked him, but you're just going to have to forget about him. He's already attached, and he has a child. You know what a mess it could turn into if you got involved with him. Besides, he doesn't look like the type to go in for extra-curricular activity.'

'And you're the expert at relationships now? Pregnant for five minutes and you're suddenly the fount of maternal wisdom?' I don't know why I said that. Okay, I do, but as soon as it was out I deeply regretted it. Laura looked stricken. I'd well and truly rained on her parade, ruined her big moment. Some kind of friend I was. 'Oh, Laura, I'm sorry,' I said. 'I'm just feeling a bit fed up, but there was no need to take it out on you.'

'It's not that,' she said, standing up abruptly. 'I think I'm going to throw up again.' And she dashed off to the toilet.

And that's how it's going to be, I thought. All this pregnancy stuff, it's going to take over: it's started already. Conveniently forgetting, of course, that a hangover would have had the same physical consequences, and I'd have been a lot more understanding (and probably suffering along with her). But, let's face it, even the worst hangover has usually gone before the evening, whereas Laura had an ailment that would last for the rest of her life, and change everything.

Almost as bad as losing Laura was knowing that I'd lost Michael Taylor without ever having had him. I've never really believed in the concept of 'Mr Right'. Which is not to say that I wasn't totally in love with Trout Man: I was. Even then, I wouldn't have said he was perfect and, of course, if he had been perfect he would have put me ahead of his fishy friends and his Celtic roots. After he'd gone, and with the help of Laura and Nic (how she would hate to be mentioned in the same breath as him), it didn't take me long to realise that, as they say, there were plenty more fish in the sea, whether trout or not. Generally, you could say I had a very modern, relationships-last-as-long-as-they-last, sort of view of romance. But I had this strange, persistent feeling that Michael Taylor had been the man for me. It was so strong it took all the breath out of me. But this Fiona person had got in first.

There was nothing for it: I'd been unlucky in love once too often. I'd have to become a nun, like Julie Andrews in *The Sound of Music*. Then I remembered that by the end of the film Julie Andrews had, against the odds, managed to set herself up quite nicely with the taciturn and blue-eyed Baron von Trapp.

A little spark of optimism asserted itself.

10

Over the next few days, I thought about Michael a lot – almost constantly, in fact. One morning while Clare was out and Veronica wasn't around I flipped through Clare's Rolodex and found his business card. His work number was on it, of course – that's the point of business cards, after all – extension number and everything. I stared at it till I had memorised it, but I couldn't bring myself to ring him. I formulated a plan to walk casually past his office at the kind of time he'd be arriving or leaving, but it was nowhere near where I lived or worked – on the other side of town, in fact – so I would have to think up a plausible excuse for being there. Maybe I could invent a friend to visit: all I would need to do would be to look at the *A–Z* for a street where my supposed friend might live ... Oh, my God, I was turning into a stalker! I put the card back, gave the Rolodex a spin so Clare wouldn't know I'd been looking, and went back to my own office.

'I'm going to ring Nic,' I announced to Laura. 'It'll be therapy for me. I need to talk to someone who's more screwed up than I am.'

Nic answered the phone on the second ring. 'Hi, Anna!'

'Nic! You have caller display, obviously.'

'How did you know?' Duh.

'Never mind. I've been trying to ring you at home since you called last week. I think I was a bit off with you.'

He snorted. 'You were indeed. I haven't been home for a while. I, like, needed to get my head together so I've been at Steve and Marlene's for a few days.' Steve and Marlene are

Nic's parents. I don't believe he's referred to them as Mum and Dad since he was potty-trained, and they like it that way. Nic's parents have never mentally left Woodstock.

'And is your head together now?' I enquired politely.

He signed. 'Not really. I've got some heavy stuff going on, Anna, you know? It really would be good if we could meet up – I need to talk to somebody about all this.'

So whatever it was he'd called me about last week was still a problem. I was very curious indeed now, and, anyway, I needed the distraction. We arranged to meet for lunch on Saturday.

11

When I opened the curtains on Saturday morning I was so glad I'd arranged to meet someone, even if it was only Nic. The sky was that glorious October blue, in brilliant contrast to the yellow and gold leaves on the trees. It looked like fresh air and optimism. Not a day to be moping around in an empty flat.

I was meeting Nic in a vegetarian café run by Buddhist monks. I arrived early, and decided to go for a walk in the park. Children were running about, wrapped in little fleeces, hats and boots, shrieking and throwing piles of leaves. An impossibly skinny girl flashed past me on rollerblades. The park was full of people walking dogs, jogging, cycling, just enjoying being in the glorious end-of-season flourish that Nature puts on before closing down for the winter. Seeing all of those people in families and couples should have made me feel sad, but somehow the whole scene was too optimistic. It felt like good things were just around the corner.

Then I pictured Michael pushing little Lily in her buggy,

walking beside Fiona, who would be wearing just a hint of makeup to accentuate her natural glowing gorgeousness. My heart felt like a stone dropping down a bottomless well.

Suddenly I'd had enough of the park, and made my way to the café to meet Nic. He was already there, gazing mournfully at the *Guardian*. I noticed that a couple of trendy-looking, student-age women were looking at him and whispering about him, and I had to admit that he looked good, all windswept and world-weary. He hadn't shaved for several days, but the dark stubble on his face only made his eyes look even more soulful than usual. He has the knack of looking tragic, lost, a man that women just want to save, and despite myself I felt quite smug watching the two women's disappointment when Nic stood up and gave me a hug.

'You're cold! Your nose is really red!' Thanks, Nic. 'I'll go and get you a coffee.'

'Proper coffee,' I said. 'Not that dandelion stuff.'

As soon as he sat down again he said, 'Something has happened, Anna, and it's completely freaking me out, I can't get my head round it at all.' He fidgeted with his cup, spilling a drop of coffee and smearing it in a trail across the table-top with his forefinger. I glanced over at the monks, but they hadn't noticed. Buddhists are probably way too spiritual to worry about things like table manners. Nic got straight to the point. 'I've just discovered I have a son.' He looked up at me. 'You can close your mouth if you want to, Anna.'

'I'm sorry,' I said. 'It was a bit of a shock.'

'You're telling me it was a shock?' He was spreading the spilled coffee into a star shape.

'How do you mean you "just discovered"?' I prompted. My immediate thought had been that he had had an affair while we were a couple, and I was gearing up for the full outrage routine. I might have dumped him, but a girl has her pride.

'He wrote to me a couple of weeks ago.' This calmed me

down. If he's capable of writing a letter, I thought, he's either an extremely precocious child or he was born before Nic and I met. 'His name is Peter, apparently. He's Danish. Eighteen years old.'

'Eighteen? He's grown-up!'

'I know! That's the bit that's freaking me out the most. I'm still waiting to feel grown-up myself, then I find that I'm the father of an eighteen-year-old.' He shook his head. 'Father. It sounds too crazy.'

'Well, how do you know he's your son?' I asked.

'His mother wrote to Steve and got my address from him. You know Steve's fairly easy to track down.'

'His mother?'

'Can you stop repeating everything, Anna? Listen. Do you remember I told you that after I left university I did voluntary work in Bhutan?' How could I forget? Nic's two years teaching in the Himalayas had given him a fund of tedious stories about lice, dysentery and other charming Himalayan customs. As a result of those two years, Nic would never go near a curry with a fork: he insisted on using his fingers in native style. This coupled with his own native lack of table manners, had been the source of much embarrassment in various Indian restaurants, some of which I still avoid. I nodded. 'I don't know if I told you but I had a thing with one of the other volunteers, a girl from Denmark, Karen.'

'Peter's mother?'

'Right. I had no idea she was pregnant when she left. I don't know if *she* did. We didn't make any plans to see each other again – it had just been one of those things that happens while you're working abroad. It's not meant to spill over into your real life when you go home.'

'Except now you find there's Peter.'

'It's too much, Anna! He's waiting for me to write back, says he wants to meet me, and I just can't make any sense of it. I can't tell Betty-Ann – she'd freak. She's only nineteen herself.' That detail got stored away for Laura later. 'I wanted to talk to Steve and Marlene about it, but how could I tell them they'd been grandparents for the last eighteen years and didn't even know it?'

'They might be thrilled.'

'Anna, Marlene would not be thrilled to learn she was the grandmother of a grown man. Talk sense.' He was right. Marlene made a living as a clairvoyant (she hadn't foreseen this, though!), giving readings by e-mail and in person from the huge, rambling 'cottage' she shared with Steve on a ley line within sight of Glastonbury Tor. Steve was a musician; he had been in a band that had had some success in the sixties, and more recently he'd become an expert in ethnic instruments of the Far East, and travelled a lot, lecturing and performing. According to Nic, Peter Gabriel occasionally popped round to bend Steve's ear about Balinese nose flutes or whatever. At the time, this had impressed me a lot. Steve and Marlene weren't married in the legal sense, but had gone through some kind of ceremony conducted by a shaman on a beach somewhere in Africa, long before such things (the beach, if not the shaman) were bookable through your local travel agent. No, somehow they just weren't grandparent material. Most of the time they were too stoned to seem like parent material. Once I'd met them, lovely as they were in their own way, Nic fell into place.

'So what are you going to do?' I asked.

'Well, I was hoping you'd tell me that! That's why you're here!'

Oh, excuse me. 'Nic, I've got no idea what you should do. It's completely outside my experience.'

'It's outside mine, too!' he wailed.

Most things on the real-world side of the doors of perception were outside Nic's experience. He just didn't watch enough soaps, in my opinion. But I did, and I drew on this well of wisdom now. 'It seems to me,' I said, 'that the person you have to think about in this isn't you, it's your son. How is *he* feeling?' He looked blank, so I carried on, drawing on my intimate knowledge of the soap opera genre: the long-lost child, or the child-you-didn't-know-you-had being a staple when the writers want to introduce a new character. 'He has questions about his identity,' I said, with Ken Barlow-style sagacity. 'He's gone through his life without a father, or maybe with a stepfather, but knowing that his real father is out there somewhere. Now he's found you, and I think the least you can do is write to him. Just tell him about yourself. Maybe that'll be enough for him.'

'And if it isn't?'

'If he still wants to meet you, you'll have to work it all out as you go along. Anyway, aren't you curious to see him?'

'I'm crapping myself,' he said.

12

On Monday morning Veronica had gone to the bank so calls were coming straight through to our office instead of via the switchboard. I was trying to write some reports, and getting annoyed because the phone kept ringing and I would forget what I'd been about to write. Laura was of little help: she was, in her words, 'a martyr' to morning sickness, and it seemed as if she had to rush to the toilet every few minutes to throw up. In between she nibbled ginger biscuits constantly. Whenever the phone rang she was either not there, or had a mouthful of biscuit and was shrugging and rolling her eyes at me in that annoying 'I can't answer the phone because my saliva has been dried up by ginger snaps' way.

When the phone rang for the hundred and fifteenth time, I picked it up reluctantly, mouthing the words 'Just . . . fuck

. . . off!' silently at the receiver. 'Caring Concern,' I said, sounding anything but. Actually, my teeth were clenched and I must have sounded like a bad (as in evil as well as crap) ventriloquist.

'Could I speak to Anna Anderson, *please*?'

'This is Anna.'

'Oh, sorry, you sounded different. This is Michael Taylor. From the Inland Revenue.' As if there could be another. My heart did the reverse of that dropping-down-a-well thing: it did the Thunderbird-One-taking-off-out-of-the-swimming-pool thing.

'Is there a problem with the tax?' was the best I could manage to croak.

'No, no problem. In fact, I'm not ringing up about business at all. I'm working quite near to your office today, and I wondered if you might be able to come for a drink after work.'

Mentally I tried out several suitable replies of the 'Oh, is your girlfriend busy tonight?' or 'Will Fiona be joining us?' or just plain 'No way, José' type. But by the time I'd engaged my vocal cords, lips and tongue these terrifically sensible responses emerged as: 'Lovely.'

We arranged to meet at the same pub at five thirty.

'I'll look forward to it,' he said.

'Lovely,' I said again, like a lovestruck parrot.

At the end of the call, Laura came back into the room, eased herself queasily into her chair and said, 'What was all that about, then?' She gave me one of her special looks, all eyebrows and exhortation, that she used when she was about to pull rank: as she was a full five months older than me and married to boot (oh, and let's not forget pregnant), she occasionally felt the need to dispense unsolicited advice.

'It was Nic, wasn't it?' she said crossly. 'Don't tell me you're seeing him again, *please*!'

I said, rather sheepishly, 'It was Michael Taylor. The tax

inspector.' It gave me a thrill just saying his name, never mind that I was going to see him again in just six hours or so.

Laura lowered her eyebrows even further and switched into self-righteous gear. 'What does he want, asking you out?' she said. 'He's got a nerve!'

'You thought he was all right the other day,' I objected.

'Yes, in a work context,' she explained patiently. 'But I can't stand men who cheat on their wives and girlfriends. Specially when there are children involved.'

'Who said anything about anyone cheating? All we're doing is going for a drink.'

'And you really don't see anything wrong in that?'

'It's not like I'm going to jump into bed with him,' I said, thinking, in my dreams, maybe.

I didn't really need Laura to spell out the pitfalls, and I'm not the sort of person who would start an affair with someone who was already attached anyway. I'm way too selfish, for one thing: I could never stand to be the woman who spends Christmas and birthdays alone because her lover has to be with his wife and kids. And I could never live with myself if I was ever responsible for breaking up someone's family.

But there was no harm in just meeting him for a drink, was there?

The pub had a different atmosphere in the evenings: it was more crowded, noisier, smokier and, obviously, darker. I found Michael sitting on the same sofa, with two glasses of red wine on the table in front of him. He stood up to shake my hand – holding it a second longer than his 'business' handshake, I thought (hoped). He was wearing a dark suit, white shirt and tie – much like a lot of the men in the pub who'd come for an after-office drink, but some of them looked like overgrown boys wearing school uniform and others looked like crumpled, shiny-elbowed backbench MPs, while Michael looked seriously good in a suit.

54

'I got you a drink.' He indicated the wine. 'I hope you don't mind.' I said it was fine, and asked him where he'd been working. He mentioned the name of a travel agent that I was pleased to note wasn't *that* close by. He'd made an effort. 'It's nice to see you again,' he said.

'And you.' Seeing him again was absolutely the very nicest thing I could think of. The wine tasted warm, fruity and festive; for the second time that month I felt like it was Christmas.

'How's Lily?' I asked. Apart from his audit of my employer's tax affairs, the encounter in the department store was our only common ground, so far, and I had to say something. Otherwise I might have started to drool.

'Oh, she's fine, really good. She's crawling everywhere, and standing up as much as she can, holding on to things. It's called "cruising", apparently, which I find quite funny. Mum reckons she'll be walking soon. Apparently I was walking by the time I was a year old so . . . I'm sorry, I'm waffling a bit, aren't I?' He paused for a long while, took a drink, and then did that fantastic little pout. I again tried not to drool. 'Actually', he went on, 'I wanted to tell you about Lily's mother.'

It caught me unawares. 'Oh, no, there's no need, I was too nosy the other day, I should mind my own business.' Perhaps this was where he was going to tell me his wife didn't understand him and suggest a sordid affair. And I was so besotted with him I would probably settle gladly for that. Forget the 'probably', in fact.

'I want to tell you,' he insisted. I felt myself tensing. For some reason, butterflies were racing in my stomach. He continued, 'Lily's mother is called Fiona. We went out together a while ago. I'd known her for years before that – I went to school with her brother. Anyway, after we'd been together for about six months, she told me she was pregnant. I didn't believe her at first – we'd always been, you know, careful.' He looked sweetly embarrassed. 'But it was true.'

'So how did you feel?' God, I sounded like a social worker.

'Well, at first I just thought, Oh, shit. Then I panicked. We weren't living together or anything, we hadn't even thought about it. We weren't really that serious, even. Then she said she was going to make an appointment to find out about a termination, and I got really upset. I'd always thought I was all in favour of a woman's right to choose, and I still am, except I couldn't get past the idea that it was my baby, and that it might look like me. Narcissistic, I suppose.' He smiled.

'Maybe that's how Nature works,' I suggested. 'Protecting your genes.' I'd seen this on a television documentary. He nodded, as if I'd just said something original, or wise, and I felt like a fraud.

'I'd never really thought about kids much before that happened. You don't, do you?' I certainly didn't. 'All I know is, I couldn't sleep after she told me she didn't want to keep the baby, I just felt sick. I told my parents about it, and I thought they'd be shocked, or angry or something, but they were brilliant. My mum told me I should go and tell Fiona how I was feeling. So I went round the next morning, and ended up begging her not to get rid of the baby, although part of me was thinking I had no right to tell her what to do with her own body. I couldn't believe it was me talking.

'I managed to stop her going for the appointment that morning, and we talked for hours. Days. The arguments went round and round, and the worst part was that I could see it from her point of view as well. It wasn't me who was being sick in the mornings and everything.

'To cut a long story short, after a lot of talking between the two of us, our families, and a counsellor at the family planning place, we agreed that she would have the baby and I would look after it. She was certain she didn't want children, never had and never would. Her career was the most important thing to her – did I tell you she works in television? She was just getting started, and she didn't want the baby to interfere with her plans.'

'So where is she now?'

'After Lily was born, Fiona gave her to me almost straight away. Completely. I've looked after her ever since she was two days old, and I had to make an application through the court to take parental responsibility for her. Unmarried fathers don't automatically have any rights over their children, I found out. Lily hasn't seen Fiona since about a week after she was born, and I haven't seen her either. She was living in America when I last heard from her, working for one of the news channels.'

That wasn't what I'd been expecting at all, and I was dumbfounded. To be more accurate, I was ecstatic. This woman, whom I'd been imagining walking and eating and sleeping beside him, was just a long-gone ex, living on the other side of the Atlantic. But there was something I still wanted to know.

'Did you love her? Fiona?'

He thought for a moment. 'I don't know. I always thought, Once she sees the baby, she'll love it and everything will be fine. I had a picture of us all being a happy family. You probably think it was really arrogant of me.' I wasn't sure what I thought. 'But in the end I couldn't love a person who could turn her back on her own child.'

'It's what a lot of *men* do,' I said, surprising myself by feeling a twinge of anger on behalf of the absent Fiona. 'It's just easier for men to avoid the responsibility because they don't have to go through the pregnancy and birth.'

Michael sighed deeply. 'I know all that, and please understand that I never underestimated how hard it was for her, and I'm incredibly grateful for what she did. But you've met Lily – how could you not love Lily, if she was yours?'

Oh. Well. I had no answer to that. I've never found any baby remotely lovable, and I've never been able to imagine how I would feel were I to be careless enough to produce one of my own. But I sensed that to say this would not be the way to impress this particular man – and I did seriously want to impress him, even though he seemed to be in line for Father of the Year, and was not without baggage, so to speak. However, I put that speedily to the back of my mind because he was utterly, completely gorgeous and I wanted him more with every minute that passed. I just nodded and smiled encouragingly, and asked him if he'd like another drink.

I stood at the bar, glad of a few minutes to think about what I'd just heard. The important thing to me, at that moment, was that he was single. I know it sounds shallow, but I was just so glad that Lily's mother wasn't a threat, or even an issue. She was just an ambitious woman who hadn't let becoming pregnant get in her way – Good for you, girl, I thought. Then I thought about Michael, and how he'd looked when he'd talked about not wanting to lose his child. It must have been a terrible situation for both of them.

'Why did you want to tell me all that?' I asked, when I sat down again.

He smiled his extraordinary smile. 'I wanted you to know,' he said. 'I couldn't stop thinking about you, and I wanted to get to know you, but you had to know about me first. You have to realise that although I'm unattached in one way, in another I'm about as attached as you can get. Lily and I sort of come as a boxed set. I know it's early to be talking like this, but it wouldn't be fair on any of us if I didn't.'

Wow.

We drank some more wine. The conversation got lighter and more flirtatious. We started getting a bit tactile – lightly touching each other's hands, arms, knees while we talked.

I could picture – I couldn't stop picturing – how he'd look undressed; I could imagine how it would feel to kiss him, and how his hands would feel on my skin. After a while I wanted to rip off his clothes so badly that I thought I was going to have to do it right there in the pub. Then he looked at his watch and said, 'Oh, God, I was supposed to pick Lily up fifteen minutes ago. Mum will be going mad. I'm sorry, I have to go.'

I couldn't believe this: we were getting on so well, everything was going beautifully, and then he had to leave? At seven o'clock?

He leaned forward and took my hand. 'I'd like to see you again,' he said. I just nodded. I wanted to see him again, of course I did, but what I really desperately wanted was to carry on seeing him now: I didn't want him to have to leave.

He gave me a lift home. I know you're not supposed to let strange men know where you live in case they turn out to be axe-wielding murderers, but what the heck? Ten more minutes with him was worth the risk.

Before I got out of the car he kissed me, very lightly and gently. Then he was gone.

13

I made myself beans on toast and sat down in front of *Coronation Street*. I know – not the most glamorous scene you can imagine, but I felt such a bewildering mixture of happiness that Michael was keen on me too, and sadness, mixed with a good old dollop of frustration, that he had had to leave so abruptly, and we hadn't even arranged properly to see each other again. I needed comfort and routine. I also needed to hear a friendly voice. As soon as *Coronation Street*'s end titles started to roll, I rang Laura.

'I didn't expect to hear from you,' she said, her voice not so much friendly as clipped and disapproving. 'At least, not this early. He didn't show up, then?'

'Of course he showed up.'

'So tell all,' she said. 'Is he offering covert nookie or just help with your tax affairs?' I told her what had happened, with particular emphasis on Fiona being an ex-girlfriend.

'And you believed him?' she said, but I could tell from her voice that her disapproval had wilted.

'Of course I believed him! You've never seen a more honest face in your life. You said yourself he didn't look the type to go in for I think your phrase was "extra-curricular activity".'

'So where is he now?' she asked, then dropped her voice to a theatrical whisper. 'Don't tell me you've left him in a state of collapse in the bedroom while you ring round all your mates!'

'I should be so lucky,' I said sincerely. 'He had to go and pick up his little girl.'

'Oh!' Laura fairly squealed. 'His baby! What's her name again? And how old is she?'

'She's . . . I don't know . . . I think he said ten months. Her name is Lily.'

'Lily. That's a gorgeous name. Dan and I think that if we have a girl we're going to call her Sera, you know, after the Elizabeth Shue character in *Leaving Las Vegas*.'

'Oh. That's nice.'

'And if it's a boy, Dan likes Travis.'

'Like Travis Bickle?'

'In *Taxi Driver*!' she said.

'Is that a joke?'

'No! Why?'

'Oh, never mind.' I wanted to get back to the subject of Michael; he was all I wanted to talk or think about.

But her mind was clearly elsewhere. 'Whereas I like Stanley, after Stanley Goodspeed in *The Rock*.'

'Slightly preferable to Travis, I would have thought. At least Stanley Goodspeed is a hero.'

'But he's played by Nicolas Cage,' Laura moaned.

'What's the problem with that?' I said. 'You love Nicolas Cage.'

'I know.' She sighed. '"The jazz musician of actors", as David Lynch called him. That's why we picked Sera, for heaven's sake. But his name always reminds me of Nic the Pric. I'm not sure I could inflict that on my own child.'

'Nic's name isn't Nicolas,' I said. 'It's Dominic. But never tell him I told you.'

'Really? Can I tell Dan, though? Brilliant. Anyway, Anna, I've got to go. If I don't eat at least every hour on the hour I get all nauseous. Lovely to hear your news. 'Bye.'

I put down the phone feeling somewhat cheated. I'd called her to have one of our in-depth-analysis talks about men, relationships and life in general, but it seemed that as soon as children come on the scene they take over people's minds as well as their bodies. Just as I'd feared, Laura was drifting out of my reach, like a huge maternal balloon.

14

The woman who opened the door was around forty, with waywardly frizzy hair, the colour of cork floor tiles, pinned in a tumbling knot on the back of her head. With her scrubbed-looking face and primary-coloured clothes she looked like a children's TV presenter from the early seventies who had been left under the hair-dryer too long. Under one arm she was gripping a small child, and was preventing several more from bursting out of the door with her sturdy green-dungareed legs. She peered in a frankly hostile way at Michael and me, but when her gaze fell on Lily she was all smiles. 'Oh, Lily! Hello! How's Lily today?' Lily stared at her. The woman wiggled her fingers. 'Can you wave? Hello, Lily! Wave at Jasper!' She grabbed the chubby arm of the tot she was holding and pumped it up and down vigorously. Jasper grunted and struggled to be released.

'I'm Michael Taylor, Lily's father,' said Michael, 'and this is our friend Anna.'

The woman continued to direct her comments at the child in the buggy. 'It's Daddy!' she confirmed. 'Granny *said* Daddy would be bringing you today, didn't she, Lily? Do come in.' We assumed this meant adults as well as child, so when she started to reverse slowly into the brood of children behind her we followed her into the temporarily cleared space. 'I'm Jasper's-Mummy-Cynthia!' she bellowed over the racket, as an after-thought.

The room we entered looked, to the inexperienced eye, like the opening scene of *Saving Private Ryan*.

Children of all sizes screamed and rushed about, leaving skidmarks of trifle and I shudder to think what else on the stripped and varnished floorboards. The older children were screeching around in an E-number frenzy, oblivious to the screams of their younger siblings as they trampled them underfoot.

The noise was incredible: at any given moment I would say that fifty per cent of those present were in tears (and I'm including adults as well as children) and balloons were bursting like artillery shells. A CD player on a shelf was proving a popular target; every five minutes some brat would wander over and whack the volume right up, causing the Spice Girls to spice up everyone's lives at a volume louder than the average land mine.

I couldn't quite believe I was in this hell-hole of my own free will.

Michael had called me the morning after our meeting in the pub. He apologised at having to leave so abruptly, and suggested meeting up the following Saturday. 'I'm going to a party,' he said, 'and I wondered if you'd like to come too?' That sounded fantastic, and I had just the most perfect little red dress I could wear. Maybe I still had time to make an appointment for a haircut in the afternoon, too.

'It's in Highgate,' he said. 'At three o'clock in the afternoon.' No time for the haircut, then. 'And I have to warn you that the majority of the other guests will be between one and three years old.'

'Sorry?'

'It's a birthday party for one of Lily's little friends from playgroup,' he explained.

Oh, marvellous. I mentally put the little red dress back on its hanger.

'My mum keeps accepting these invitations on my behalf and only telling me about it at the last minute,' he said – by way of apology, I presumed. 'It's a complete set-up. I'm usually the only man there for a start – most dads have got football or the pub or something blokeish to do on a Saturday. So all these mums either look at me like I'm an escaped child molester, or else they try to Brady Bunch.'

'They what?'

'You know, they get the idea I'm there to find a "lovely lady" to get together with to form a lovely ready-made family. That's what my mum's hoping for, anyway.'

This was all I needed to hear to persuade me to go with him. Although the idea of spending part of my precious weekend at a children's birthday party was less appealing than sharing a nice bottle of Chianti with Hannibal Lecter, I couldn't leave Michael to the mercy of these predatory single females. What if he fancied one of them? And anyway, I reflected, it mightn't be so bad: probably all the kids would play quietly in one room and the adults could get to know each other. Two of them in particular.

So here we were, in the living room of Jasper's-Mummy-Cynthia; probably a beautiful home in normal times but today knee-deep in wrapping-paper, food, and upturned infants, and with an overwhelming smell of poo.

Michael's mother had supplied him with a gift for Jasper, the 'birthday boy'. Jasper, an unprepossessing infant, grabbed the proffered package and toddled away, flinging it under the table unopened. Michael shrugged and sat down in a corner with Lily, who appeared wisely to have a limpet-like reluctance to be separated from him, and attempted to fend off the attentions of a small boy wielding a dangerous-looking toy train around her head. I perched as near as I could to Michael, smiling wanly at a lumpen female child who was staring at me and pushing a hank of her hair up one of her nostrils.

'If you keep doing that, your head will disappear up your nose,' I advised her. Her gaze didn't waver, and she never seemed to blink (oddly reminiscent of Tony Blair), but she responded by shoving another inch of hair up her nose. Then she pulled it out and examined it closely. I felt sick.

Suddenly there was a piercing scream, which cut through the ambient racket. A small boy bearing the legend 'Gap' on every article of his clothing was screaming as if he'd been bitten. Which, it turned out, he had. The biter was a slightly larger girl, who was looking quite satisfied with her afternoon's work until Gap's mother descended on her.

'What did you do that for, you horrible child?' she squawked, at which the biter's mother got involved, resoundingly informing anyone in hearing range, which probably embraced most of the N6 postal area, that her daughter couldn't possibly have done anything wrong because she wasn't 'that type of child', and even if she had been, Gap's mother had no right to refer to her as 'horrible' as this was 'destructive to her self-esteem'. Michael rolled his eyes at me and attempted to divert Lily's attention from the fascinating sight of two warring adults. Meanwhile, the biter's mother had removed her offspring to the side of the room where we were sitting, and was trying to point out to her the social benefits of not biting people.

'Why are you always bossing me around?' the child grumbled sullenly.

'Because you're little, and I can,' was the reply.

The next sideshow was the official one: a 'clown', a seedy old guy smelling strongly of mothballs. One thing I remember from my own childhood is that most kids are terrified of clowns. This one's appearance duly set many of the younger children off crying, while the older and braver ones took it as a challenge to try to ruin his tricks. He seemed myopic and borderline senile: in fact, I wouldn't have been surprised to discover that he was one of Dan's clients. He went down a storm with the mothers, though, who applauded the production of a toy rabbit from a hat as if it was God's sixth-day party trick.

I hadn't had lunch, and was starving. I wandered over to the table to see what was on offer. There was plenty of food, but most of it had little faces on – jelly with faces, tiny pizzas with faces, cakes with faces. I always try to follow Paul McCartney's rule of never eating anything with a face. Particularly if it also features thumbprints.

Then one of the mothers approached me. Like many of the others, she seemed to be dressed as a toddler herself, apart from the combat boots.

'Hi!' she squeaked. 'I'm Rosie's-Mummy-Pippa.'

'I'm Anna,' I said, wondering if Rosie was the little charmer with the snotty hair.

'Lily's-Mummy-Anna?' she asked. It was a naming system that Tolstoy would have felt at home with.

'Lily's-Daddy's-Friend,' I said, attempting to enter into the spirit.

'Oh', she said. It seemed I'd killed that piece of social interaction stone dead in the water by not being a *bona fide* mummy, but Rosie's-Mummy-Pippa recovered well and asked if I'd like a glass of wine. I nearly bit her arm off: there was civilisation in this place, after all. I followed her into the kitchen. The 'glasses' were paper cups featuring that horrible Disney version of Winnie-the-Pooh, but the contents were pleasingly alcoholic. I grabbed two cups and took one back for Michael. Rosie's-Mummy-Pippa had excused herself to deal with some territorial dispute involving Teletubbies.

'Are you having a really awful time?' Michael asked.

'No!' I said, perhaps a touch too brightly. 'It's . . . interesting.'

He laughed, and drank his wine in one go. 'It's a nightmare,' he said. 'I love kids, but there should be a ban on them gathering in groups of more than three. To make up for it, I thought you might let me cook you dinner later?' He was looking at me as though, if we hadn't been sitting on the margin of a highly competitive game of Pass the Parcel, he would rather be licking Häagen-Dazs out of my navel. Or, at least, that's how I interpreted it; it made me feel all kinds of incredibly rude things anyway, so of course I said dinner would be lovely.

He held that look for a few seconds longer, then glanced fondly down at Lily, who was curled up on his lap fiddling with a large piece of gaudy wrapping paper. 'Well, Lily looks tired, so I think we can reasonably make our excuses and leave.'

'Oh, you're not leaving before Jasper has blown out his candles, are you, Lily?' cried Jasper's-Mummy-Cynthia, overhearing the end of Michael's sentence. So we sat stoically through the most discordant rendition of 'Happy Birthday to You' I've ever heard, as well as the ensuing tantrum when the birthday boy realised his miniature guests were going to ruin his Thomas the Tank Engine cake by actually eating it. We made our excuses as Jasper and friends began applying themselves to the cake.

As we were leaving, they had started applying the cake to the furniture.

15

We beat a hasty retreat back to Michael's house in leafy Crouch End. I knew that Laura would be expecting quite a bit of detail about this, since it was my first visit to his place and you can always tell a lot about someone's personality from their surroundings (witness the studied Bohemianism of Nic's mattress-on-the-floor, candles-in-bottles mess of a flat), but it didn't help that I was viewing it through a headache the size of Manchester.

Perhaps Michael sensed that I had had enough of children for one day (for one and a half incarnations, actually) because fairly swiftly he took his off for her bath and bed.

Equipped with a large mug of tea and a couple of Hedex, I shoved aside a blue plush whale with a zip-up mouth and a couple of books about some kind of creature called Spot, and sank on to the sofa. My head was still buzzing in the aftermath of all those screaming kids. It had been too horrible.

I've lived most of my life in an almost totally child-free environment. As an only child, even my own childhood was fairly child-free. My parents' friends were all the same age as them and had kids the same age as me, or older, or none at all. None of my close schoolfriends had tiny brothers or sisters, and since I've been living on my own and working, all the people I know just happened to be childless (if you don't count the traitor Laura). So I had no idea how little kids worked; they were an alien species. And I had had no idea they could be so loud.

By the time Michael came back down the stairs the Hedex were kicking in and I was beginning to resemble a human being again. He picked up the blue plush whale and the Spot books, dropped them on the floor and sat down beside me. 'Sorry,' he said. 'That was a bit of a baptism by fire.' I struggled to find something positive to say, and failed.

'Did you see the party-bag Lily got when we left?' he said. 'When I was a kid you used to get a piece of birthday cake wrapped in a paper napkin to bring home, with a candle in it if you were lucky. These days you're no one if you're not handing out designer accessories. I'm not sure what my mum put in that parcel for Jasper, but I'm fairly sure Lily came out of the deal with a net gain.'

'I didn't know kids could make so much noise,' I said.

'Did they?' Michael said. 'I didn't notice. Every time I looked at you it was like there were only the two of us in the room.'

My heart did a little tap dance, and then when he kissed me it was like drinking a delicious, very alcoholic cocktail: fruity and rich and luscious, and it did incredible things to my insides. Apparently I had the same effect on him, and it wasn't long before we were tugging at each other's clothing, all thoughts of dinner temporarily forgotten.

Sex in the movies is not like it is in real life. In the movies it's all fuzzy-focus and choreographed, or else it's oily and athletic and choreographed, either way with saxophone accompaniment. In real life, there's too much to worry about before you can abandon yourself to passion: you're worrying about your cellulite, your breath, your underwear. Had I done a good enough shaving job with my legs, I wondered. Was I wearing A knickers or B knickers? The most worrying thing was: where and how did he like to be touched? How would he know where and how I liked to be touched? But we solved that problem easily, by touching each other everywhere, and it wasn't long before I felt myself melting away in a flood of passion.

Until we were rudely interrupted by howling from above. Michael instantly leapt up, leaving me sprawled on the sofa like something that had recently fallen from an aeroplane. He smiled apologetically as he rapidly rearranged his clothing. 'I won't be long,' he said. 'She's probably just dropped her dummy. Sorry.' He disappeared upstairs.

I sat up, rearranged my clothes and tried not to feel annoyed. It wasn't his fault, after all; that's what babies were like. That's why they were so damned inconvenient. If only they came supplied with an off switch, so you could leave them on standby when they weren't required to – to what? I couldn't actually think of any practical reason you'd want them *not* to be on standby. Switch them back on when they're seventeen would be simplest.

But I wasn't going to let it spoil the evening: it was time for assertive action. I went into the kitchen and discovered a bottle of wine in the fridge. I filled a couple of glasses, then tiptoed upstairs with them. Michael's bedroom was obviously the one that didn't have a picture of Little Miss Sunshine attached to the door, though if that was supposed to be some kind of representation of Lily, Little Miss Centre of Attention would have been more appropriate.

His room was perfect: a nice spacious double bed, plain white walls, simple furniture, no distractions. On the bedside table was a book, *Air and Fire* by Rupert Thomson, which I'd also read and loved; I approved of the fact that the bookmark showed he was well over half-way through and hadn't creased the cover or broken the spine: a man who knew how to take care of books, bless him.

Michael was saying goodnight to Lily so I undressed, kicked my clothes under the bed and slipped beneath the duvet, which was cool and soft. I'd left the door open, and he glanced in as he was about to walk past. When he saw me his face lit up in a huge grin, and his clothes had soon joined mine on the floor.

For the longest time we lay face to face, our bodies pressed together, skin against skin, just kissing and kissing, until I couldn't tell where I ended and he began, like the two prongs of a tuning fork vibrating together, then everything was hands, mouths, skin, all warm and everything fitting into the right place as if one body had been designed specially to fit the other.

16

At some point during the night I woke up, needing to go to the bathroom. I eased myself from under Michael's arm, and stepped quietly out of the room. There was a nightlight glowing a soft blue-green light on the landing, and I found the bathroom easily. (In the past I have taken a few embarrassing wrong turns when staying in strange places.) On the way out, I heard a squeak from Lily's room. The squeak turned into a little cry: I must have woken her up. I started towards her door, then remembered I was naked. It seemed improper somehow to let myself be seen naked by a child (I had vague worries that the sight of my cellulite could scar her for life) so I tiptoed back to Michael's bedroom and found his shirt on the floor. I put it on and went out on to the landing, where I could clearly hear Lily snuffling.

I pushed her bedroom door gently open. She was sitting peering through the bars of her cot, looking tearful. I made a rapid and shrewd assessment of the situation. Her blanket was on the floor so I picked it up, then laid her down and covered her with it as I'd seen Michael do earlier. She kicked at it with her toes – she was wearing one of those little pyjama jobs with integral feet. A little girl in the film *City of Angels* tells the angel played by Laura's hero Nicolas Cage that pyjamas with feet are the best thing about being alive. I could see what she meant: they looked like the ultimate in cosiness, and I wondered whether they were available in adult sizes. They also looked, I was forced to admit, adorable on Lily. She picked sleepily at the ribbon-trimmed corner of the blanket and held it against her nose, regarding me solemnly.

'Sleep tight,' I whispered, and tiptoed out of the room, feeling something that bordered on a glow of fondness for her, and satisfaction that I'd sorted out her problem without having to wake Michael.

I shook off the shirt, got back into bed and snuggled up against Michael's warm sleeping body.

Then Lily started to scream like the proverbial stuck pig.

'Anna, I need your help.'

Needless to say, it was Nic. Historically, a lot of my conversations with Nic had started 'Anna, I need . . .'

'I'm fine, thanks, Nic. How are you?' I said. Whoosh! Straight over his head.

'Peter's coming to England!' whined the voice at the other end of the phone. 'I can't meet him on my own. Please say you'll come with me, Anna! Please!'

'What about Peggy-Sue? Wouldn't she like to meet him?' I said, a touch scathingly.

He sighed dramatically.

'Betty-Ann, and if you must know, we've split up.'

'Oh dear. Whose idea was that?'

'It was a mutual-consent thing. Okay, it was me. I told you, she's only nineteen. She couldn't handle this. I couldn't have handled her handling it even if she could've handled it, anyhow.'

'So I take it you didn't tell her about Peter?'

'No! Are you crazy? It would have been all around the college in hours.'

'And we couldn't have that, could we?'

'Anna!' He sounded genuinely pained.

Apparently Peter had sent Nic an e-mail, informing him that he would be arriving the following weekend, and that he planned to stay for a week so he could really get to know his father. 'Please come with me to the airport,' he begged.

Which is how I came to be standing at Heathrow Terminal Three unreasonably late one evening. We took our places in the loose circle of people around the Arrivals gate. According to the flickering screens, the Copenhagen flight had already landed, and as the minutes ticked past Nic was getting increasingly jumpy. He started pacing up and down like a madman, desperate for a cigarette. He won't normally smoke anything you can buy legally, but I had absolutely refused to allow him to bring a spliff to an airport that must have been crawling with customs officials and drug-sniffing dogs.

'What if he hates me? What if I hate him? What am I going to say to him? He might be, like, really straight,' he moaned. 'I'm not ready for this, I can't deal with this . . .' In desperation I told him to go and get a drink, maybe some alcohol and nicotine would 'chill him out', as he might say.

This left me to hold the little placard on which Nic had written 'Peter Jørgensen'. He had been very specific about the slash through the 'o': apparently it made a world of difference pronunciation-wise, though he wasn't quite sure how. He'd barely gone when people started to pour through the gate. Many were young, carrying rucksacks. There was a preponderance of blond hair and purple garments, and several were wearing those shoes that look like Cornish pasties. They were Scandinavians, all right, and any one of them could have been Peter. I turned round to see if there was any sign of Nic but he'd vanished. Not wanting to leave my post in case I missed Peter, I held up my sign a bit higher, figuring that he was expecting to be met by a man (his father, no less! It was still a spooky thought) so he wouldn't be looking for me.

I didn't register for a few seconds that someone had materialised out of the crowd to stand in front of me. Then I glanced up, and I was looking into the image of Nic's intense grey eyes. I would have known him anywhere.

'Peter?' He was well over six feet tall, and he had to stoop a little to shake my hand.

'Good evening,' he said. 'I'm Peter Jørgensen. You are . . .?'

A little flustered, if the truth be known, but I told him my name, and that I was a friend of Nic's.

'My father is not here?' he asked, gazing around.

'Well, yes, he's here somewhere. Shall we get a trolley for your rucksack and go and look for him?' We trooped off into the milling mass of people in the airport concourse. I was aiming for the bar where I'd last seen Nic heading. My plan was to find him as quickly as possible, get the introductions over with then leave them to it. I'd had enough of Nic's histrionics for one day. Peter strode beside me, apparently unhampered by the weight of his backpack – he had rejected my offer of a trolley – or by any apprehension; indeed, he looked a picture of serene confidence for a person who has just arrived in a foreign country to meet their father for the first time. It crossed my mind that, in the family tradition, he might be stoned out of his brain, but he looked far too full of health and vigour and hadn't said 'man' or 'wow' once.

There was no sign of Nic in the bar. I told Peter to stay there and wait.

'You'll recognise Nic if you see him,' I said. 'He looks just like you only more . . . crumpled.'

'Excuse me?'

'Never mind,' I said, 'He looks like you. You'll know him.'

I retraced our steps back to the Arrivals gate. No sign of Nic. I did a couple of circuits of the place, checking back with Peter on each lap. Nothing. Nic had obviously done a runner.

I wasn't surprised. It was entirely in character: Nic just wasn't equipped to deal with responsibility. He was the worst

73

person I'd ever met for remembering people's birthdays and paying bills. But this was in a league of its own. All the times I'd defended Nic to Laura came back to haunt me. She'd been right all along: he was totally selfish and completely spineless, if that wasn't an insult to invertebrates. It crossed my mind that he'd planned this all along, and that had been why he'd been so keen for me to come with him. And, like a mug, there I was, left as usual to deal with the fallout of Nic's inability to cope with adult life.

My first problem was how to break the news to Peter – I'd already wasted over half an hour looking for Nic. When I returned to him he was sitting on his rucksack, looking perkier than anyone who's just got off a plane has a right to. 'I think he has gone home,' he suggested. 'It must be very difficult for him to find that he has a son after all this time. I have had many years to prepare for this meeting. My mother told me that my father was in England when I was only a little boy. But she would not tell me his name or let me look for him until I was eighteen. For him, it is more of a shock.'

It was a shock to me that any progeny of Nic's could be so sensible, and it was just as well that I was warming to him because it seemed that I had immediate responsibility for him now. I thought of going to Nic's place, but had the feeling that if he'd chickened out of meeting Peter at the airport he wasn't going to be sitting at home just waiting for him to appear. Which was a shame, as I'd dearly have loved to throttle him. But it was getting late, and I didn't have the energy for a midnight wild goose chase around London with a teenage backpacker. I wondered what to do with him. Of the few solutions that suggested themselves, the best idea I could come up with at that late hour was for Peter to stay at my flat for the night and we could try to contact Nic in the morning. He readily agreed to this plan because, despite his youthful vigour, he was tired after all.

74

We got home just before midnight. On the tube Peter had told me about his mother, who was a teacher in a small town not far from Copenhagen. The bit that I really wanted to be around for was when he told Nic that she had lived for the past sixteen years with another woman. They had brought Peter up together. That explains why he's so sensible, I thought. Another titbit tucked away for Laura.

When we got in, my answering-machine was flashing. I expected it to be Nic, and was ready to click off the machine quickly if he started to say anything Peter shouldn't hear. But it wasn't him.

'Hi, Anna, it's Michael. Just wanted to say I'm missing you, and I'll ring you at work tomorrow to try to arrange something for the weekend. 'Bye.' Just hearing his voice made me tingle.

'This is your boyfriend?' asked Peter.

'Erm, yes, I suppose he is,' I said. The truth was, things were all so new with Michael that I didn't really have a word for him. It was certainly too early to refer to him as my 'partner' or, heaven forfend, 'other half'. 'Boyfriend' didn't seem quite right either: it sounded trivial, impermanent, and a bit young.

'We've not been together long,' For some reason I felt the need to elaborate.

'But you like him a lot,' Peter said. 'You looked so happy to hear him.' I admitted that he was right, and found myself telling him all about Michael, how we'd met, how he made me feel. There was something calm and soothing about Peter: I forgot I was talking to an eighteen-year-old I'd just met, and we talked into the small hours like old friends.

I woke up the next morning to the smell of cooking. In that vague state between sleeping and waking I'd been dreaming that Michael and I were having breakfast on the balcony of a beautiful hotel overlooking a topaz mirror of a lake that reflected mountains and glaciers in perfect inverted images. I felt so happy I decided to fly off the balcony into the cool mountain air and over the lake. I kept laughing because I could see my reflection in the water, and I was wearing big fluffy slippers. I looked back at Michael, who was sitting on the balcony waving a piece of toast at me.

Then I realised I was in my own flat, in bed, alone. So who was making toast? It took me a second or two to remember my house-guest. When I emerged from my bedroom I found that the sofa-bed had been put away, the bedding neatly stacked on the floor beside it. The table had been laid with a cloth (I didn't know I even had a tablecloth – maybe he'd brought it in his purple rucksack for just such an eventuality), a jug of orange juice and a teapot. Peter was scooping omelettes on to plates.

Despite appearances, I was having serious doubts as to whether this could really be a relative of Nic's. The only time I'd ever known Nic try to make an omelette, I'd had to throw away the pan afterwards, and the kitchen curtains were never quite the same again.

'Good morning!' Peter said, frighteningly chirpy for eight a.m. 'I hope you don't mind me making breakfast?' I said I didn't mind at all, and in fact he could stay with me for ever if he wanted to.

'That's kind of you, but I'm afraid today I really should find my father,' he said seriously. 'I wonder, can you direct me to his address?'

I wasn't at all convinced he would find Nic at home, so I also told him how to find the college where Nic taught. Finally I gave him my work phone number and my spare set of keys. 'If you don't find Nic you must come back here,' I insisted.

'I think the English phrase is, "You only love me for my omelettes,"' he said.

21

'It's Nic for you, Anna,' Veronica's voice chirped from my phone, and she added unnecessarily, as she sometimes does when she's feeling droll, 'Putting you through!' I prepared myself to give Nic the north edge of my tongue. I'd almost forgotten how pathetic he could be sometimes, but running off like that in the airport was the worst thing he'd ever done. Before he could start making excuses, I launched into him. 'What the hell happened last night? I didn't think even you could be such an arsehole.'

There was a long pause.

'So you'll not be wanting any fax rolls today, then?'

It was Mick, from the stationery company.

22

As he'd promised, Michael rang me in the afternoon. I was so thrilled to hear his voice that the world turned into a mass of clichés – sun out, birds singing, bells ringing, violins playing. You get the idea.

'I was just telling my mum that I'd met this wonderful woman,' he said.

'What are you doing, going out and meeting wonderful women behind my back?' I said.

'I meant you, of course.'

'I know you did.'

'Oh. Well, anyway, she's taken the unprecedented step of offering to look after Lily tonight so we could go out somewhere – see a film or something,' he said.

'I'd love to,' I said. And then I remembered Peter. 'Except . . . it might be a bit difficult tonight. Maybe tomorrow?'

'Tonight's the only night Mum can do,' he said, sounding disappointed. 'She's got her bridge club, and the Neighbourhood Watch and so on all the rest of the week. Ever since she gave up work she's been a social whirlwind.'

I explained the problem to him. I'd already told him a bit about Nic, but obviously I had emphasised all the negative aspects, and let him think that there was hardly any contact between us any more. It wasn't that I was trying to deceive him, it's just what you do when you first start sleeping with a new man, isn't it? They want to know about your history, but you don't want to fuel any insecurities they might have so you tinker with the truth and leave out huge chunks altogether. I hadn't even mentioned Peter to him. I expected him to be annoyed with me or at least a bit jealous – Nic would have been going off the roof in the same situation – but Michael seemed mainly concerned for Peter.

'Of course you'll have to make sure he's okay,' he said. 'I just hope he's managed to track his father down. He'll feel terrible if he hasn't. Poor Anna, it sounds as if you've been left holding the baby.'

'Big baby,' I said. 'And, actually, he's a very nice baby – a great deal nicer than his father, if I'm honest.'

'Well, why don't I come over and keep you company? If he's been reunited with Daddy, all well and good and we can go out. Otherwise we can take him out with us, or stay in and order a takeaway and let him have a good cry, or whatever seems appropriate.'

78

'Michael Taylor, you are too good for this earth,' I said, meaning it.

'Rubbish,' he said. 'It's just that I can't possibly last another day without seeing you, and if it means sharing you with a legion of ex-boyfriends and their offspring, well, fair enough.'

'Enough of the "legion" business,' I laughed. 'I'd love you to come, but it might get a bit messy if Nic turns up. He does tend to emote. And he's not likely to be terribly thrilled with you.'

'I'm used to the emoting of a ten-month-old child and it can't be worse than that. We'll just handle it the way I handle Lily.'

'Which is?'

'We'll give him a drink of milk and let him watch a *Teletubbies* video.'

'I can imagine that working for Nic,' I said.

When I got home the flat was in darkness. I sincerely hoped that Peter had been happily united with Nic and that they were sharing a family moment over a pint somewhere. As I tried to unthaw my fingers enough to get the key into the lock, I noticed that my downstairs neighbours already had a plastic holly wreath pinned to their door. 'Noël' was emblazoned underneath it in red foil. It was only mid-November, for Christ's sake.

I'd left work early because I wanted to tidy the flat before Michael came. It was going to be his first visit to Anderson Towers, and before he arrived I had a bit of work to do, because housework is not one of my priorities. Something else I got from my granny: she always said that it's criminal to waste your time dusting skirting-boards when there are books you haven't read. My flat is living proof that I've still got a lot of reading to do.

However, I didn't want Michael thinking I was a total slob, so my plan was to skim round the worst of it and let low lighting, wine and my own desirability distract him from the rest.

But when I switched on the light, I was amazed to see that not only had Peter washed up the breakfast things he'd also practically spring-cleaned. The place looked so tidy it was almost unreal, like a set for a breakfast TV show; I had to resist the urge to throw a couple of magazines on the floor just to stop the breathless, dizzy feeling all this cleanliness was inducing in me. A glance into the bathroom confirmed that he'd 'done' the entire place. Even the brownish murk that normally encrusts the base of the taps, which I'd long thought of as a 'period feature', had gone. He'd stopped short of regrouting the tiles, but it must have been a close call.

What a star. And now that I didn't have to worry about cleaning the flat, I could concentrate on making myself beautiful. I had a long soak in the bath, luxuriating in the gleam and sparkle of everything. I could actually see my face reflected in innumerable shiny surfaces! I exfoliated, moisturised and perfumed like a mad woman. Then I spent ages choosing something flattering-yet-casual to wear. The aim was to look gorgeous without looking like I'd made an effort. Then I hunted among my CDs for something kind of romantic but not too much, something I might have been listening to anyway had Michael not been about to arrive. (Oh, come on – we've all done it.)

The doorbell rang, and my heart pounded. Just time to lay a book casually on the sofa so that it looked like I'd been reading calmly (I know, I know) and check my hair. Then I went to let him in.

It wasn't Michael, of course, it was Peter. He looked tired, miserable and very, very cold. Trying not to show signs of disappointment, I ushered him in, closing the door quickly to stop any more cold air getting in; it was absolutely freezing outside.

'Thank you for cleaning up in here. You're a complete angel,' I said, as I put the kettle on. 'Did you find Nic?'

'There was no one at his house when I went there this

morning, and then when I went to the college they said he is away on vacation, they won't say where or for how long. I walked around all day, and sometimes I tried to ring his number but always the answering-machine was on. I went back to his house again, after it was dark, and still no one was there.' He sighed deeply, and wrapped his fingers around the cup of tea I handed to him, blowing it gently so that the steam rose and warmed his face.

'I'm sorry,' was all I could think of to say. I felt so angry and hurt for him: if Nic had walked in just then I could quite cheerfully have punched him hard. Peter looked crushed, like the lost boy he almost was. The optimistic perkiness of the previous evening had gone. I was unable to say anything to cheer him up, and was feeling a bit awkward, and somehow responsible for Nic's behaviour, as if that had ever been something I had any control over. Then inspiration struck. 'Look, would you like to ring your mum? She's probably wondering if you're okay, anyway.'

'Yes, I would like to, if you don't mind. She will probably say she told me so. For some reason, she never had a very good opinion of my father. I guess she was right.' He took his tea and went to make the call from my bedroom.

The doorbell rang again, and I went to let Michael in, though it did cross my mind that it might be Nic. Wouldn't that be turning things into a farce? Or even more hilariously, it might be George Preston, come to declare undying love. I could hide him in the cupboard, where he would be found later, for some hysterically funny reason without his trousers, by an enraged Michael.

But this time it was Michael. He was smiling his wonderful smile and holding a huge bunch of white chrysanthemums nestling in green tissue paper like fat snowballs.

'Well, look at you,' he said. 'You look beautiful.' Oh, I do love it when one's efforts are noticed. He kissed me, and his lips were so cold I thought there was a possibility I might freeze right on to him and stay there, like when Arctic fishermen get their bare fingers stuck to cold metal railings on the deck. Being permanently attached to Michael's face would have its compensations, but I wouldn't be able to look at him, because if you look at someone when your faces are that close together they look as if they've got one big eye.

We went indoors.

'Who's here, then?' he whispered.

'The son,' I said. 'The father, it seems, has disappeared without trace.' While Michael was taking off his layers of coats and scarves Peter reappeared. I introduced them and they exchanged a few polite remarks. Then Peter said to me, 'I'm sorry, I didn't know you were expecting someone. I'll go.'

'No, it's fine,' I said.

Michael agreed. 'You can't go back out into that awful weather,' he said. 'I knew you might be here anyway. Honestly, it's fine.' He looked more convinced than I felt – at that moment I would have had only a twinge of conscience about pushing Peter out into a blizzard in his socks – I was so desperate to be alone with Michael.

But there he was, and it seemed that for now I was sort of responsible for him. So we stayed in and ordered a pizza. It was actually a really enjoyable evening: we drank a lot of wine, and once again Peter proved to be really good company. He told us he had plans to become an architect; he would be starting university in Denmark or Germany (his mother's partner was German and Peter was fluent in German as well as Danish and English) the following year.

'I was going to be an architect,' Michael said, surprising me: he hadn't mentioned this before. 'It wasn't my idea, actually. My father's an architect, and everyone assumed I would follow in his footsteps. I didn't really think about it, I just went along with it.'

'So what happened?' Peter asked.

'Well, I started the course,' Michael said. 'I didn't have any better ideas at the time, so I just took the path of least resistance. I studied for two years, but you have to do a phenomenal amount of work. I don't know about Denmark, but it was a five-year course I was doing, plus a year in practice. I just didn't have the motivation to finish it.' He poured out some more wine. 'My dad went a bit mad when I told him I was dropping out, but my mum talked him round. Then I had no idea what to do next. I had some vague thought about travelling, so I was doing various jobs to raise the money – you know, warehouse work, some office jobs, that sort of thing. But things were taken out of my hands when my daughter was born. I had to get a sensible job.'

'Do you regret it?' Peter asked.

'What, dropping out of university? Not at all.'

'No, I mean having your daughter.'

Michael looked amazed that the idea could ever occur to anybody. 'Absolutely not. Never. She's the most precious thing in the world.'

I felt a bit put out. How could I compete with that?

But Michael and Peter were warming to their subject, and Peter was asking about Lily's mother. Michael didn't show any of the embarrassment he had when I asked the same questions, and told Peter the story he'd told me.

'This is different from my situation,' Peter remarked. 'My father didn't even know I existed until I contacted him. I can understand why he is nervous to meet me, but I can't understand how your girlfriend could leave her child like that. Maybe she will come back?' That was my worst nightmare, but Peter seemed oblivious to my horror.

Michael noticed, though, and said quickly, 'No, I'm certain she won't. She made it quite clear.' He was sitting next to me, and moved his hand slightly so his fingers brushed mine reassuringly. I felt a little consoled, but I wanted to be alone with him, so I said I was tired and asked Peter if he wanted any help putting up the sofa-bed. He said no, and went into my

83

room to get his bedding. While he was gone Michael said, 'Do you want me to go?' I shook my head. Definitely not.

After everyone had had their turn in the bathroom, and I had made sure Peter was comfortably installed on the sofa bed, Michael and I were finally alone in the bedroom. We kissed as soon as the door was closed, a warm, loving kiss that quickly turned passionate. We fell on to the bed, wriggling out of our clothes. As I pulled my sweater over my head Michael grabbed my arms and held them above my head.

'Is this what they teach you at the Inland Revenue?' I asked, squirming pleasurably, and submitting myself to a thorough auditing and several shades of bliss.

It turned into one of those nights where nobody gets much sleep; even when I was so tired my eyes felt like they were full of grit and my head was aching from the need to sleep, we wanted to stay awake and talk or just look at each other. Eventually we gave in to tiredness, and I fell asleep in Michael's arms.

Only one thing stopped everything from being perfect: it seemed like wherever we made love, at my place or his, we had to be quiet so that we didn't disturb somebody's child.

23

Normally, as I've said, I love shopping. It's a hobby rather than a necessity, and apparently this is true for most of the population of Great Britain. On Sunday mornings people up and down the land are putting on their Sunday best ready for a trip to Ikea or Homebase.

To me this is not shopping in its pure sense. It's all far too practical – and how can you enjoy it when you know it's going to be followed by several hours or even days of self-assembly or DIY torment?

Just about the only other situation where shopping doesn't work for me is when it's got to be done. I'm talking birthdays and, particularly, Christmas. How come all the rest of the year I can see any amount of things that I know this or that person would love but when I have to buy them a gift I'm devoid of inspiration and the shops are full of crap?

The only way to cope with Christmas shopping and keep your marbles intact is to plan it with military precision: make a list, map out your route, then get in and get out as fast as possible before you're driven mad by festive cheer, screaming kids and Christmas music blaring in every shop.

This latter phenomenon is a real problem for me: certain Christmas songs make me cry, and I'm not talking about a delicate tear poised on my milk-white cheek but a collapse into racking sobs complete with bright red face and pints of snot. For the record, these songs are 'Have Yourself A Merry Little Christmas' – I'm filling up just thinking about it – and 'Joy To The World.' I know my dad has a bit of trouble with 'When A Child Is Born' by Johnny Mathis (I always mix it up with 'Mary's Boy Child' by Boney M, a confusion that Dad says should be filed under 'sublime/ridiculous'), so it must run in the family. Occasionally I have to march out of a shop mid-purchase when one of these tunes is playing, just to avoid embarrassment, which sets my itinerary back somewhat.

I always mean to start Christmas shopping in October, but invariably I'm out there in the scrum just a week before the Big Day, cursing and spending ludicrous amounts of money on highly improbable rubbish just to get it all finished.

This Christmas was no exception. At least I had the excuse that I'd been spending a lot of my free time in those late autumn weeks falling in love. Or, rather, falling in love had taken very little time at all; it was being in love that was occupying me.

A week of November had also been spent in looking after Peter. Nic had vanished; no one seemed to know where he was. I even called his parents to see if he was there. Peter wanted to

85

speak to them – they were his grandparents, after all – but I persuaded him that it wouldn't be fair on them or Nic (not that he deserved any consideration). When I rang, Nic's father answered.

'Hi, Steve, it's Anna Anderson.'

'Hey, Anna! How's it going?' Steve spoke in an American hippie mumble, like Val Kilmer pretending to be Jim Morrison, even though he was from Colchester.

'Fine, thanks,' I said.

'You guys back together again, then?' he asked hopefully. For some reason, Nic's parents thought I was the best thing since king-size Rizlas and had been quite upset when Nic and I finished.

'Erm, no,' I said. Fat chance. 'But I'm trying to get hold of Nic, and he doesn't seem to be around at home or at work. Have you seen him?'

'Um, well, we did,' he drawled. 'When was it? Marlene, honey, when was it we saw Nic?' I heard Marlene's voice in the background. 'Oh, yeah, that's right. 'Bout two, three weeks ago.' The visit he'd made after Peter had been in contact to get his head together. What a shame it hadn't worked.

'Steve, if he contacts you, can you tell him to ring me? It's urgent,' I said.

'Anything wrong, Anna?' Steve asked. 'You're not pregnant, are you? You're not going to tell me I'm about to be a grandpa?' Cue dope-fuelled hilarity. Oh, if only you knew, Steve.

'No, nothing like that,' I said, thinking that it would serve Nic right if I told his father the truth. 'I just need to speak to him, that's all. He'll know what it's about.'

'Okay, honey. You take it easy, now.'

'Yeah, thanks, Steve, you too. 'Bye.'

Needless to say, Nic didn't call. I took a couple of days off work, using up my precious annual leave (a good thing I hadn't wasted any sick days – I was really going to need them now), and showed Peter around London.

We did the obvious touristy bits, like St Paul's and Tower Bridge, and my favourite walk from the Tate Gallery along the river to the Houses of Parliament, Trafalgar Square and Covent Garden. Peter was fascinated by all the different architectural styles of the buildings we passed, and shamed me by knowing more about London than I did after five years of living in the city.

He was as enthusiastic about shopping as I was, but being on a student budget he was more interested in street markets than Oxford Street. We spent a whole Sunday at Camden Market; Peter wanted to look at every stall and go into every shop. The streets were dark, gloomy and cold, which only made the market stalls look more inviting, brightly lit and festive. We bought roasted chestnuts to nibble while we shopped, and drank mulled wine. It was years since I'd been to Camden Market – I'd loved it when I first came to London, then after a while I got tired of the crowds and the laboured alternative trendiness of the place. But it's hard to be cynical when you're with someone who's so enthusiastic, and we didn't leave until most of the stalls were being packed away for the night.

We eventually retreated, with tired feet, to a bar where loud salsa music was pounding out. We drank hot coffee and brandy, and started to thaw.

'This is great!' Peter said.

'What is?'

'This place. London. Everything.'

'You're not too disappointed about not seeing Nic?'

'I'm not thinking about him. I'm just having a good time.' He gazed at me with those amazing grey eyes: he really was the new, vastly improved version of his father. Like Nic, he'd been attracting his fair share of admiring glances as we walked around, but unlike Nic he didn't seem to notice. He was quite adorable.

Michael invited us for dinner one evening, and Lily was still up when we got there. Peter was charmed by her. He spent the whole time sitting on the floor with her and making up little games. On my previous encounters with Lily she'd clung to Michael like a little monkey, but she seemed perfectly at ease with Peter: he made her laugh, and he didn't mind when she pulled his hair. He sang little songs to her in Danish, and read stories. It was the happiest I'd seen him all week.

Finally it was time for him to leave. He still hadn't entirely given up hope of seeing Nic, but the longer time went on the less positive he was feeling about how things would go when it did happen. Naturally he'd asked me a lot of questions about his absent father, which I'd done my best to avoid or to which I had given the vaguest replies. 'I'm really not the best person to ask,' I told him. 'I suppose it says something that we're still . . .' I had been going to say 'friends' but I wasn't sure that that was the right word '. . . in contact with each other. When people split up, they often don't even keep in touch.'

'Why did you two split up?' Peter asked. I sighed: how long have you got?

'I suppose we weren't really meant to be a couple. We're just better as . . . friends.' I couldn't think of another word that time.

'Had you already met Michael?' As usual, just the mention of his name made me go all warm.

'No,' I said, 'Nic and I were long finished when I met him.'

'I like him,' he said. 'You two make a good couple.'

I went with Peter to the airport, and waved him off, making him promise to keep in touch.

'Thank you for everything, Anna,' he said. 'This was not the way I expected things to turn out, but it's been really good to meet you.' He gave me a hug, the back-patting kind that men do. I realised, with some surprise, that I was going to miss him. The Salvation Army were playing carols in the airport concourse. I heard the opening bars of 'Joy To The World' and beat a tactical retreat to the ladies'.

24

I'd been neglecting Laura badly recently. You'd think that we'd have enough of each other's company working together five days a week but, like schoolgirls who sit next to each other all day in class then ring each other as soon as they get home to 'catch up', we never ran out of things to talk about. We'd usually have one of our 'girls' nights' at least once a fortnight, and more often in times of crisis, as well as get-togethers at the pub with Dan's workmates and other mutual friends. But I realised, with a guilty feeling, that the last time I'd seen Laura outside working hours was the evening after Michael had been working in our office.

And, to tell the truth, my oldest and bestest friend had been getting rather boring of late. Okay, maybe I was fairly boring myself, when every other sentence I uttered seemed to contain the word 'Michael', but Laura just went on and on about her foetus. I was constantly updated about its size ('It's the size of a kidney bean!/Jersey Royal potato!/fairly large satsuma!'). She moaned constantly about how tired she was, and punctuated the working day by sending me out to the shop for snacks. I'm sure the owner of the convenience store across the road was developing his own theories about why I was in there at least once a day buying Quavers and tins of fruit cocktail. And it didn't help that I was the only person at Caring Concern who knew that she was With Child.

Laura was now just over twelve weeks' pregnant. She hadn't told anyone except me about her 'condition' because, she told me, most miscarriages occur in the first twelve weeks and she didn't want to tempt fate. Clare and Veronica seemed happy to accept that her frequent puking was the result of a close encounter with a dodgy prawn (I wouldn't have been that harsh about Dan, myself). But now that the magical twelve weeks had passed without anything dreadful occurring, reporting bans were lifted and Laura couldn't have broadcast her news more thoroughly or widely had she appointed Max Clifford as her agent.

The effect on the office was incredible. Clare (married, post-menopausal, two watery-eyed little dogs who holidayed in a dog hotel) and Veronica (single, tedious and, as far as we could ascertain, terminally celibate) positively gushed with enthusiasm. Laura's every appearance was greeted with (a) queries about her health, (b) requests for confirmation of Dan's presumed joy at impending fatherhood, (c) questions about gender preferences – though this latter was always swiftly followed by a tripartite chorus of 'Of-course-it-doesn't-matter-as-long-as-it's-healthy.' Apparently the most riveting and engrossing topic of all was (d) possible names.

'Travis?' queried Veronica. 'I would have thought that's more of a surname.'

'Tubby has a cousin called Alvis,' Clare offered, 'and when I heard that I said, "Tubby, surely Alvis is the name of a car?" "Well," he said, "maybe that car has connotations."'

'What did he mean?' Veronica asked.

'Veronica, to this day I have absolutely no idea. Tubby can be rather deep sometimes.'

It was most depressing.

But when Laura told me that the few of Dan's workmates who hadn't already rushed off for Yuletide skiing trips down the Amazon would be convening in their usual pub one Friday night just before Christmas, I was looking forward to the chance to spend some time with her, like in the good old pre-pregnancy days. Michael couldn't come – his mum was presiding over some charitable fund-raising meeting and no other babysitter could be found for a Friday evening. However, while I would have loved the opportunity to show him off, and just to be with him, I felt I owed Laura my undivided attention just for one evening. Plus there was a slight risk that George Preston might be there. I hadn't seen George Preston since the night of the 'Christmas party', so it was going to be slightly awkward when we did meet, and very awkward if I had Michael to worry about too.

After work Laura and I went straight to the pub. Dan was already there, with Sadie and a couple of other women I knew vaguely.

'Sit next to me, Anna,' Sadie said, as soon as we arrived. 'Then you and Dan can act as a buffer between my smoke and the mother-to-be, who apparently is Not To Be Exposed to my fumes.' So much for an evening just like pre-pregnancy times. It was the topic of conversation before we'd even sat down.

'Oh, come on, Sadie,' Dan said, 'there's no need to sulk. You know cigarette smoke can be harmful to an unborn baby.'

Sadie rolled her eyes heavenwards. 'Dan, I'm sympathetic, darling, you know I am. But, for God's sake, it's a pub! People smoke in pubs, it's what they do.'

Laura tried to be conciliatory. 'He's just being over-protective.' she said. 'I don't mind you smoking, as long as you don't blow it right in my face. And I'm certainly not going to spend my entire pregnancy avoiding pubs.' She glared meaningfully at Dan, which signalled to me that this was part of some Ongoing Dialogue that it was best not to get involved in. Dan looked a bit annoyed, and he and Laura started a whispered conversation of their own.

Sadie turned her attention back to me, a cigarette poised between fingers tipped with talons glossy with dark purple polish. 'So, Anna, apparently you're seeing a new man?' she said. I nodded, smiling at the thought of him. 'Does he have a name?' Sadie enquired.

'Michael,' I said. God, I loved the sound of that name; only a few weeks earlier it would only have made me think of the most controversial member of the Jackson Five, but now, well, say it loud and there's music playing, say it soft and it's almost like praying. If you see what I mean.

'And he's a tax inspector?' she asked. I nodded happily. 'Well I'm sorry, darling,' she said, exhaling smoke ostentatiously away from Laura, 'you're going to have to work hard to convince me that a tax inspector is an object of desire. I've seen the advertisements – aren't they all stumpy little men in bowler hats with Hitler moustaches?'

I laughed. 'Some of them are women.'

'Probably still have the moustaches, though,' she said.

I secretly rather hoped they did. 'He hates those little-bowler-hat-men ads,' I said.

'As well he might. So, come on, what's so wonderful about him?' she demanded.

'Well . . .' I pondered. 'He's got a really lovely bottom.'

'Is that it?'

'No, it's just the first bit of him I saw.' She looked puzzled. 'Never mind,' I said, 'it's a long story. No, I think what I like best about him is that he's got a sort of quiet confidence, like he doesn't have to put on any kind of show or pretence. He's just . . . comfortable in himself.'

'No, stop right there, darling. "Quiet confidence" just isn't doing it for me. The last thing I look for in a man is "quiet" anything!' I could imagine that Sadie would probably terrify the majority of men. 'You're making this Michael sound like George Preston,' she continued. 'Speaking of whom . . .' She was staring pointedly over to the door, which had just opened with a rush of cold air. Oh, God, George Preston was here. How embarrassing.

I glanced furtively in the direction she was looking at. It wasn't George Preston at all; it wasn't even anyone I knew.

'Oh, very funny, Sadie!'

She sniggered: possibly the only person I know who could produce an authentic snigger. 'We never did get any detail on your affair with G.P.,' she said.

'There was no detail,' I informed her. 'And no affair. Just a desultory snog because I was depressed and, yes, I did feel bad about it afterwards.'

'Whatever for? Say what you like about young George, and I have, over the years, but he is a decent snog.'

'What? Sadie, you haven't! When?'

'I couldn't really say now.' She yawned theatrically. 'Oh, I remember. It was Hallowe'en, rather appropriately. You remember, Learning Disabilities had that fancy dress party? Well, there was our George, all done up as Dracula and looking rather desirable in a Christopher Lee sort of way. It was destiny, dear. His widow's peak had found its special purpose.'

'And who did you go as?' I asked.

'Well, since I spend what passes for my normal life looking like Morticia Addams, I decided to go as Marilyn Monroe. Bit of padding, blonde wig, luscious pout and a faint greenish tinge to the complexion. It was Hallowe'en, after all. But enough of this, and back to your stumpy little man in the bowler hat. Dan informs me he's a single parent.'

'Yes. He has a daughter. She's nearly a year old.'

Sadie crumpled up her face. 'Darling, you must be a saint. Personally, I'd rather chew my leg off than do the reproduction thing, but putting up with a kid who isn't even yours . . . Well, all I can say is you must have it bad.'

I couldn't really tell her that I was right with her on the leg-chewing; somehow it sounded disloyal to Michael. So I said nothing, turning my attention to the other side of me where Laura and Dan seemed to be warming up for a full-scale row. The other two women who had been at the table when we arrived had wandered off tactfully to the bar. Laura looked close to tears, stood up abruptly and marched towards the ladies'.

'Is she all right?' I asked Dan.

'I don't know, these days,' he said. 'Ever since she's been pregnant I'm almost terrified to say anything to her. Is she like that at work?'

'Erm, no, I don't think so.' The truth was that I tended to glaze over as soon as Laura started talking about anything to do with her 'condition', and always changed the subject as fast as possible, so I couldn't really say how she was.

Dan sighed. 'Half the time she makes me feel guilty for getting her pregnant in the first place.'

'But she's really happy about the baby,' I pointed out.

'Well, if that's true, why does she keep bursting into tears the whole time?'

'Hormones?' I said lamely.

'You're telling me. It's like one long bout of PMT.' He sighed again. 'Go and see if she's all right, would you, Anna?' He looked cross and tired.

A ribbon of toilet paper wafted across the floor as I opened the door of the ladies'. There was a strong smell of something that probably advertised itself as pine fragrance, with an underlay of old cigarette smoke. The wooden surround to the washbasin, and indeed any other horizontal fixture, was peppered with cigarette burns. Why do people do that? There was no immediate sign of Laura, but one of the cubicle doors was closed, so I said, 'Laura?'

'Anna, is that you?' The bolt clunked and the door swung inwards. Laura was sitting on the toilet with her jeans around her ankles. Her eyes were bleary and wide open; she looked pale and sweaty.

'Are you okay?'

'Anna,' she said, in a small, frightened voice, 'I'm bleeding.'

'Oh, my God.' She began to sniff.

'I don't want to lose the baby,' she said, 'Dan thinks I don't want it, but I do.'

I tried not to panic and summoned the full resources of the two-day first aid course I had been on five years previously. 'I'll go and get Dan and come straight back,' was the best plan I could come up with. 'We'll take you to the hospital. Stay there.'

'Don't worry, I'm not about to go anywhere.'

Dan was watching the door as I came out, and leapt up as soon as he saw my face, closely followed by Sadie. I told them what was happening. Dan froze. I froze. We stared at each other helplessly. Luckily Sadie assumed control. 'Have you got your car?' she asked Dan. He nodded. She told him to go and bring it to the front door of the pub, then she and I went back to Laura.

'I feel like I'm fucking haemorrhaging or something,' she wept. I really didn't want any details, I was seriously afraid I'd faint. Sadie was shoving coins into the sanitary products machine, and came back with a handful of pads.

'Come on, shove these down your knickers and we'll get you to the hospital,' she said, and helped Laura to stand up. We walked either side of her, our arms round her protectively, as she shuffled towards the door.

Dan was waiting in the car right outside the pub, his face an anxious, pale moon in the window. Laura started sniffing again when she saw him.

The drive to the hospital was awful. Of all things, we got stuck behind a hearse, which I fervently hoped Laura hadn't seen. She clutched my hand the whole time, still crying.

Luckily A and E wasn't too busy. Dan found a nurse, and insisted that Laura was seen immediately. Sadie and I sat down in the waiting area. 'Maybe we could use the time to pull a couple of gorgeous doctors,' she said, glancing around for possibilities. I was too worried to say anything in reply.

'I had a miscarriage once,' Sadie said. I looked at her, 'Hurt like buggery, but it was just as well, under the circumstances.'

'How old were you?'

'Oh, God, seventeen or something. I would have been the proud mother of a nine-year-old by now. Can you picture that?' I couldn't. 'So it was for the best. Definitely.' The subject seemed to be closed, and we sat in silence again.

After a while, Dan came back, without Laura. I felt a sharp pang of fear, but Dan's face was reassuring. 'They're sending her up for a scan,' he explained, 'but the doctor examined her and thinks her cervix is still closed.' I barely suppressed a shudder (why do impending parents always feel the need to offer all this detail?), but Dan didn't notice. 'Apparently that makes it more likely that the baby is all right.' He looked weak with relief. 'So if you two want to go, it's okay.' We both said we would stay. Dan hurried back to where he'd left Laura.

Waiting in a hospital is like waiting at a bus station or a (fairly seedy) airport. There's the same sense of time being dislocated, like real life is happening elsewhere. There's the same stale, recycled air that makes your mouth and the inside of your nose feel dry and gluey, the same bizarre mix of people, and that peculiar we-got-through-the-Blitz-we-can-cope-with-this camaraderie. No wonder it's such a ripe setting for TV drama.

Sadie went outside for a cigarette. I got a Coke from a machine, and wished I'd brought something to read, although I wasn't sure I'd be able to concentrate. I tried to imagine how Laura was feeling, but I couldn't envisage the anguish of losing a baby. I knew in my head, but not in my heart, and that's where Laura would feel it. I took a mouthful of icy Coke, savouring the almost painful sensation as it burned down my throat. I just hoped that Laura would be all right. The look on her face as she'd sat in the car, too frightened to hope but too frightened not to, had made me realise what being pregnant meant to her. I think it was the first time she'd properly grasped it herself.

Sadie came back, smelling of cold air and tobacco. I didn't know about pulling a doctor, but a male nurse and a couple of porters were looking quite impressed with her already.

Finally, Laura and Dan reappeared. Relief was evident in both their faces. Laura was clutching a piece of paper, which she thrust at us. It was a grey, grainy picture, that looked like the surface of the moon. 'Our baby,' she said, pointing at a little blob in the top right-hand corner. It looked like a peanut. 'We saw its heart beating.' Her voice was giddy and tearful.

'So everything's all right?' I asked.

Dan and Laura beamed widely. 'Everything's fine,' Laura said. 'The doctor said it happens sometimes – you get bleeding like this for no apparent reason. He said he gets at least three people in a week with the same thing. But the main thing is that the baby looks fine and the placenta looks normal.'

'Okay, enough of the medical detail. But I'm so glad for you!' I hugged her, and for the first time since she had told me she was pregnant I felt truly happy for her.

Sadie was still peering at the scan picture. 'It says here it's a singleton,' she said. 'What's that mean?'

'It means it's not twins,' Dan said. 'Just a little singleton, all on his own. Or her own.'

'So nothing to do with Valerie Singleton on *Blue Peter*, then?'

'Or Mary-Ann Singleton in *Tales of the City*,' I suggested.

'No, but we'll bear those names in mind if we decide against Travis or Sera,' Laura said.

'Or Buck,' added Dan.

'Buck?' Laura shrieked.

'Damn. I thought I'd be able to get that one past you in your weakened state,' he said.

Laura was looking exhausted, and the doctor had advised her to spend the weekend in bed.

Dan dropped Sadie off at the station and then took me home. I waved at them as they drove away, and went indoors.

Parenthood. You'd have to be mad.

25

Nic's self-styled 'clairvoyant' mother, Marlene, once told me that, when they get to thirty or so, everybody goes through what's called a 'Saturn Return'. The theory goes that around your thirtieth birthday the planet Saturn has made it's way back to where it was in the heavens when you were born. This, for reasons best known to the planet Saturn, prompts you to get into a serious re-evaluation of your life: 'a celestial spring-cleaning', Marlene calls it. After your Saturn Return your life might continue as it was, but it's likely that some major changes will have occurred and life will never be quite the same again.

Most of the things Marlene says are mad, but that one has the ring of truth, in that I've seen one friend after another go all wobbly around the time they hit their thirties – look at Laura, for heaven's sake. We put it down to the intimations of mortality we see in the bathroom mirror the morning after a heavy night, not being able (or wanting) to shop in Miss Selfridge or Top Shop any more, or go clubbing without feeling ancient, or the 'biological clock', when actually it's none of those things. It's the ringed planet that we have to blame. Maybe, one day, someone will come up with the astrological equivalent of HRT to ease us through our Saturn Return without pain or embarrassment, but until then it seems that around thirty we all get a bit distracted.

I don't know if it was anything to do with Saturn, or everything to do with Michael, but for the first time in my life I was feeling perilously close to wanting to be settled and domestic. I couldn't imagine anything more lovely than chestnuts roasting on an open fire with Michael and me snuggled on a sofa in the firelight. I wanted to frolic in the snow with him, like Ali McGraw and Ryan O'Neal in *Love Story*. I wanted to shop for cushions with him, and start baking cakes. My visions were alarmingly homely except at work, which was enlivened by daydreams of Michael wearing nothing but a strategic scrap of tinsel, doing unspeakable things with me under the mistletoe.

This year, at least, Yuletide debauchery was not on the cards. My mother booked me months in advance for Christmas.

Actually, that's being a bit harsh. At the time of the booking, which normally occurs as soon as the final notes of 'We Plough the Fields and Scatter' have died away at St Thomas's Harvest Festival, I was only too glad to know that I would be in the bosom of my loving family over the festive period; since I'd finished with Nic several months earlier, it didn't seem that there would be any rival claims on my time. Of course, things looked different after I'd met Michael, but once you've made a promise to your mother about Christmas it's iron-clad and you can't get out of it without masses of tears, sulking and probably being written out of the will, so that was that.

Michael was planning to cook Christmas dinner for his parents, his brother and his brother's wife. I've never cooked a meal for more than three people before, and certainly not a Sunday/Christmas kind of dinner, so this struck me as very impressive and grown-up. Although I was invited, I was quite glad to have an excuse not to face such a family gathering just yet.

I wondered if it was just Michael, or whether having a child meant that you naturally got good at things like hosting family celebrations, and made a mental note to observe Laura and Dan closely to see if their near-legendary reliance on pizzas, Chinese and M&S ready meals would alter after their baby arrived.

26

In many novels and biographies, particularly American ones, you get a lot of colourful cross-cultural family history before you even catch a scent of the person you really want to hear something about. 'Momma's grandpappy, Theodore H. Drexl, arrived from Lithuania as a small boy with only the clothes he stood up in. By virtue of his sunny personality and juggling skills, he soon became a favourite with the Italian community of the Lower East Side.' And so on. Personally, I find that stuff boring and always flick through to where the person I'm really interested in is starting to do the stuff that made me interested in them in the first place.

However, Yorkshire families have tended to stay put for generations, so you don't get so much of that, although you do get exotic names like Shufflebottom and Crapwick. With my family, you get neither exotic ancestry, peculiar names nor colourful history. Both of my parents, and their parents before them and so on, were born and bred in York and the surrounding villages. You can see why I caused such a stir when I moved to London: my parents' friends and neighbours never tire of asking me suspiciously what it's like 'down there'. Which always sounds a bit gynaecological to me.

I made the journey north for Christmas by train, as I had almost every year since I left home at eighteen. When I was a student, finances forced me to travel by coach, and around Christmas time it was all quite jolly and festive, with a charabanc-to-the-seaside bonhomie and lots of northern, working-class cheer. The downside was that the journey took forever and it wasn't unknown for me to spend several hours in a broken-down bus by the roadside, knowing that my parents would be waiting for hours at the bus station (note for younger readers: this was in the days before everyone had a mobile phone permanently attached to the side of their head).

Trains, while quicker and a tad more reliable, are generally full of what my granny would have called 'miserable buggers'. Everyone seemed to be travelling 'home' for Christmas out of a sense of weary duty: goodwill to all men it certainly wasn't. This particular train was horribly crowded, with every seat full and people sitting on piles of luggage in the gangways. Luckily I'd reserved a seat, but I had to pile most of my luggage on the table in front of me. There was no leg room: the woman diagonally opposite me, who was strangely reminiscent of Po-faced Vo in a grey-perm-and-Shetland-wool sort of way, had put a cat basket under the table, from which a constant yowling emerged. She didn't seem to notice as she was too busy trying to engage other passengers in conversation. Trying not to make eye contact with her (I was in no mood for small talk, and you could tell just by looking at her that God was on the agenda at some point), I leant my forehead against the cold window and watched as King's Cross slid away into the background, followed by the landmarks I always looked out for – the art deco Arsenal football stadium on the right, the strangely squat Alexandra Palace perched on its hill on the left: cultural cathedrals that marked the leaving of the city that I'd lived in for most of my adult life but still didn't think of as home.

This time was different, though. If home is where the heart is, my home was now behind me, back in North London where Michael was. From his back garden you could see Alexandra Palace apparently floating on the rooftops at the end of the street, and as it disappeared from my view I already missed him so much. It was hard to believe I'd known him for less than two months and could probably just about count our time together in hours.

To divert myself from sad thoughts, I opened my bag and took out a parcel that had arrived that morning. It was book-shaped so I was particularly careful about removing the paper, not wanting to damage the contents. Turning it over, I read the title: *Frøken Smillas Fornemmelse for Sne*. There was a card inside the front cover.

Dear Anna,
I didn't want to write on the book, because you told me you don't like people writing on books. I know you have read *Miss Smilla's Feeling for Snow*, but I hope you will like to have it in the original Danish. Maybe I can teach you some Danish one day and you can read it for yourself.

Thank you again for all you have done for me. You were

very kind. You probably guessed I still heard nothing from my father, so maybe I'll forget this idea of meeting him for now – until he grows up, my mother says! But I would like to keep in contact with you, and of course you are always welcome to visit us in Denmark.

Good wishes for Christmas and the New Year, and please pass on my regards also to Michael and Lily.

Love, Peter.

I settled back in my seat, holding the book open in front of me, my eyes skimming unfocused across the exotic-looking words, thinking about my parents, and about Peter and Nic, Laura and Dan, Lily and Michael. My thoughts returned again and again to Michael.

The woman sitting opposite must have assumed from the book that I was a foreigner so, mercifully, I didn't have to speak to anyone till I got to York.

27

At the station I had to wrench out my bags by brute force over a clump of people sitting in the space next to the doorway on top of what seemed to be their entire household contents. I was hot, sweaty and irritable by the time I was on the platform, where I was instantly smacked by air so cold it felt as though I wasn't wearing anything. The city of York is built in the middle of a vast, flat plain, and seems to capture the coldest air streams passing from any direction and clutch them there in a damp mist.

My dad was standing at the end of the platform, dressed in a beige overcoat and a tartan scarf. Every time I saw him he seemed to be a little bit smaller, his moustache a little bit whiter, although that could well have been frost, if he'd been standing in that cold for very long. We hugged in the slightly awkward way that fathers and grown-up daughters do, exchanged greetings, then he insisted on taking the heaviest of my bags and led the way to the car.

As usual, it was one of the cleanest in the car park; my dad prides himself on maintaining it in 'tip-top' condition. He took a little tool out of the glove compartment and scraped at some frost that had settled on the windscreen. I didn't know anyone among my friends in London who had any special little tools for anything, but Mum and Dad had a gadget for everything. Maybe that was something else that happened when you underwent that mysterious process of becoming an adult. I was still waiting to find out.

When we got home, the house was ablaze with fairy lights, on the Christmas tree in the window, around the front door and decorating the now otherwise naked laburnum at the side of the house. My mum opened the front door as we were getting out of the car, and came out to greet us. Dad shooed her back in. 'You'll catch your death outside in those slippers, Margaret,' he chided her gently. We followed her inside. The kitchen was warm, and fragrant with the smell of roasting meat. Mario Lanza was booming out from the stereo as he had every Christmas Eve since I was small, and the whole thing was so cosy and familiar that I felt like a child again, waiting for Santa Claus.

When Mario started singing 'Joy To The World', with his luscious voice that seemed to owe more to natural exuberance than technique, it was too much. If I heard one bar more I would be in paroxysms of weeping. I had to be brutal or I would lose it.

'Can we kill Mario?' I said.

My mother pursed her lips. 'Mario has already passed away, Anna, as you well know,' she said. The late tenor had occupied a special place in my mother's heart for longer than my father had, and was not to be treated lightly.

'I meant, can we put him off, or I'm going to cry?' I said, wobbling a bit.

Mum tutted loudly, and clicked off the stereo. 'I don't know why you can't say that in the first place, instead of using your silly slang expressions,' she said.

'Why do you want to cry, anyway, love?' Dad asked. 'Is there anything wrong?'

I smiled a bit damply at him. 'No,' I said. 'It's just that song. It's the same as with you and "Mary's Boy Child".' He looked confused for a couple of seconds, then said,

'Ah, you mean "When A Child Is Born". You're getting the sublime confused with the ridiculous, Anna.'

'What on earth are you two going on about?' Mum said, clattering roasting tins in and out of the oven.

Lunch was every bit as lavish as most people would be sitting down to on Christmas Day itself, but I knew Mum was keeping her best work in reserve for the big day, although there would be only the three of us again. My parents filled me in on the hot item of local news: Mum's hairdresser had run off with a temporary barman from the village pub, an Australian with 'Antipodean charm in bucketloads'. The move was not entirely unexpected, as said hairdresser was known to be a 'flighty piece'. This was supported by less sensational stories about the car, next year's holiday plans (Jersey, apparently, which was classified as 'abroad'), the garden and, of course, the traditional run-through of the neighbours' children, most of whom were my ex-schoolfriends. I hadn't kept in touch with anyone from school, since we'd all gone our separate ways to university, and had lost contact fairly quickly. But Mum had them all mentally catalogued, even remembering to use the nicknames they'd had at school, which even I had forgotten long since.

'Do you remember Sneck?' she asked. I looked blank; she looked irritated. 'You must remember Sneck,' she insisted. 'Sharon Patterson.'

'Oh, yes. I can't remember why we called her Sneck, though,' I said.

'I'm not sure I'd want to know,' said Dad.

'Anyway,' Mum continued. 'Mrs Patterson, her mother – you remember, at the post office – she was telling me Sharon is expecting triplets in March. They live in Belgium, you know.'

'I thought they lived at the post office.'

'Not her parents. I meant Sharon and her husband. He's something to do with the European Parliament, doing very well for himself, Mrs Patterson says.'

'He'll need to be, with three bairns to support,' Dad observed. I had no comment to add to this, although the news of her fecundity was hardly surprising: the only thing I could remember about Sneck was that she was hardly ever seen without a lovebite. And now I remembered. Her nickname was short for 'Spam Neck', which had seemed hilarious when we were fourteen, particularly in its abbreviated form. We ate in silence for a couple of minutes, until I realised I had something of my own that Mum would find newsworthy.

'Laura is having a baby in June,' I said. Mum and Dad looked thrilled, considering they hadn't seen Laura for years.

'That's wonderful!' Mum said, and demanded the usual details: due date, names, gender preferences. 'I must send them a card.' My parents send cards for any reason under the sun. I'm convinced they have shares in Hallmark. 'You must tell me when she's had it. Don't forget, now.'

Dad helped himself to some more gravy. 'And what about you, young Anna?' he said, beaming at me over the gravy boat, as if Jimmy Stewart had joined the Oxo family. 'Any eligible young man on the horizon for you? We're getting on a bit to be still waiting for grandchildren, you know.' My customary annoyance at this question was now tempered with guilt: I hadn't spoken to my parents for so long that they didn't know about Michael.

'Ooh, look, there is somebody,' Mum said. 'She's gone all introspective.' I'd been wondering what Michael was doing at that very moment, and whether I should ring him today or leave it till tomorrow. 'I hope you're not back with that Nic,' Mum was saying. 'I didn't really like him, Anna. I can say it now you're finished with him. I always thought he was a bit full of himself.'

When I was going out with him she kept telling me how marvellous he was. She always does that.

'No, I'm not back with Nic,' I said. 'But I have met someone.' My parents were all attention; cutlery was laid down on plates, the better to concentrate. 'He's called Michael.'

'And what does he do?' Dad asked, always his first question.

'He works for the Inland Revenue. He's a tax inspector.'

This met with approval. 'It's a good steady job, is that,' Dad said. 'Where's he from?' This was always his second question.

'London.' This didn't go down as well, my parents harbouring a deep suspicion of anyone born further away than Harrogate. 'His parents live in Hampstead. His dad's an architect.' This swung Michael's approval-rating back up to the positive score that his southern upbringing had threatened.

'And you're fond of him?' Mum asked.

'I think I'm in love,' I said. 'In fact, I know I am, and I'm pretty certain he is too.'

'So can I start looking for a hat for the wedding?' Mum wanted to know, only half joking.

I said I didn't know about that yet, but she'd be the first to know. Now she'd mentioned it, the idea of marrying Michael was pretty appealing. Except for one thing. I smiled brightly, hoping to sound more positive than I felt. 'He has a daughter,' I said. 'Her name is Lily and . . .'

'Lilian?'

'No, Dad, Lily. As in water lily. She's nearly a year old. She lives with him.'

'Oh. Very nice.'

Mum started to clear the plates away, scraping the leftovers on to a saucer for the cat, clattering cutlery into the sink. Dad hurried to help, running hot water into the sink for the washing-up. They seemed to be trying to work out what their viewpoint was going to be, but had started talking between themselves about trivial subjects on which I was not expected to have an opinion.

There was no point in offering to help with the washing-up: I would only be met with 'Oh, no, love, you've had a long journey, you relax a bit.' The earliest I would be able to get away with helping was tomorrow tea-time.

I went into the front room and sat gazing at the Christmas tree lights. It didn't matter how old I got, or how cynical (and I'd been through some very cynical years in my teens and early twenties), a Christmas tree still looked magical, holding the promise and excitement of all the Christmases of my child-hood. I started thinking about Lily, and wondering if she was old enough to appreciate Christmas yet. I'd bought her a doll, a little Eskimo with a furry hat and clothes and big furry boots, which I'd wrapped and given to Michael to put under their tree. I was surprised to find I felt a little bit sad that I wouldn't be seeing her opening it.

Mum came into the room. 'So where's the baby's mother?' she asked, as if there hadn't been any break in the conversation. Dad joined us while I was telling her about Fiona.

'Well, I must say, I think young people these days take things a bit too lightly,' Dad said. 'Imagine a mother abandoning her child like that. It's not natural.'

'In our day there wouldn't have been any question of it,' said Mum. I didn't want to get into any debate with them about the politics of reproduction, so I didn't say anything. Mum said, 'Mind you, this Michael must be a decent sort of a chap to want to bring up a kiddie on his own.'

'But he'll not be bringing her up on his own for long, will he?' Dad said. 'He's going to have our Anna to help him. He knows which side his bread's buttered. Are you sure you want to be landed with another woman's child, love? It's a lot to take on.'

'Oh, Dad,' I said, 'it's not got that far yet. I've only known him a few weeks. All I know is he's the loveliest man I've ever met – apart from you, of course. We'll just have to wait and see what happens. But you'd love him if you met him, really.'

'That's what you said about that Nic,' Mum pointed out.

28

'Oh, my God, Michael! It's enormous. You should have told me! I'm going to be completely overwhelmed.'

'You'll be fine,' he said, patting my arm. 'Just relax. Try to enjoy yourself.'

'It's easy for you to say. You're used to it.' I got out of the car, and my feet scrunched into deep gravel. Michael was unbuckling Lily from her little seat in the back while I gazed around at what could only be described as the grounds of his parents' house. 'Garden' was too small a word. The house itself was icing-sugar white, Georgian in style with a portico around a front door the same deep, oily black as the door of number 10 Downing Street. The downstairs windows glowed warmly in the thickening gloom.

Michael had hoisted Lily on to his hip and locked the car. He took my hand. 'Really, don't worry, they're not frightening at all,' he said. 'Well . . . maybe my dad is a bit,' he conceded. As he spoke, the front door swung open and a woman rushed down the steps towards us. She was slim and several inches smaller than me, with a shiny cap of beautifully cut blonde hair; her movements were light and she seemed to skip rather than walk. Michael had told me that she had been a dance teacher until she gave up to look after Lily and pursue what seemed to be a hectic social life. She hugged Michael and plucked Lily from his arms in one movement. Lily was delighted and chattering loudly in baby language, waving her arms happily.

'Mum, this is Anna,' Michael said.

She turned to me, with a smile that was so much like Michael's I couldn't help grinning back. 'It's lovely to meet you at last, Anna,' she said. 'Michael has talked about very little but you for weeks.' She reached up and pinched his cheek and he squirmed like he must have done when he was a boy. 'You must call me Jean,' she went on. 'Anyway, Lilykins, let's get you inside where it's warm.' She led the way into the house.

The hallway on its own was the size of my whole flat (okay, I'm exaggerating a bit), with chequered tiles leading to a staircase at the far end. Jean went through a half-open door on the left, into what could probably be described as a drawing room.

The room was full of things: plants, cushions, ornamental whatnots and books piled upon every horizontal surface. The walls were encrusted with framed paintings and prints. My mum would have thrown up her hands at the thought of all the dusting it would entail, but the effect was cosy and comfortable. Michael's father was sitting in a huge leather armchair in the middle of a pile of newspapers. Jean had put Lily down on the floor, and she showed off her recently acquired walking skills by tottering towards her grandfather, who gathered her up in his arms as he stood up to greet us.

'You must be Anna,' he said, shaking my hand. Michael was right – he was a bit frightening, nothing like my sweet old dad. The word 'formidable' came to mind: he was very tall, athletically built, like a rugby player, solid and somewhat stern. Jean left the room to make some tea, closely pursued by Lily, who seemed attached to her granny.

'Could you give me a hand, darling?' Jean called. Both Michael and his father seemed to realise that this was directed at her son rather than her husband, so Michael got up and followed his daughter out of the room, I was left with his father. It was a bit like being in the headmaster's study.

'Michael tells us you work for some sort of employment

agency,' he said. I told him about my job at Caring Concern. 'And what about the future? Any plans to move on?' he enquired.

I thought about this for a minute. 'Well, I'm quite happy there. The work is interesting, and I like the people I work with. It pays the bills,' I added lamely.

To my surprise, he looked pleased. 'So you wouldn't really describe yourself as a "career woman" then,' he said, more a statement than a question. And a statement most people had stopped making about women at least a decade ago. I didn't know how to reply, but evidently a reply wasn't needed and he carried on regardless. 'That was Michael's problem the last time,' he said. 'It was obvious that that girl wasn't the sort to settle down to family life. Obvious to everybody except my son, that is. He tried his damnedest to persuade her, but parenthood's either in your nature or it isn't, I reckon. And it obviously wasn't in hers. Ambitious sort of girl. We found her a bit cold, to be honest. But, on the other hand, I can't say I blame her. I remember what a bloody shock it was to us when Michael was born: one minute we were newlyweds, still getting used to the idea of being man and wife, and then, bingo, there's this little demanding bundle,' I couldn't help smiling at the thought of Michael as a little bundle, but he didn't seem to notice, 'and nothing's ever the same again. And we were married, we planned to have kids, admittedly not quite so soon, but there you go.

'To me, it's a sensible woman, or man, who can admit upfront they don't want kids. Even though it broke Michael's heart at the time, I had to admire Fiona for the way she stuck to what she wanted.' He nodded slowly. 'When Michael told us about the baby, I don't mind admitting now I was furious. Of course, his mother was all for it, but I always hoped he would change his mind about being an architect. He certainly had the talent and the brains for it.'

He paused in this monologue, and looked at me hard. 'Never

underestimate what my son will do for that child,' he said. 'She means the world to him. She will always come first.'

Again, I didn't know what to say. The phrase 'It broke Michael's heart' stuck in my head: I'd thought that New York was far enough away for this Fiona to be, but sometimes I wished her right off the face of the planet. It was the first time I'd ever felt like this about the ex-girlfriend of someone I was going out with: Nic had had quite a history before me, but I never felt remotely threatened by it. In large part that might have been because I never felt for Nic what I felt for Michael, and there had been a lot less to lose, but there was more to it than that. Fiona was always going to have that direct link to Michael via their daughter, and Lily would always be there as a reminder of her mother.

A spatter of little footsteps, a crash and her trademark piercing shriek heralded Lily's reappearance. Michael was close behind her, scooping her up, rocking her, calming her, until about thirty seconds later she'd stopped crying and was wriggling to be free. He set her down and she tottered back out of the room again in search of her granny.

'It's okay, darling, I've got her,' Jean called, from a distant room. Michael shifted some newspapers and sat down next to me on the sofa opposite his father. They started talking about something that was going on in the news, and I tuned out.

I was relieved when Jean and Lily came back, and the atmosphere lightened. Jean and Michael were obviously close, and their conversation was filled with a lot of teasing and jokes. His father's mood also lifted, but several times I caught him looking at me. I felt as if I'd undergone a test, but had no idea whether I'd passed or failed.

Lily was in her element with four of her favoured adults to show off to, and she had a whole different set of toys at her grandparents' house, which were soon strewn across the floor.

'Sometimes I look at her and think she's so sweet that it's almost a shame she ever has to change,' Michael observed.

His mother smiled. 'I remember you saying that when she was two days old,' she said, 'and now look at her. She did change, but I bet you love her more.' Michael had to agree that he did. 'And you'll keep on loving her more,' his mother said. 'I know I do with you.' Michael looked embarrassed, as he had outside when Jean pinched his cheek.

'What used to freak me out most,' he said, 'was the thought that it was up to me to teach Lily everything about everything. I looked at her lying in her cot, and I realised she didn't know anything about English, or sums, or the weather, or sheep and cows, or blowing her nose, never mind right and wrong and having good table manners. It felt like such a huge responsibility to have to teach someone all that from scratch.'

'But they have such a capacity to learn built in,' his father observed. 'They just pick things up the whole time from whatever's going on around them. It's incredible just watching the process.'

I had little to contribute to this conversation, and it was all I could do to stop myself yawning. It was little comfort to know that, in a few short months, Laura and Dan would be finding these topics equally riveting. There would be no escape from baby talk then.

29

Soon after the milestone of Meeting the Parents, there was another test to be faced. If the relationship with Michael was going to go anywhere, then it was obvious I was going to have to do some serious bonding with Lily.

With Lily it was the communication I found most difficult. At a year old, she could say the odd word (mainly animal noises: 'Ssss' for snake and a sound like 'Ap!' to signify a dog barking) but nothing that made much sense. She still communicated her needs mainly by crying. Michael seemed able to tell from the context of the cry roughly what was going on, but it left me flummoxed.

It was with some trepidation that I offered to take her shopping with me one Saturday so that Michael could play squash with a friend from work who was always asking him. 'That's a great idea,' he said – doubtfully, I thought. 'But are you sure you can manage?'

'Of course I am,' I said breezily. 'We'll have fun.'

I couldn't contemplate trying buses or taxis with the buggy, which left all the retail delights of Crouch End at our disposal. Lily sat impassively, looking cute in a lilac fleece hat with earflaps. I actually felt quite proud pushing her along, and enjoyed the admiring glances she was getting from passers-by.

One of the things I needed to buy was a birthday present for Dan. I remembered seeing an interesting looking shop near the clock tower, so I headed for that but no sooner had we got inside than Lily started to whinge. I tried shoving a dummy in her mouth. She spat it out and the whingeing got louder. She flapped her arms pitifully and shrieked. Eventually I realised she'd spotted a puppet, a dog-like creature held together with nylon wire, which she'd obviously decided was just the thing her already overflowing toybox needed.

'No, I don't think you need that,' I said confidently. 'It looks a bit come-apartable for babies.' At this she produced her top-volume scream. The other shoppers, trendy well-dressed twentysomethings, looked appalled. Recognising that look as one my own face had worn on innumerable occasions, I hit on retreat as the best course of action, and attempted to reverse out. In doing so I bumped into several people and a display of pottery which swayed threateningly before righting itself.

Out on the pavement again, Lily's crying magically stopped. She even started chattering happily in that Martian way she had. I decided to ride my luck, and crossed the road to the bookshop.

If you spend any amount of time in London you quickly become adept at dashing across roads through the merest sliver of a gap in the traffic. With a small child it was a different story. I hovered and wavered on the pavement as the cars tore by, never finding a gap big enough to risk my precious cargo. Haunted by visions of having to break the news to Michael that I'd caused his beloved child to be mashed, I retreated meekly to a crossing three hundred yards away.

It was fairly difficult manoeuvring the buggy into the bookshop, but I found that looking helpless (not difficult) brought someone to hold the door for me. Once inside, I took a deep, calming breath of that wonderful smell of new books, and prepared for a good browse. Three point five seconds later, Lily started crying again. I decided to take her out of the buggy and carry her for a while – this always worked beautifully for Michael. Unfastening the various buckles and straps with only moderate difficulty, I lifted her up. Unfortunately I'd forgotten that my bag was hanging on the handles at the back, and the sudden redistribution of weight made the buggy tip over backwards with a crash. This time the shelf it hit fell over, and three dozen slim volumes by local poets went slipping across the floor. Several people rushed over to help, one of them displaying as much ignorance of buggy engineering as I had by trying to stand the buggy upright with the bag still attached to the handles. It immediately fell backwards again, almost braining the person who was scooping up the slim volumes, and knocking off his glasses.

In the middle of all this, Lily was looking on with interest. In fact, she had a somewhat fixed and concentrated expression.

'Sorry,' I said to the man who was scrabbling for his glasses, and grabbed my bag off the buggy which was up on its wheels for another go. Order was restored but Lily's linguistic development was about to take a major step forward.

'Poo!' she shouted, sounding pleased. 'Poo! Poo! Poo!' And I realised, belatedly, that there was a familiar stink about the place.

I gave up on shopping – I could always pick up something for Dan on my way to work.

30

Laura had a book called *Nine Magical Months for Mandy*. It dealt month by month, in stomach-turning detail, with every aspect of pregnancy and birth. A quick glance through it convinced me that the NHS should distribute it to every woman of childbearing age: it was the most powerful contraceptive I could imagine.

The disgusting things that happened to poor Mandy! Not least of which was her repellent husband, John. It was a crime against humanity to let John procreate at all, never mind have the process photographed and turned into a manual for expectant mothers. Mandy had probably needed a general anaesthetic for conception to take place. I can't imagine that she would have gone through it willingly if she'd had to stare up at those cavernous nostrils during the 'act'. Though it was likely that Mandy was several sandwiches short of a picnic anyway, as no one in their right mind could suffer the hideous indignities she experienced at the hands of the medical profession and keep smiling and producing chirpy, positive comments invariably followed by chirpy exclamation marks. Even worse, John seemed to feel the need to be a supportive presence, and thus his repulsive visage appeared in almost every photograph, looming over Mandy's ever-swelling abdomen like a particularly ugly moon rising over Jupiter.

Laura was now sixteen weeks pregnant. The sixteen-weeks' pregnant Mandy was reporting entering the 'blooming' stage.

Apparently her complexion and hair were more lustrous and beautiful than at any time in her life; she felt full of energy and wellbeing, and had stopped puking her breakfast up (or 'No more morning sickness; thank goodness!' as she put it herself in her characteristically brisk style).

Laura, too, was managing to keep her cornflakes down, and most days was following them with a full English breakfast followed by a full continental breakfast, followed by brunch, then lunch . . . I believe it's known as eating for two.

'It feels as if the baby's in there demanding food constantly,' she grumbled. 'It's not like normal, when you think, Ooh, I feel a bit peckish. It's like, give me food NOW! And meat, it's got to be meat. I don't usually eat bacon, but I can't get as far as the bus stop these days without having to duck into the greasy spoon for a bacon sarnie. I've just got this mental picture of the baby sort of crouching in there with rows of teeth, spitting out bones.'

'Oh, yuk. It's not a baby, it's Henry the Eighth.'

'Anyway,' she went on, 'Mandy says it's time I got fitted up for a support bra.'

'Is it?'

'Well, I should say so. The upside of all this pregnancy business is I've got hooters like you wouldn't believe.'

'Well, that's a compensation.'

'Dan would be in seventh heaven if only I wasn't so knackered all the time. Plus they get all hypersensitive – sometimes I scream if he so much as glances at them. But I'll tell you another interesting thing. I haven't had to shave my legs once since I got pregnant. Hormones are mysterious things indeed.' There you go, then, girls: one good reason for getting knocked up is you can throw away your Ladyshave.

Laura insisted that I accompany her for her bra fitting. Say the words 'bra' and 'fitting' and my instinctive response would be 'John Lewis' or 'Marks & Spencer',' but Laura felt that only a specialist would do.

'What about Rigby and Peller, then?' I said. 'They do the Queen. You can't get much more specialised than that.'

'I meant a baby specialist,' Laura said. 'Mothercare.'

Mothercare? I had never been in one of their shops in my life: I had had no need to. But, like a dutiful friend and in a spirit of adventure, I accompanied Laura to Mothercare to obtain what she described as a 'support bra' (I thought that all bras were for support, but maybe I'm missing something).

God, that place is weird. For a start, they have nursery rhymes and children's songs playing constantly, at something louder than background volume, and you can call me cynical if you like but the only time you hear music like that in the normal world is as the soundtrack to a movie where either (a) the spawn of the devil is poised to wreak childlike havoc on its unsuspecting human parents or (b) someone's beloved child is about to come a cropper under the wheels of a large recreational vehicle.

'I feel completely bogus in here,' Laura said, eyeing two hugely pregnant women, who were pondering something described on the box as a 'breast pump'. I tried not to think about it. 'I just don't feel pregnant enough.'

'There aren't degrees of pregnancy,' I pointed out. 'There's either up the duff or not up the duff. And you most certainly fall into the former category.'

'I suppose . . . But I just don't look very pregnant.'

'So, are you worried people will think you're buying this just for kicks?' I asked. I held up a heavily reinforced cotton and elastic job that looked like an exhibit from a foundation garments museum.

Laura looked suitably horrified. 'What's that?' she said. I looked at the label.

'"Support bra" it says. "Thirty-four B."'

'Bloody hell. Only Thirty-four B? It looks . . . industrial.' She pondered the other available choices. Things got even more heavy-duty on the row marked 'nursing bras'.

'Don't you want to try somewhere else?' I suggested queasily. 'See if you can get something a bit silky, with underwiring?'

Laura shook her head firmly. 'Can't have underwiring. I can't remember why exactly, but Mandy was quite insistent. No,' she said, 'I reckon it's time to bite the bullet and find a woman with a tape measure.'

She marched off purposefully to find an assistant, and disappeared with her into a cubicle. I wandered around trying to find something interesting to look at, but the specialised nature of the goods on offer failed to excite my finely tuned shopping instincts. I overheard an assistant asking someone if she wanted to keep the hangers from the tiny garments she was buying. The hangers were minute, and I wondered if Lilliputian wardrobes were available to accommodate them.

The other customers generally had small, unpleasant children in tow, and there was a constant traffic to and from the nappy-changing room. I thought about the first time I'd seen Michael, hovering outside the women's toilets with a smelly, screaming Lily, and smiled.

Laura showed no sign of emerging from her cubicle so I amused myself watching a woman trying to prise a child off a Postman Pat ride; the child clung on screaming like murder, the ends of its fingers bloodless but unyielding. One of the assistants, who was reorganising something on the shelf beside me, nodded in the direction of this spectacle. 'We get some proper little horrors in here,' she said, 'but don't worry – I'm sure yours will be a little angel.' She breezed off, leaving me horrified that I'd been mistaken for a mother-to-be. I hastily rearranged my posture, pulled in my stomach muscles and resolved to spend the entire first half of *Coronation Street* doing sit-ups.

I was relieved when Laura reappeared, looking very self-satisfied.

'Thirty-six D!' she shrieked. '*D*! I'm turning into Pamela Anderson! I can't wait to tell Dan.'

31

Michael, as I think I may have hinted, had many wonderful qualities. He was kind, considerate, charming, tolerant, sexy, optimistic, practical . . . The adjectives could go on and on, and frequently they did.

But an unexpectedly wonderful thing, which I discovered only after I'd known him for two months, was that, like me, he loved the films of Danny Kaye. Previously this had been a lonely obsession of mine, pursued on solitary Sunday afternoons in front of the television with only a bar of chocolate for company. Even my dad was mystified by this – he's more of a Bob Hope man. To me, Danny Kaye is one of the greatest entertainers in the history of cinema (okay, I'm getting a bit over-excited now), but I had never met anyone who shares my enthusiasm, let alone anyone who can recite the 'vessel with the pestle' routine from *The Court Jester*, though a quick Internet search one dull afternoon at work proved that such people do exist. Imagine my utter joy when Michael rang me one evening to ask if I fancied going to see a double bill of *The Court Jester* and *The Secret Life of Walter Mitty* at the NFT. If I hadn't already fallen in love with him I would certainly have done so at that moment.

The National Film Theatre is part of that sprawling, wind-blasted concrete confusion on the South Bank of the Thames that most people can't stand. Perversely, I've always quite liked it, because however unlovely the buildings are on the outside, they're fantastic within. The Olivier Theatre has the comfiest seats and best sightlines of any theatre I've been to, and the Royal Festival Hall does excellent snacks.

But I have to admit that, as a decorative item, the South Bank is . . . Well, the only word for it is grey. However, almost anything can look beautiful when it has a river beside it, and the South Bank is one of the few places apart from the Members' Terrace at the House of Commons where London makes the most of its river. There are cafés with long tables overlooking the water, rows of stalls selling secondhand books; there are buskers and skateboarders, and a stunning view in every direction.

We came out of the NFT feeling warm and happy from the sweet, innocent humour of Danny Kaye and from the gorgeous sexual tension of sitting in the dark for almost four hours just holding hands. The afternoon had almost gone, the winter twilight bringing a biting wind pitching icy drizzle into our faces; not the kind of weather to hang around in.

'I thought you'd want to stop and look at the books,' Michael said, pointing across at the ranks of tables covered in second-hand books.

'Michael Taylor!' I said in mock-horror. 'Me look at secondhand books? Books that have been thumbed through, and sneezed on, had coffee cups rested on them, and their spines broken? You might as well ask me to join a library.'

'You're weird, you are,' he said. He wrapped both arms around me and kissed me. 'I suppose that's why I love you.'

'You do?'

'I definitely do.'

He definitely did; he loved me. I gave him the kiss he so richly deserved.

'The thing is,' I said, smiling up at him, the person who'd just said he loved me – hurrah!, 'that if I say "I love you, too," it'll just sound like I'm saying it because you've said it first.'

'And would you be?'

'No! I'd be saying it because I love you.'

'Only now you can't say it?'

'No.'

'But you just did say it.'

'Did I?'

'Like I just told you,' he said, 'you're weird. And I love you. And I'm going to take it that you love me, otherwise it's all getting too complicated. Is that okay?'

'That's perfect,' I said, and we walked along with all that grey concrete on our left and the grey-green river on our right, and somewhere a busker was playing a penny whistle and I didn't think life could ever be so lovely again.

We decided to cross the bridge and find somewhere to eat in Covent Garden: Michael's parents had Lily overnight, so we were looking forward to a rare night on our own and planned to make the most of it.

Michael paused to give some change to a young man who was begging on the steps of the bridge. He found it almost impossible to refuse anyone who asked him for money; not your standard tax inspector at all. As he turned back towards me, he collided with another man, who was rushing past him, going in the same direction as we were. The man paused to apologise, and then glanced at me. All the blood drained from his already gaunt face. 'Ah . . . Hi, Anna,' Nic said.

He seemed about to continue on his way, and I almost let him because I was lost for words, but as he turned away I shouted, 'Wait!' in a commanding voice that made me think maybe I should have been a schoolteacher. He stopped and turned back. Understandably, Michael was looking a little confused, so I said, 'Michael, this is Nic – you've met his son.'

Nic looked like a rabbit caught in headlights. 'I'm sorry,' he said, after a moment, 'I'm in a real hurry. I'll call you, Anna, okay? Nice to meet you, Mike.' He rushed off.

'Nic!' I shouted uselessly, as he disappeared into the people scurrying across the bridge.

Michael was laughing. 'So that was the famous Nic,' he said, as the rapidly retreating figure disappeared into the gloom. 'He didn't expect to see you, obviously.'

'He's such a bastard,' I said. 'I could kill him for how he's treated Peter. I want to run after him and just chuck him over the side of this bridge.'

'Okay, go on, then,' Michael said.

'What?'

'Well, I hate being called "Mike". He deserves to die.'

'Too right. He deserves the chalice from the palace.'

'The chalice from the palace got broken, remember.'

'So where did the pellet with the poison end up?'

'In the flagon with the dragon, I think.'

'The flagon with the dragon, then,' I said. 'And let's hope the poison is a particularly painful and slow-acting one.'

32

The amazing thing was, Nic *did* call me, the very next day.

Michael and I had spent a heavenly morning in bed, having breakfast, conversation, sex, at one point all three simultaneously.

Later we'd gone to his parents' for lunch. His father was less frightening this time, and didn't refer again to my career ambitions – or lack of them. His mother was as delightful as before, and even Lily seemed quite pleased to see me. She was even attempting to say my name. 'Na', anyway; although she also said that when she meant 'banana'.

When I got home late that evening, Nic had left a message on the answering-machine, but while I was replaying it the phone rang again and it was him. 'I guess you're a bit pissed off with me,' was his opening gambit.

'"Pissed off" comes nowhere close,' I said. 'I don't even know where to start with what I think of you.' I was so mad at him I was gripping the telephone receiver as tightly as if it was his throat. If he'd been in the room, I'd have kicked him.

'Peter turned up, then?' he asked meekly.

'Oh, for heaven's sake, Nic, of course he turned up! Not everyone in the world is as spineless and self-absorbed as you are! He said he was coming and he came. You said you were going to meet him at the airport, and you pissed off. And then disappeared for weeks. Can you even begin to imagine how that made him feel? Never mind me! I was just the mug who got landed with sorting out your mess, as usual.' There was a long pause, during which I could hear the clicking of Nic's ancient and unreliable Zippo lighter.

'I don't know what to say,' he said. 'I panicked, that's all.'

'And you stayed panicked for the whole week? And ever since?'

'I'm just not parent material, Anna. He's better off not knowing me.'

Ain't that the truth, I thought to myself, but said, 'That's not how he sees it. Just for once in your life, couldn't you try to put yourself in someone else's shoes?' Another pause, during which I hoped this was sinking in.

'What's he like, then?' he asked.

'He's great,' I said, and told him that Peter was lucky that nurture had won out so splendidly against nature and that he'd been fortunate enough to inherit his father's looks but not his personality. Of course, I couldn't resist telling him about his former lover's current partner.

'Karen's a lesbian?' he said. 'Wow. Freaky.' A pause. 'Do you think he'll ever forgive me?'

'It's up to you,' I said. 'You have his address.'

'Yeah, okay.' Another pause. 'So . . . who's this Mike guy, then?'

'His name is Michael,' I said. 'And he's my . . . We're together.'

'How long have you been seeing him?'

'That's none of your business, Nic. So, are you going to contact Peter?'

'I don't know.' He sighed. 'I haven't made it any easier for myself, have I? It's embarrassing.'

'Embarrassing? What kind of an excuse is that?'

'Jesus, Anna, I didn't call you just to be given a hard time. I'm not very good at heavy emotional stuff,' he said. And then added, 'But tell me more about Mike.'

I gave up.

33

By May, Laura was enormous. Every day when she came to work I was amazed at her sheer bulk, as if my memory reset itself to the old template of Laura as soon as she was out of sight. She had always been fairly slim, but now evidence of her pregnancy was obvious all over her body, not just her huge belly: her ankles were swollen, her face was puffy, and she looked (I'm about to sound a bit harsh) quite literally gross.

When they'd gone for a routine scan, Dan and Laura had both been pretty sure they'd seen a little penis bobbing around in the grey blur. The person doing the scan (are they called 'scanners'? Or is that just a film where people's heads explode?) had refused to be definite about anything – they're always so worried they'll get sued for one reason or another – but said she was 'eighty-five per cent certain' it was a boy.

'Obviously takes after his dad,' Dan was boasting in the pub that night, and showing the picture to anyone who would look. 'I mean, it's a bit blurred there, but you could see it quite clearly on the screen, couldn't you, love?' He looked at Laura for confirmation. She nodded, and shifted her weight to the other buttock.

'I'm fucking fed up of this,' she confided to me, while Dan was still eulogising his child's manhood to anyone who would listen. 'I just want it out! I can't sleep, I can't walk more than twenty yards, I can't go more than an hour without needing to piss. Honestly, you were right, Anna. This is mad. Never, ever get pregnant. Have you ever heard of Braxton Hicks contractions?' I looked blank. 'No, of course you haven't. It's just another of the horrors they don't tell you about until you're already too far gone to change your mind. Braxton Hicks contractions are like your womb limbering up for the Big Push. I lie in bed at night, and suddenly my belly goes tight, like those things they put on your arm when they do your blood pressure.'

'I haven't had my blood pressure done for years,' I said. She gave me a look. 'I know what you mean, though,' I added quickly. 'I watch *Casualty*.'

'I have my blood pressure done about every five fucking minutes,' she grumbled. 'Anyway, there I am, lying in bed with this belly you could bounce coins off, then it sort of subsides, and I'm just dropping off to sleep when the little horror starts kicking me in the liver or somewhere. It's bloody painful, wherever it is. Dan's going, 'Ooh, isn't it a miracle?' and I'm thinking, Yeah, right. It's a miracle that human skin can stretch that tight. I keep expecting a little arm or leg to come busting through. I've got stretch marks that look like purple flames from my pubic hair nearly up to my tits, and down my thighs as well. I'm never going to be the same again. My bikini days are gone forever.' She took a swig of her Guinness, which her midwife had said was not only allowed but positively to be encouraged – in moderation – because of the iron.

'You're looking forward to having the baby, though, aren't you?' I said cheerfully.

She gave me a withering look. 'There's the fucking birth before that!' she said.

'You're swearing a lot these days.'

'You'd bloody swear! They say it's the worst pain of any, worse than being tortured. They've tested people with agonyometers or something. Electrodes attached to the testicles

125

apparently doesn't even come close to the horror of childbirth. Which is a shame, because that's what I'd dearly love to do to Dan for getting me into this shit in the first place.'

Half a pint of iron-rich Guinness later she got even more cheerful. 'Dan gets really cross with me for this, but I can't help thinking about all the things that could go wrong. We can more or less rule out spina bifida, they would have seen that on the scan, but it could still have Down's syndrome. The first thing I'm going to do is look at the palm of its hand. Apparently they only have one little crease across the palm if they've got Down's instead of the usual heart line and life line and all that palmistry crap. Or it might have cerebral palsy! Or a harelip!'

'All those things are very rare,' I said, not entirely sure what a harelip was. 'You should try not to worry.'

'I honestly don't think I ever will stop worrying. Even once it's born there's cot death, and meningitis, and sex perverts roaming the streets. My mum says she worried even more about me when I was arranging my first mortgage than when I was a baby. She says it never, ever stops.'

'She can't be that worried,' I pointed out. 'She manages to live thousands of miles away in Canada and only sees you once every two years.'

'She still worries, though,' Laura said doggedly.

34

The Saintly Clare had decided to throw 'a bit of a party' to celebrate Laura starting her maternity leave. She had decided it would be 'jolly' if we invited 'the boys', i.e., our partners.

'Would it be all right if I bring someone?' Po-faced Vo asked. Laura and I stared at her: this was unprecedented. After Clare had retreated to her office to whip up some catering, we demanded details from the woman we'd always thought of as existing in a social vacuum. 'His name's Dennis,' she confided, a faint blush spreading under her slightly spotty, makeup-free skin. 'I met him at church.' Of course she did.

'And?' Laura wanted to know.

'And he's very nice. He's a divorcé, but I'm not worried about that. No children, though, which is a bit of a shame.'

'Is it serious, then?' I said.

'He generally comes round for a bit of lunch on a Sunday,' she said, blushing again, ever so slightly, and turning to her switchboard to indicate that the conversation was over.

Lunch? And the rest, Laura and I both thought.

Ugh.

It was an odd but not unamusing assembly. Laura and Dan, of course; Clare and the small, rounded mass that was Tubby; Michael, Lily and me, and Veronica. Dennis hadn't appeared, and Laura and I were taking bets that he was going to turn out to be fictional after all. Veronica was looking tense.

Predictably, most of the attention was focused on Lily. Michael had brought her at Laura's insistence, and she was thoroughly enjoying herself. She had changed a lot since Christmas; she could now walk without falling over so much, and was beginning to say a few words (mainly 'Daddy', the only word she could articulate perfectly).

'It seems funny being here again,' Michael said to me, while his daughter held court over the others. 'I remember sitting at that desk and looking at you, and thinking how beautiful you were.'

'I was thinking exactly the same about you,' I admitted.

'Were you really? You never told me that before.' He looked pleased. I was enjoying this spot of romantic reminiscing, but Clare was determinedly circulating and it was our turn.

'How is life at the Inland Revenue?' she asked Michael heartily. He gave his standard reply. 'Well, I must say, I think it's marvellous that you two got together,' she said. 'I certainly didn't expect that to happen when I heard they were sending someone to go over my books.' She beamed brightly at Michael in her best hockey captain manner. 'And your daughter is charming. She's a complete credit to you.' Michael thanked her, and the conversation went off on to the endlessly fascinating subject of Lily, as it was wont to do.

Then the phone rang. Apparently and incredibly, it was the not-so-mythical Dennis, to say he was running late but would be with us in five minutes.

Exactly five minutes later the entryphone buzzer sounded, and Veronica pranced off, her greying perm bobbing joyfully around the shoulders of her sensible blouse. She reappeared with a fireman.

Laura and I gawped, and even Clare looked as if her HRT was kicking in, big-time. The men in the room didn't seem to notice the effect that a uniformed fire-fighter had on grown women.

'This is Dennis,' Veronica said proudly, introducing us all to him. He wiped the back of his hand across his forehead and apologised for being late and arriving in such a mess. It seemed he had just come from what he thrillingly called 'a shout'. He bore a faint whiff of smoke.

'I don't believe this,' Laura muttered in my ear. 'You realise the shock could send me into labour?'

35

It was strange not seeing Laura at work every day. Clare had had no problem finding someone to cover her maternity leave – we were an employment agency, after all. The new bloke, Colin, had worked for Caring Concern for some time, mainly covering emergency calls at weekends, so I knew who he was but didn't know him well. Although he turned out to be good at his (Laura's) job and was rather sweet, he just wasn't and never could be Laura. In fact, the only thing they had in common was that they both had partners called Dan.

'I'm that pigged off,' he said to me one morning. 'You'll never guess what Daniel's done now?' I couldn't, but it had outraged poor Colin. 'He's only gone and put me on a diet!' Admittedly Colin was on the rotund side, but which of us isn't? I clucked sympathetically. 'We've got a fortnight booked in Puerto del Fandango, or similar anyway, I'm useless at names, and he says he'll die if he has to look at me in swimming trunks all day.' I suggested that, since they lived together, this was surely a sight to which he was accustomed. Colin nodded furiously. 'You'd think so, wouldn't you? And that's exactly what I said to him. But apparently what's fine in private is just plain embarrassing when there's a beach full of young lovelies for comparison.'

'But that's terrible,' I said. 'I wouldn't stand for that. He should love you for yourself, not for your six-pack.'

'Or lack of. But that's queers for you. Very superficial.'

36

One morning, I was dialling Laura's number as Colin left the office to go to a meeting. I was desperate to talk to her. It rang for ages, and I was waiting disappointedly for the answering-machine to switch on with it's none-too-friendly 'If you want Laura or Dan – tough. We're not answering!' message, but then the receiver clicked and a bleary-sounding Laura mumbled, 'Uh?'

'It's me!' I said.

'Oh, hi, Anna. I was asleep.' She yawned. 'That's all I have the energy to do these days. Except at five a.m when I could be awake for bloody England. Can't get back to sleep till Richard and sodding Judy. This woman at Antenatal reckons the baby'll be born at five a.m. It's obviously when he's liveliest. He's practising by kicking me awake, little bastard. God, I'm going to have to stop swearing before too long: he'll be repeating it all at school, and the next thing I know I'll have Social Services on the doorstep.'

I had even less tolerance for baby talk than usual. There were more important things to discuss. 'Michael has asked me to marry him,' I said, and held the receiver a couple of inches away from my head while Laura shrieked in a congratulatory manner. She then wanted to know if he'd done the proper, down-on-one-knee thing. This was a bit of a sore point with Laura – Dan had proposed to her by e-mail, which had left her feeling a bit cheated. She was mollified to hear that knees hadn't featured as we'd been in bed at the time.

It had been romantic, though. We were lying together, you know, fairly sweaty and breathless, and Michael nuzzled his face into my neck and sort of murmured, 'Let's get married,' in a voice so low, husky and post-coital that I had to ask him what he'd said, just so I could be sure. He repeated it.

'Wow,' I said, stunned. 'I'm stunned. That came out of the blue!'

'I know,' he agreed, laughing. 'I didn't know I was going to say it till I said it, but now I have I'm glad I did. I meant it. Will you marry me?'

I put my head on his chest, inhaling his clean-but-freshly-exerted smell. 'I'll have to think about it,' I said. 'It's such a new idea.'

'Okay,' he said, sleepily. 'You think about it and tell me when you're ready.' He was falling asleep. 'Lily would love it,' he said, and pretty soon his chest was rising and falling steadily as he slept. I, on the other hand, couldn't sleep for hours.

'So have you said yes?' Laura wanted to know.

'No,' I said.

'You said no? Are you crazy?'

'I didn't say no. I just didn't say yes.'

'Well, why the hell not? You're mad about the bloke, he's mad about you, he's absolutely gorgeous—'

'It's Lily,' I said. 'I just don't know if I'm ready to be somebody's stepmother. I didn't say that to him, of course. That's the one thing he wouldn't understand. He's such a natural parent, it's unbelievable to him that anyone else could have a problem with it.'

'But she's a lovely little girl,' Laura said.

I sighed. 'I know. Everybody says she is, and sometimes I even think so myself. She's really cute and funny and stuff, but I only see her once or twice a week, and even then, most of the time I can't help resenting the way Michael has to work his life around her – babysitters, bedtimes, mealtimes. Sometimes I just want to be able to be spontaneous – you know, go away for a weekend, or go out somewhere on a whim, or even just to have a morning shag sometimes. We'd have to start at about five a.m. to fit it in before Lily's awake and wanting her breakfast.'

'Well, that's something for me to think about the next time Travis/Stanley kicks me awake at the crack of dawn,' Laura laughed.

'And when he asked me to marry him, part of me was really happy, but at the same time it was like I could see my misspent youth flashing before my eyes – that holiday in Portugal with Trout Man when we ended up sleeping on the beach because we'd run out of money, clubbing till six a.m. and getting home with the milk. I wouldn't be able to do any of that if I was having to be all couply and responsible.'

'But you're too old for that kind of thing anyway,' Laura pointed out, somewhat cruelly, I thought.

'God, that's too depressing even to think about,' I said. 'But honestly, Laura, do you think I sound selfish?'

'Yes, I do,' she said. 'But I know what you mean about Lily, and I'm sure I'm going to feel some of it myself in a month or so when Junior is born. But that'll be different because he'll be mine. And Lily isn't yours, and you don't really like kids.'

'You have such a gift for summing things up.'

'Thank you,' she said. 'Do you know? Dan was telling me just the other day he'd read that step-parents are much more likely to kill their step-kids than natural parents their own children. It's all to do with genetics. Pushing the cuckoo out of the nest.'

This was depressing. Even worse, Laura had reached the same conclusion I had.

'You're going to have to tell Michael exactly how you feel,' she said.

37

How did I feel?

Number one: mad about the boy. I loved every inch of Michael, everything about him. I couldn't imagine life without him.

Number two: marriage? No problem. I've always thought if I met a person I felt right with, that marriage would definitely be a Good Thing. The thought of a wedding made me balk a bit – all hats and stress. But marriage itself was a lovely, cosy idea. Eek! My Saturn had well and truly returned!

Number three: children. Babies, kids, infants, offspring, issue, progeny. Whatever word I used, that was the sticking point every time. My ordered life had been turned upside down. When I was with Nic we often spent almost the whole of Sunday in bed – after all, bed was really the safest place for Nic to be. We wouldn't surface till early evening when we emerged to search out some food and a drink. On Saturdays we usually went to the theatre or cinema, or just sat around watching old black and white movies on BBC2, or having a leisurely row and a luxury four-hour sulk.

None of this was possible with Michael. Come rain or shine, high days or holidays, at six forty-five a.m. on the dot we would be woken with a siren call of 'Daddaddaddadda!' when Michael would give me a sleepy kiss and haul himself out of bed.

The weekend consisted of pushing Lily in a trolley around Safeway, feeding her grapes we hadn't paid for to keep her from screaming the place down, pushing her on the swings in the park. But Michael and Lily came as a done deal, and did I really want to throw out the bathwater with the baby? Laura was right. I'd have to talk to Michael about some things I'd done my best to hide from him.

I was despondent. I was going to lose him, I was sure of that. I couldn't forget his father telling me not to underestimate how much Lily meant to him, what he'd given up to have her. Laura had told me that only that morning on *Richard and Judy*, Judy had been saying that before she married Richard she had warned him that she and her children came as a 'package', and if he wanted her he'd have to have her children too. Of course, Richard had been only too happy to oblige. But obviously enough, I was not Richard Madeley.

If only I'd met Michael a couple of years ago, before he and Fiona had had the chance to reproduce. Things would have been so much simpler.

Then I realised that I was wishing Lily didn't exist. What kind of love could I have for Michael if I could think like that?

And the fact was that Michael was a father. It was as much part of him as the colour of his eyes or the shape of his hands, and had he not been a father, maybe he wouldn't have been the same person, and maybe I wouldn't be in love with him at all.

It was too confusing.

38

After work, I went to Michael's house, stopping at an off-licence on the way for a bottle of wine. However the evening went, I thought we'd need it. I walked along the street, as I had so often in the last six months, but thinking this time that either one day it might be my home, or I might never be welcome here again.

As he answered the door Michael looked a bit tense. He kissed me and gave me a warm hug, as usual, but after that things felt strained. I knew I'd made him nervous by not accepting his proposal immediately.

'Could you watch Lily for a couple of minutes?' he asked. 'I'm at a crucial stage in the kitchen and I'm going to be getting stuff in and out of the oven. It's safer if you could just amuse her in the living room. I won't be long.' He disappeared in the direction of the kitchen, and I hung up my jacket and went to find Lily.

She was playing with a large silver balloon. When she saw me, her face squashed into a smile that showed off her row of astonishingly perfect little teeth and wrinkled up her nose. 'Hi-ya!' she said, in her singsong baby voice, grasping the balloon firmly between two pink fists and toddling towards me. The balloon escaped her grip and floated up to bump softly against the ceiling. She threw back her head further than was necessary to look where it had gone, and giggled delightedly when I grabbed the string and pulled it down for her. After several repetitions of this hilarious game, she forgot about the balloon for a moment, and came over to where I was sitting. She laid her cheek against my leg. 'Aah,' she said, patting me.

I stroked her hair a bit, and said, 'Your dad's put you up to this, I bet.'

'Put her up to what?' Michael asked, coming into the room with knives and forks.

'Oh, she's just being sweet, aren't you?' I said, but Lily was already off, her arms stretched up to Michael for him to lift her up.

After our meal, Michael asked if I wanted to help him bath Lily. Now that did sound like a set-up, because I knew how cute she could look in the bath. I said I'd do the washing-up instead.

When he came downstairs again, I was half-heartedly watching the news and sipping wine. I'd poured him some, and the sight of the full glass of red wine standing on the table made me think of those meetings in the pub when we first got together. An 'Our Tune' in alcohol form. Michael sat down opposite me, picked up his glass and said nervously, 'Shall I let Mum know she needs to buy a hat, then? Or not?' He reached for the remote control and turned down the TV volume. I put my wine glass down, and moved to sit on the floor by his feet. This was partly so that I could touch him, and partly so that I didn't have to look directly at him while I was talking.

'I love you more than anything in the world,' I said.

'You sound like one of those American talk shows,' he said. 'There's a "but" coming now, isn't there?' I nodded. 'But . . . Lily?' he suggested. I nodded again, relieved I didn't have to say it myself.

'Dan says there's a far higher incidence of children being killed by step-parents than by natural parents,' I said.

Michael gave an exasperated snort. 'So you're worried you might kill her, then?'

'Of course not!'

'Well, stop talking such rubbish. Tell me how you really feel.'

'I'm . . .' I struggled to find the words. 'I think I'm too selfish to be a parent. You always put Lily first —'

'I have to.'

'I know, and that's what I mean. I'm fond of her, but mainly because she's yours, and I love you. And I don't know if that's enough.' I glanced up at him for a reaction, but he wasn't looking at me. He'd leant his head against the back of the sofa and was gazing in an unfocused way at the point where the wall met the ceiling. He took a deep breath as if about to reply, but before he could say anything I was grabbing the TV remote control.

'Shh! Wait!' I said.

I knew the face on the screen. You don't normally see people you know in real life on television, so when it happens it feels a bit like a dream. The newsreader was saying that a British musician, Steve Goldman, was among the passengers of an aircraft that had gone missing in a remote part of Indonesia. It was feared that there would be no survivors. The newsreader was adding some background about Steve's career, but I wasn't listening.

'Oh, my God,' I said. 'I have to ring Nic.' You can imagine how well that went down with Michael. I explained to him that Steve Goldman was Nic's father.

For once, Michael's endless patience failed him, and he looked very irritated indeed. 'Isn't it time Nic found someone else to hold his hand? Does it have to be your job all the time?'

'I'm not sure what you mean by "all the time"', I said. He didn't reply, just made an exasperated gesture with his hands. 'Nic's father could be dead,' I said. 'I just think I ought to at least ring him and see if he's okay.'

'All right,' he conceded, 'but couldn't you wait ten minutes? We're in the middle of a serious conversation. It would be nice if we could sort out whether you're going to marry me or not, before you dash off to comfort your ex-boyfriend.'

'Michael! I can't think about that now.'

'I'll take that as a "no", then, shall I?' he said irritably. 'Obviously Nic is more important to you than I am.'

'Now you're being unreasonable and stupid and jealous,' I shot back. 'And that's three good reasons for not marrying you right there!' That's not what I had meant to say at all, but once

136

it was out there didn't seem to be any way to take it back. We just looked at each other for a few seconds, then I grabbed my bag and my jacket and was out of the door before he could say anything else.

As I walked away I expected him to come after me, and dearly hoped he would.

But of course he couldn't – Lily was in bed so he couldn't leave the house.

39

About an hour later I arrived outside Nic's flat. I hadn't been there for months, and it was strange to be standing on the step ringing the bell, not having my own key any more. The street was the same as it had been the last time I was there: like Nic, it was fashionably scruffy, but you could tell that if someone really made an effort it would scrub up nicely. It crossed my mind that Peter was just the person to make vast improvements to Nic and his lifestyle, if only he was ever given the chance.

I glanced up at the window on the second floor and saw Nic looking down. He disappeared, and a second later the entryphone buzzed. The flat was in its usual state of chaos: clothes, sheet music and CDs scattered around the floor, overflowing ashtrays, unwashed mugs and glasses on the coffee table and bookshelves. The only thing in the room that looked clean and cared-for was his beautiful toffee-coloured cello, which was propped carefully in a corner.

Nic had been in the middle of throwing clothes into a bag. His face was strained and wretched. I gave him a hug.

'You heard?' he asked.

'Just saw it on the news. I came straight round. Where are you going?'

'To Marlene's,' he said. 'She's totally freaking out. There are reporters out in the back garden and all, it's crazy.' He laughed humourlessly. 'Must be a slow news day.'

'Are there any more details?'

'Well, it's fairly certain he's dead. It's just a case of finding, you know, a body . . . Apparently it could take years. The place where the plane disappeared is pretty remote.'

'Oh, God, that's terrible. Poor Steve. Is there anything I can do?'

Nic tucked a small, black, lacquered box among the clothes in his bag: his stash box. He immediately thought better of it, took it out again and sat down to roll a joint.

'I don't know what I'm supposed to feel,' he said. 'I'm hearing that my father is probably dead. It's meant to be a big deal, right? And I have no idea what I'm supposed to feel. It's not like my family is at all normal.' He lit up the joint and inhaled deeply. He looked confused and sad.

'What do you mean?' I asked, although I had a rough idea.

'Oh, Steve and Marlene and their universal love trip. Love the planet, love your fellow man, love the one you're with. All that sixties schtick. All the time I was growing up I just wanted normal parents. Parents who were too embarrassed to let you see them naked – do you know what I mean?' I certainly did: I think my parents are too embarrassed to see each other naked. God knows how I came about. 'Do you know,' he continued, 'they never said no to me, about anything? They never said, "You can't do that, put that down you'll break it, be in by this time, do your homework first," any of that stuff normal parents say. I grew up like a flower in their garden – you've seen the state of their garden, sort of fondly beheld but left to get on with it.' He sat forward with his head in his hands, smoke hazing around his head. 'I know I'm a mess,' he said. 'I'm amazed you put up with me for so long. I'm truly amazed that you're still my friend, after all the shit I put you through. But the thing is, I don't know how to be any other way. See what I mean? I had no blueprint. I don't even know why I'm going. Sod the pair of them.'

'They're your parents.'

'I told you, I've got no idea what that's supposed to mean.'

'They love you.'

'Me and the rest of the planet.'

'No parents are perfect,' I said. 'Mine aren't.'

'Your parents are great,' he said. 'They're really kind, and solid and reliable. You know you can trust them.'

To try to give him what Oprah would call a 'reality check', I said, 'My mum thinks you're a bit full of yourself.'

'She does? Wow. She never said that to my face. But she's right, and maybe I wouldn't have been so full of myself if my parents had ever said stuff like that to me.' He stood up and finished packing his bag. 'I'm sorry, Anna.'

'What for?'

'For being a self-absorbed wanker . . . and just generally.' After a pause he said, 'Could you do me a favour, though? Sorry to lay this on you, but could you contact Peter for me? I guess he ought to know. He is Steve's grandson, after all. It's just a shame I was so stupid that they never even got a chance to meet—' His voice stalled and he concentrated hard on the packing.

Soon he was ready, and we went outside and found a cab.

'Thanks for coming, Anna. You're a true friend. Really.'

'Just give my love to Marlene,' I said, 'and keep hoping for the best. I'll talk to Peter. I'll call you.' He kissed my cheek, and got into the cab. I waved as he drove off, then set off to get the tube home.

It was one of those warm, early summer evenings that smells of cut grass and the first barbecues of the season; still early enough in the summer for London to look fairly fresh. Later on, the city would get that parched, sandblasted look, all dust and car pollution. But this evening the weather felt happy.

I, however, was anything but.

40

The day was already hideously hot. My head felt fuzzy and thick from lack of sleep, my eyes were sticky and tired, and I was glad of the sun so I could legitimately hide behind dark glasses. I would have had to wear them anyway, or risk frightening people who were presumably upset enough already.

As we got to the rise of the hill, we began to hear jazzy, percussive music, and the sound of . . . I was going to say a crowd, but it was more the sound of a lot of people – a street market sound rather than a football crowd sound. I couldn't believe the sight as we got to the top of the hill and looked down at the field.

'Wow,' I said. 'Woodstock.' It was like the last thirty years had never happened.

Steve's body hadn't been found and, unless you've heard any different, it hasn't been found to this day. So, instead of a funeral, a 'celebration' had been arranged. Knowing Marlene, I couldn't imagine her having any truck with a conventional funeral anyway.

As a memorial, this was anything but conventional but certainly reflected Steve and his life. In a field near to the place where the Glastonbury Festival takes place, a stage had been set up under a white awning. A band was currently playing jazzy rock, and even through my bleary eyes and sunglasses I could recognise a few famous faces among the musicians. People sat in front of the stage and listened to the music, or wandered around. Children ran about, shrieking happily, dirt-streaked, face-painted and barefoot. I almost said, 'Lily would have loved this,' but let the thought hang unspoken.

We sat down on the grass at the edge of the crowd. The air smelt of parched grass and patchouli oil, dope smoke and, incongruously, the fresh, lemony scent of Eternity for Men.

'Is that you smelling of Eternity for Men?' I asked Peter.

'Why? Don't you like it?' he said.

'Yes, it's just that you're probably the only person here who doesn't smell like a hippy'

'*You* don't smell like a hippy.'

'Why thank you, kind sir,' I said, and wondered whether someone knowing you don't reek of patchouli oil means you've let them get a little too close. I looked at him; he was wearing a pigeon-grey T-shirt and soft, faded jeans and looked as bright and fresh as morning. I was lost for words.

The night before, we'd arrived late and booked into a hotel in Bath. We were both tired after a very emotional journey. Peter had just arrived from Denmark to meet the father who'd bottled out of meeting him on the previous occasion, and mourning the loss of a grandfather he'd never met. I was upset because of Steve, too, but mostly I was feeling mixed up and worried about Michael.

Neither of us felt like sleeping, so we sat in my room and got companionably drunk. And in amongst being tired and emotional and having far too much to drink, at some point Peter kissed me.

I don't think it was him being too young that had stopped me from responding, in fact Peter almost made me wish I was nineteen again. Most of the time I'm far happier being thirty than I ever was when I was nineteen, but I couldn't help envying the kind of life Peter had. All the choices in the world were still open to him: he was young and intelligent and had no ties or commitments, free to just come and go whenever and wherever he wanted to. He was everything I'd found attractive about Nic without any of the drawbacks.

But when he kissed me all I could think of was: why isn't this Michael?

Trying to think of something to say, and vaguely scanning the crowd, I spotted Marlene and Nic. They were talking to the musicians who had just come off the stage. Marlene looked suitably ethereal, her long greying hair fanning out around the shoulders of a flowing white dress. Beside her, Nic looked tall and slim. He was dressed almost formally, compared to the rest of the assembly, and he hovered protectively close to his mother, though from what I could see she didn't seem too overcome by grief. That was the advantage of being a clairvoyant, I supposed.

Peter was now looking in the same direction as me. 'Is that them?' I nodded. 'Oh shit. I'm suddenly very nervous, and wondering if this was a good idea.'

'Of course it was a good idea,' I said. 'Nic wanted you to know about Steve. They'll be very happy to meet you.'

Peter looked unconvinced, and I thought for a moment he was going to do a disappearing act like Nic had before. But he'd started to smile. 'You were right,' he said.

'About what?'

'At the airport – when I first arrived last year? – you said I would know him when I saw him. We do look alike, don't we?'

Nic and Marlene were wandering through the crowd, talking to people, hugging them, all the time moving closer to where we were sitting.

Then Peter made a silent decision and stood up. He brushed some blades of dry grass off his jeans, and walked deliberately towards his father and grandmother. I saw Nic glance at him, do a double take; then he saw me, and obviously made the connection. Marlene was simply staring at Peter, her eyes fixed on his as if she'd seen an apparition.

I have never admired Nic more than at that moment (which, I admit, isn't saying much). He stepped towards Peter, his hand outstretched, then turned to his mother and said, 'Marlene, this is Peter. He's my son.'

Marlene continued to stare, as did anyone within earshot

who had heard what Nic said. Then she clasped her hands, heavy with rings, together and said, 'Of course he is. He has your father's eyes.' She held out her arms wide, and Peter went to her. Everyone ended up hugging and crying.

41

Marlene, of course, insisted on getting to know Peter, and said he absolutely had to stay in the house with her and Nic.

'And you must stay, too, Anna,' she said, giving me yet another hug. I couldn't remember her being so tactile before, but losing a husband and gaining a grandson in such a short space of time had obviously affected her.

'That's very kind,' I said, 'But I really should be getting back.'

She took my hand and held it tightly. 'It would mean a great deal to me if you would stay,' she said. 'Steve always looked on you like a daughter.' This was news to me. 'And Nic has told me how kind you've been to Peter. This is a very healing place,' she said, in her best Mystic Meg voice, and glanced towards the surrounding hills, 'and I sense that you're in need of some space to think about some choices in your life.' Well, that much was true: I still hadn't sorted out in my head whether I was ready to settle down to cosy family life, and I hadn't spoken to Michael since we'd had the row on the night of Steve's disappearance. The thought of a breathing space and time to think was appealing, and one day turned into two turned into several.

Various other people were staying, mainly old friends and students of Steve's. The atmosphere wasn't gloomy at all, but – as everybody said Steve 'would have wanted' – celebratory. This was assisted by copious quantities of drugs and alcohol: everyone seemed to be in a permanent haze, but that had been the case on my previous visits to the house when Nic and I were a couple. It had always amazed me that Nic had been interested in going out with someone who was so, as he put it, 'straight'. But there's no accounting for tastes.

There was always someone around with a guitar, strumming away and singing old James Taylor songs and that sort of thing. A frail-looking blonde girl in a kaftan, who looked like the Mama who wasn't Cass, flitted in and out of the kitchen producing wholemeal bread, substantial soups and carrot cake at all hours of the day: there was always someone complaining of the 'munchies'. Despite her own thinness, she seemed to be on a mission to feed everybody as much and as often as possible.

Her name was Debbie and she had been one of Steve's students. She seemed more upset than anyone by Steve's death: her room was next to mine, and I frequently heard her weeping softly. I also heard her play the same piece of music over and over again. It started with a noise like a little bell ringing, then a soprano bellowed the single word 'Sanc-tus!' The singing gave way to a sort of breath-holding cacophony, before crashing into the most immense wave of drums and brass and unfettered grief and despair and hope all mixed together. It made me shiver. I asked Debbie what it was.

'It's from Benjamin Britten's *War Requiem*,' she said, and explained that it had been Steve's favourite piece of music, and the inspiration for him to start learning about Indonesian music (the breath-holding cacophony apparently). She felt it was a requiem for Steve, too. I wondered exactly how close she and Steve had been. Like father like son, after all. And grandson . . .

'You and Nic are together?' she asked.

'No,' I corrected her. 'We used to be. Not any more.'

'That's funny,' she said. 'Whenever I heard Marlene and . . .' her voice faltered '. . . Steve talking about you, I always got the impression that you and Nic are a couple. They spoke of you like part of the family.' So I told her about Michael because I was fed up with people assuming things about me and Nic, but also because I was missing Michael and I was glad to have the excuse just to mention his name – it made him feel present in some way.

I didn't see much of Peter, or Nic. They seemed to be constantly with Marlene, helping her through her grief and bonding with each other. I was glad to have time on my own to think.

Most of the time I went for walks, or talked to Debbie or the other people who came and went in the house. Or I sat in my room, like Flora Poste at Cold Comfort Farm, looking out of the window amazed at how rural it was. I didn't ring anybody, and no one rang me. No one knew I was there, and even if they'd guessed, Marlene was ex-directory and no one had the number.

'No one', of course, meaning Michael.

42

'No one' also included Laura and Dan. When I got home, accompanied by Peter who was due to fly back to Denmark the next day, there were ten messages on my answering-machine. Two were from my mother, and eight were from Dan, in various stages of hysteria.

Laura had had the baby some days earlier. It was a boy, as they'd expected, but they had been banking on him arriving a couple of weeks later – apparently the nursery was still in a state of chaos. They were calling the baby Ben, 'after Nicolas Cage's character in *Leaving Las Vegas*,' Dan said. Ah: the one who drinks himself to death. Nice.

I rang them immediately, and Laura answered. 'Where have you been?' she demanded. 'You just disappeared, we've been going frantic, and then Ben arrived and everything.'

'I'm sorry,' I said. 'I didn't think he was due yet or I would have phoned, you know I would. How are you? How's the baby? Is everything all right?'

'Oh, it's fine. He's fine. Eight pounds, eight ounces, bless him. Absolutely painless birth, you wouldn't believe. They just stuck an epidural in, and every time I felt even a tiny twinge, they put some more stuff in. Brilliant! I just sat there all day, reading magazines and eating. Then forty-five minutes of painless pushing and out he plopped. Easy as having a crap – though, of course, I ought to say "poo" now there's a child in the house. Loads of stitches, though, and I'm bleeding like a stuck pig.' Lovely.

'Was Dan okay?'

'He was a natural.' She laughed. 'He was down there at the sticky end, getting in the midwife's way, screaming, "Push! Push!" like he's seen them do on *Casualty*. He even helped me sit on a bedpan because I couldn't feel my legs properly and they wouldn't let me walk to the loo. Then I couldn't pee, so I had to have a catheter! I felt like one of Dan's elders!'

'It sounds revolting.'

'I know. I couldn't believe I was doing it all either. And absolutely never again, so don't even ask. When are you coming round to see the baby?' she demanded. I said I'd go the next morning, because I'd just got back and needed to unpack and wash my clothes and sort myself out.

'Well, just come soon, or he's going to be a grown man before you see him. Ooh, what a horrible thought. So where have you been, anyway? Somewhere nice with Michael?' she wanted to know. I said I'd tell her all about it when I saw her, and hung up.

So this baby was real now. Laura wasn't just my friend who happened to be pregnant any more: she was somebody's mother.

I was very tired, and getting home had been depressing. I'd expected at least one of the ten messages on the answering-machine to be from Michael, but apparently he wasn't interested in talking to me.

I just wanted a cup of tea and an early night. I turned round, and Peter was coming out of the kitchen carrying two cups, which he placed on the table. He lifted his backpack off the sofa, propped it up by the door and sat down. 'Back to real life,' he said. 'Gran's house is like another world, isn't it?'

I nodded agreement. 'I feel like I've been in a time warp,' I said. 'London is such a shock after Somerset.'

Peter laughed. 'Gran says that's because of all the concrete and cars in London. "Negative energy conductors", apparently. They "block the psychic flow". And the very worst place is the underground, she says. That's why everyone looks grumpy on the tube: all the concrete and metal. Psychic energy was obviously invented in olden times, when the biggest obstacle was a wood hut or a cave.'

'I'm amazed she lets you call her Gran,' I said. 'Nic only ever calls her Marlene.'

'I know,' he said, sipping his tea. 'He's sad that they never liked him calling them Mum and Dad.' This was news to me, but made sense in the light of the conversation I'd had with Nic on the night of the news of Steve's plane crash. 'Gran says being a grandmother is making her feel "part of the Goddess's eternal ebb and flow". She gets a kick out of it.' He smiled to himself. 'I think I probably have the most unconventional family in the world, if you consider my Danish family and my English one,' he added. He finished his tea, put the cup down on the floor then stretched out luxuriously on the sofa. He looked beautiful: long-limbed, tanned a deep gold from being outdoors so much recently, his hair streaked blond by the sun. His feet were bare; he had long, beautifully shaped feet, and on the middle toe of one he was wearing a narrow silver ring, a present from Marlene. It looked incredibly sexy, and I couldn't stop myself thinking about the night before Steve's memorial; the hotel in Bath. It wasn't something I really wanted to think about just now. It was unnerving.

'I'll go and get your bedding,' I said. 'You remember how to do the sofa bed, don't you?' He nodded, and we both stood up. He put his hands on my shoulders and kissed my cheek lightly.

'I guess tomorrow you need to sort things out with Michael,' he said softly, and began to unfold the sofa bed.

43

This time Peter didn't want to be seen off at the airport, so I said goodbye to him at the tube station. After he'd gone I felt sad but, I have to admit, somewhat relieved. Things had felt too complicated with him around.

I wondered about ringing Michael at work. I even picked up the phone a couple of times and started to dial the number, then hung up. It could wait until later. Somehow I felt it would be easier to talk to him once Peter was right out of the country.

Instead I went round to Laura and Dan's.

I could hear wailing from outside the door. It turned out not to be baby Ben but Laura, who was having what Dan, when he came to let me in, confidently described as 'the baby blues'.

'The midwife took me aside yesterday and told me to expect it,' he informed me chirpily: he was clearly loving his new role. 'It's because of the milk coming in,' he said, and added, perhaps unnecessarily, 'Hormones.'

'Never have a baby. Have yourself sewn up,' was Laura's welcoming remark. She blew her nose and threw the tissue into a bin, which was overflowing enough to show that that the baby blues had been going on for some time. I was amazed to see her looking almost as pregnant as before: I'd expected her to be all flat and normal-looking. Of course, I was far too tactful to say anything. 'Ooh, flowers!' she said, and I handed over the freesias I'd brought, while noticing that every horizontal surface in the room bore a container of blooms in varying stages of wilt.

'I've also brought these,' I said, holding up a large box of chocolates. 'I thought you deserved them.'

'You're a darling!' she said, ripping it open and offering me one. 'People only ever bring things for the baby.' (It hadn't occurred to me to bring a present for the baby. What do you need when you're less than a week old?) 'I'm sitting here feeling like my insides are likely to drop out whenever I stand up, and am I being pampered? No, I am not. I am being expected to breastfeed, for God's sake. It's like having your nipples napalmed, and does he know how to do it naturally? Does he bugger. I've had the midwife sort of aiming his face at my tits for over half an hour, like trying to teach a Scud missile where to go, and still he hasn't got the hang of it, and every attempt is deeper agony for me than the last. Do you want to see the state my nipples are in?' I shook my head vigorously. 'No, I wish I didn't have to, either. So I said to Dan, "Fuck that," and sent him out to buy some formula milk.'

'Isn't breastfeeding supposed to be good for the baby?' I asked, and was horrified to see her burst into tears again.

'Don't you start!' she wailed. 'Everybody's trying to make me feel guilty!' I tried to be reassuring, which was difficult as I wasn't sure what was going on. I was glad when Dan came back into the room and took charge.

'No one wants you to feel guilty,' he said, with the air of someone who has repeated the same speech many times only recently. 'You know the midwife said that what's best for you is best for Al.'

'Al? I thought the baby was called Ben.' I said.

'Oh, no,' Dan said. 'We changed our minds this morning. We're calling him Al, after Al Pacino—'

'After Nicolas Cage's character in *Birdy*,' corrected Laura, who seemed to be cheering up again and was reaching for the chocolates. 'Plus it's easy to spell.'

She cheered up even more with the arrival of Sadie, who brought a bottle of champagne. 'Well, thank God I'm not breastfeeding or I couldn't have had much of this!' Laura said, almost happily. A piercing cry from another room alerted us to the presence of Ben. Sorry, Al. Dan went off and returned some minutes later proudly carrying his son and a bottle of formula milk. He sat down and proceeded to feed the baby as if he'd been doing it for years. Sadie and I cooed obligingly at the baby, who was rather cute – not wrinkly at all – and then I noticed that tears were sliding silently down Laura's face. I asked her what was wrong.

'Dan's so good at it!' she said. 'I'm no good at all and I'm supposed to be his mother!' Dan shoved the baby and the bottle at Sadie, which took her aback, and went to comfort Laura. Baby Al, realising what was expected of him, continued to suck contentedly at the bottle, enabling Dan to make the point that Al didn't care who was feeding him as long as he got fed. Laura was calming down again, and mumbled tearfully, 'He even prefers Sadie.' She seemed to find this funny, and picked up her champagne again.

44

'Bloody hell. Hormones,' Sadie said. We were sitting in a café, having left Laura, Dan and offspring as soon as we reasonably could.

'I know,' I agreed. 'Rather her than me.' We raised our coffee cups to the exalted state of motherhood, and the even more exalted state of childlessness. This had the effect of silencing both of us for several minutes.

'So . . .' Sadie said eventually, 'Dan was saying that you just vanished off on holiday somewhere. Been on a "tax break"?' She laughed at her own joke. I said I hadn't been anywhere with Michael, and then, because if I didn't talk to somebody I would probably explode, I told her everything that had happened, from Michael asking me to marry him right through to meeting her at Laura's. She listened in silence, raising her pierced eyebrow now and again but otherwise not making any comment. When I'd finished, she said, 'So what's the state of play now, then?'

I sighed, and thought for a moment. 'I don't know,' I confessed. 'I feel like shit. I just can't work it out. One minute I'm totally in love with Michael, and then I'm being kissed by my ex-boyfriend's son.'

'Hang on,' Sadie said. 'Rewind that last bit. *Kissed*?' I nodded and explained about Peter.

'What the notice at the side of the swimming pool used to call "petting"?'

I shook my head. 'Not even that,' I said. 'Really. Nothing that would get you thrown out of a swimming pool.'

'Oh, for heaven's sake,' Sadie grumbled. 'I'm sitting here keeping my face all straight like a priest in a confessional, and you've done nothing at all? Exactly what is the problem here, because, frankly, I'm failing to see it?'

'I thought Michael was the love of my life,' I said. 'I can't believe I could even look at another man, never mind for one second . . . Sadie, I feel like I've betrayed him.'

'Darling, I do think you're overreacting. For one thing, I don't believe there is one perfect man for anybody. Do you think Lauren Bacall has been living the life of a nun since Bogie passed on? I think not. Romance is just nature's way of saying, "Give me your sperm and stay with me until the offspring's at least able to tie its own shoelaces." There's no magic to it. It's all humping, put whatever romantic gloss on it you like.'

'That's very cynical even for you, Sadie.'

'I'm a realist, darling. And I must say that having heard all about your dreadfully nice tax inspector and his charming child, and then about this nubile Norwegian fanny magnet, I know which I'd go for.'

'He's Danish.'

'Who cares? He's nineteen. That's when men are at their peak, sexually, trust me. You must be an absolute nun to resist that when it's offered! But here you are, moping around and feeling all guilty, because you've fallen for the Barbara Cartland myth of romantic perfection. And it can't have been perfect, or you wouldn't have been tempted by your Scandinavian.'

I sighed again. I had been doing a lot of sighing lately.

'I doubt if Michael would have me back anyway, after the way I talked to him and then just vanishing for nearly two weeks.'

'Well it seems to me you're going to have to give it a try, if that's really how you feel,' Sadie said. 'Personally, *I* would be on the next plane to wonderful Copenhagen to give the Dane a proper try-out.' A thought occurred to her. 'So what was it that made little Hamlet resistible in the end? You said yourself he's a bit of a hunk, and it sounds like he was up for it, as it were.'

'It was just a weird night, very emotional and we got very drunk,' I said. 'It would never have happened otherwise. Peter's lovely, he really is. He's kind and interesting and really nice looking and everything, and even though he's a lot younger, a while back I certainly wouldn't have said no. But things are different now, because I'm in love with Michael.'

'So why had you and perfect Michael had this argument then, if you're so much in love with him?' Sadie asked.

'I suppose I was scared: if I commit myself to him, it's so final, because there's Lily to think about and everything. I'd be settling down to family life, and if you'd said this time last year that that's what I'd be doing I'd just have laughed at you.'

'But if you care about him as much as you say you do, where's the problem?'

'Well, at the time I thought it was because of him having a kid, you know, I wasn't ready to be a stepmother? But all the thinking I've done since, I think I'm just scared by Michael's *certainty*. Everything is so straightforward for him. But it's not like that for me. And now I've completely blown it anyway.'

Sadie blew out a plume of cigarette smoke impatiently and said, 'I don't see how anything's changed, frankly. In fact, in your romantically warped view of the world, I would say that the whole thing has turned out rather well.'

'How do you make that out?'

'Well, you've repelled the advances of a horny nineteen year old Scandinavian, and maintain that the love of your life is indeed the man from the Inland Revenue. I would say you are now suffering from just about as much "certainty" as he is.'

'So what do I do?'

'You go and get him.' She ground her cigarette out in the ashtray, pausing to add, 'And give me the Danish babe's phone number.'

I still wasn't convinced, and continued to feel so mixed up that I couldn't face ringing Michael. My phone rang twice after I got home that evening. Both times my heart practically leapt out of my body and I hoped yet feared so much that it might be him.

It wasn't, and I went to bed and lay sleepless for most of the night. It didn't help that I couldn't shake the thought that my granny would have been so proud that, even without ever being an air hostess, I had almost managed to bag myself an international man.

45

There was no getting away from the fact that the next day I had to go to work. When I arrived, Po-faced Vo was in her gun-turret as usual. I noticed, with only a touch of *Schadenfreude*, that regular rogering with Fireman Sam hadn't done anything to improve her mood. Or her complexion.

'Oh, what a surprise!' she said. 'Didn't you used to work here?' Scathing. I gathered that she'd had to cope with some extra duties as a result of my absence, and wasn't best pleased with me. I braced myself to hear her account of the hardships she'd had to endure, but fortunately Clare summoned me straight in to her office and closed the door.

'How are you, Anna?' she asked, all solicitude and concern. I said I was fine, thanks. 'How was your friend's funeral?' she wanted to know. I'm slightly ashamed to admit it, but to get leave at such short notice, I'd had to lay it on a bit thick about how close I had been to the deceased. Before I could reply Clare said, 'I saw some of it on TV, of course. We've got digital now. Tubby does love his armchair sport, and I must say they have quite a wide choice. Even beach volleyball, would you believe? Some of those girls are so skimpily dressed I can't believe they take the sport seriously, but Tubby seems gripped. Though personally I'm more of a reader than a TV viewer. Sci-fi's my bag, believe it or not. I can get absolutely lost in an Iain M. Banks.' Clare is a constant revelation, she really is. 'However, Tubby spotted your friend on one of those news channels and gave me a shout. I must say, it looked like quite a jolly event. Quite a jamboree.' I wasn't sure what a 'jamboree' was, but allowed that Steve's family were a little unconventional.

'Well, I'm glad you're bearing up. Funerals can be very trying,' she said, then added, 'Though I was surprised that your young man didn't seem to know where you'd gone.'

'Michael?'

'Yes, our lovely man from the Inland Revenue. We had quite a little chat. Absolutely adorable, such lovely manners. I told him you'd gone to your friend's funeral in Somerset.'

Michael had called! That meant he wanted to talk to me, which had to mean he didn't hate me. That was good. But it meant he had known where I was. And had probably made all sorts of assumptions about what I was doing and who with. That was bad.

I went back to my office, trying to ignore the hate rays that Veronica was projecting from beneath her newly permed fringe. I closed the door behind me, and was greeted by the sight of Colin's bottom looming at me as he rummaged in the bottom drawer of the filing cabinet. 'Fucking bastard!' he was muttering.

'Problems, Colin?' I asked. He stood up quickly, his face red with inversion and exertion.

'Oh, Ms Anderson! Thank God you're back!' he said. 'I'm in such a fucking mess with this paperwork. Clare'll have my guts for garters. And that thing outside,' he nodded towards where Veronica was sitting, 'is about as much help as a mop on the *Titanic*.'

I spent the rest of the morning overhauling Colin's paperwork, which was in a bit of a woeful state, while he answered calls and took bookings.

I offered to treat him to lunch as a thank-you for covering for me while I was away. Strangely, I had no such generous impulse towards Veronica.

'Forbidden, I'm afraid,' Colin said, and produced a large brown paper bag from his rucksack. 'Daniel is packing healthy snacks for me these days.'

I was amused. 'So you've succumbed to his diet plan, then?'

'Well, I could do with losing a few pounds. And it wasn't worth fighting over it. Anyway, Daniel's healthy lunches are huge – care to share it with me?' He passed me an enormous sandwich, and plonked a Tupperware bowl filled with salad on the desk.

'How long have you and Daniel been together?' I asked as we ate.

He picked some pieces of salad from the bowl and inserted them into his sandwich. 'Oh, let's see . . . it must have been USA 'ninety-four.'

'You met in the USA?'

'No, that's where the World Cup was that England weren't in. Yes, it was nineteen ninety-four.'

'That's quite a long time. You must get on really well.'

'He's the love of my life,' Colin asserted, not at all ironically. I smiled. 'No, he is,' Colin said. 'I haven't even looked at another man since I met Daniel. Except Veronica's Dennis. Have you seen him? He's a fireman! I nearly died! He's got the uniform and even the little axe! I thought he was a strippergram the first time I saw him. But, of course, he's straight – or what passes for straight, if you're reduced to screwing that thing out there – so he doesn't count, and I wouldn't consider it anyway because, like I say, I am one hundred per cent monogamously in love with Daniel for my sins.' He delved into the brown paper bag again and brought out a large piece of chocolate cake. 'Look at that,' he said admiringly, breaking it in two and offering me a piece. 'Low-fat. Baked it himself. How could I not adore him?'

I can never eat chocolate cake – whether low-fat or not – without coffee, so I went to make us some. When I came back there was something I wanted to know. 'Colin, if Daniel was ever unfaithful, or even thought about it, would you be able to forgive him?'

He paused for a second to flick crumbs from his shirt before replying. 'I'd kill him. Quite literally. I'd kill him in the most painful and lingering way I could devise. Not that I'm a jealous person or anything.'

'Clearly. And would he feel the same about you if you were to stray?'

'Anna Anderson!' he said. 'Are you propositioning me just because I've spent the morning being fetchingly helpless about my paperwork? Seriously, no, he knows it wouldn't happen. But what's this all about, anyway? Just healthy het curiosity about my gay lifestyle? Or,' he peered at me meaningfully, 'has someone been having a bit of a lost weekend?'

'No, sorry,' I said quickly, making a big thing of sweeping away crumbs from my desk and collecting up the cups. 'I was just being nosy.'

Colin rummaged in the brown paper bag one last time and produced some sugar-free mints. 'Have an after dinner mint,' he said, scrunching up the bag and tossing it expertly into the bin, 'and then you can pop off to the ladies' and chastise yourself with Veronica's *Woman's Realm*.'

'Pardon?'

'Well, someone has some guilt to assuage, and I'm guessing it's not your other half.'

46

You can rehearse something over and over in your mind until you think every possible outcome has been explored, and every possible emotion you might potentially feel has already been felt, and coped with. Then real life turns out to be different again, and you could have saved yourself the worry.

Buddhists call worrying about the past 'clinging'. Worrying about the future is 'craving'. You're not supposed to cling or crave: you're supposed to live entirely in the present, and thus you'll be happy . . . or enlightened? Unworried, at any rate. I would have a spectacularly hard time being a Buddhist because I spent the rest of that week clinging and craving like mad.

Then on Saturday morning my doorbell rang, and when I opened the door, there was Michael.

'Oh,' was all I could say, but I hoped it came out as a happy, pleased-to-see-you sort of 'oh'. I wanted to hug him, but I wasn't sure if that would be appropriate: there was no way of telling his mood from his face. I'm fairly sure that he'd spent the walk along my street composing a noncommittal expression for himself. (That's what I would have done. Men always say they're above that sort of thing, but I suspect not.)

I invited him in, and he followed me upstairs. My mind raced ahead: what sort of state was the flat in? It actually wasn't too bad: Peter had given it the once-over before he'd left a week ago, and there's only so much mess one person can generate, even if the one person is me. The biggest embarrassment the flat offered was the smell of bananas slightly past their best. I'm never very good with fruit: I buy lots, and there it sits on the table until it smells too bad or grows fur. They I throw it away.

'Where's Lily?' I asked.

'My parents have taken her to Brighton for the day.'

'That's nice. How is she?'

'She's fine, thanks.' It wasn't like Michael not to volunteer extra information when asked about Lily.

'And . . . how are you?' I asked, guessing this was the signal for the Serious Conversation to start, rather earlier than I'd hoped.

Michael sighed, and looked at his hands. (Did I ever mention he had beautiful hands?) He cleared his throat, and said, 'I wasn't sure what I was going to say to you when I got here. I just thought I'd come over, see if you were in, play it by ear, I don't know. But now all I can think of is how much I've missed you.' He looked up at me. 'You look really lovely,' he said. 'All brown.'

'I've been away.'

'I know. Clare told me. You went to Nic's dad's funeral.'

'Yes.'

'For two weeks?'

'No,' I said. 'I stayed at Marlene's for a week. I've been back here since last weekend.'

'You didn't think to let me know?'

'I didn't know if you wanted to see me,' I said.

He reached out and took my hand. 'Why would I not want to see you?' he asked. If the question wasn't meant to be loaded, the answer have been, but I said, 'You were angry with me

158

about Nic, and about what I said to you. Which I apologise for. I was angry and upset.'

'I apologise, too,' he said. 'I had no right to get annoyed that you wanted to talk to Nic when the news came about his father. You're a kind person; and that's one of the things I love about you. I had no reason to be jealous, did I?' He gazed at me intently, making me feel confused and confessional. He must have seen something in my face, because he repeated, 'I didn't have any reason to be jealous, did I?' He sounded alarmed. 'You're not back with Nic?' I felt so relieved that I could answer this one honestly. I shook my head, squeezing his hand. It nearly killed me that he looked so happy.

Then I looked him straight in the eyes and realised there was only one absolute and important truth. 'Why would I want anybody else? I love you.'

He smiled his beautiful Michael smile, and put his arms round me. I snuggled my face into his neck, loving his warm, familiar smell. He stroked my hair. 'I'm sorry,' he said. 'I was wrong to ask you to marry me so soon, especially with Lily and everything –' I cut his words short with a kiss: I just wanted him to kiss me for at least the next five days without stopping. His hands slid down my back and under my T-shirt. Just the feel of them on my bare skin made me shiver. He pulled the T-shirt over my head, and the rest of our clothing was soon in a loose heap on the floor, while we made love desperately, pressing our bodies together tightly as if we wanted to be the same body and never to separate again.

Afterwards we lay sprawled on the floor. I started to laugh. 'What's funny?' he asked.

'I'm just happy,' I said. I was thinking that sex with Michael was just a frank exchange of love; it was the physical expression of everything we felt about each other. What might have happened with Peter just wasn't significant any more, compared with the pure joy of lying there with Michael. It was just love.

The doorbell rang. We ignored it.

It rang again.

'Ignore it,' Michael said.

It rang again.

'Oh, fuck off!' I said, to whoever was disturbing our moment.

Then we heard a voice outside shouting up, 'Anna! I know you're in! The window's open!'

'It's Laura,' I said. 'I'll have to let her in.' I kissed Michael again briefly, once on the mouth and once on the nipple, where he was really ticklish. He clapped his hands to his chest and rolled away, then gathered up his clothes and disappeared into the bathroom. I put my T-shirt back on, and stuck my head out of the window. Laura was standing in the street looking agitated. I threw down the keys and she let herself in while I finished dressing and brushed my hair.

'I knew you were bloody well in!' she said, as soon as she got through the door. 'What were you doing?'

'Michael's here,' I said pointedly.

She rolled her eyes in an 'Aha!' sort of way, and said, 'I remember the days when Dan and I used to be able to have a shag on a Saturday afternoon.'

Apparently she didn't remember how annoying it was to be interrupted, but she was obviously upset, so I just said, 'Where are Dan and the baby?' (I'd forgotten his current name.)

Laura flung herself down on the sofa and said, 'I've escaped. I've left them both to it. Have you got any vodka?' I hadn't, but I opened a bottle of wine. (I mightn't have fresh fruit, but I usually have a bottle of wine in the house for emergencies.)

'Things not going well, then?'

'Huh!' she said. 'That's an understatement. I stand next to that sink every evening, making up about fifty bottles, literally wanting to lie down right there on the kitchen floor and go to sleep. My bones ache from tiredness. I've got no life any more, I'm just at the beck and call of this little thing that cries and demands and shits. Dan goes off to work every morning and I'm terrified, I never believe I'll be able to get through the day. Then I'm counting the hours till he gets back.' She went on and on with her list of woes: there didn't seem to be any positive side to this parenting business at all, as far as she was concerned. Even I was thinking she was being a bit negative.

Laura held out her empty glass for a refill. 'I knew as soon as he was born that it had been a serious mistake,' she said.

'What?'

'Having him.'

'You don't mean that,' I said. I was shocked: they always say that the birth of your baby is the most wonderful moment of your life. They even say that seeing the baby makes you instantly forget all the pain and trauma you just went through.

'Oh, I don't know what I mean,' Laura said. 'I'm incapable of rational thought. Too tired. But, honestly, in the hospital the night he was born, after Dan had gone home, I was so tired and aching, I felt like I'd swum the Channel with a heavy period. I'd just dropped off to sleep, and he started crying. All these brisk nurses appeared and started propping me up with pillows so I could feed him. I just wanted to say, "Piss off, you feed him, I've just been through the biggest physical upheaval of my life and I need some fucking sleep."' She took a big slug of her wine. 'I realised then that this is it. For the next few years what I need or want isn't going to count at all.'

I couldn't think of anything constructive to say or do so I made sympathetic little clucking noises and kept topping up her glass. What I could have said was, 'You knew all this, we talked about this, but you still went ahead and did it,' but that wouldn't have been very helpful under the circumstances.

I was glad when Michael reappeared from the bathroom. He looked dressed, washed and tidied up, but still somehow very post-shag: something about his eyes. Whatever it was, it was madly sexy and I wanted to drag him to bed immediately, but frustratingly that wasn't an option.

'Hi, Laura,' he said, calm as usual. 'This is a nice surprise.' Laura rallied quite remarkably now that she was faced with a nice-looking man (and I'm underselling him here), but fairly soon she lapsed back into her woes-of-motherhood routine.

Michael, of course, was something of an expert in this area, and he began to tell her confidently that he had survived all of these traumas except for the painful breasts. 'It passes,' he said. 'One day soon you and Dan will be looking back and saying to each other, "Do you remember those days when we used to get hardly any sleep?"'

'No, we won't,' she said sulkily, 'because I'll have divorced him before that happens. And he can have custody of the Tyrant.'

'You don't mean that,' I said again.

'I bloody well do mean it. I want my life back!'

Michael was sitting on the floor at Laura's feet. He leant forward and patted her knee in a gesture that somehow reminded me of Lily. 'I've thought that sometimes,' he said. 'Like when I've wanted to go out somewhere with Anna, just the two of us, and I couldn't because there wasn't anyone to babysit. Or if people at work are going down to the pub on a Friday night. I can't do that either. Or in the middle of the night, when I'm knackered and the bed's nice and warm and Lily has a nightmare or something and I have to get up. Having to live my life to a routine of naps and nappies and bedtimes and making sure the cupboard is always full of Weetabix and full-fat milk. It gets you down sometimes, when you think of how free you used to be.' Laura and I were looking at him like he was the Oracle of Delphi, but for different reasons.

'But it gets better, truly, and having Lily is the most wonderful thing I've ever done,' he said. 'It's true life's never the same again, but it's better in a lot of ways.'

'How do you make that out?' Laura wanted to know.

'Well . . . I think I'm a nicer person now. I'm more settled, and more calm and philosophical about things. And Lily reminds me of how funny things are, like when she laughs at the bubbles in her bath, or when she's giving her dolls a talking to in baby talk. Just simple things. She's seeing everything for the first time – it's all fresh and new and interesting to her. Yesterday a little fly landed on her arm, and she was looking at it like it was a rare and beautiful thing, and I looked at it as well, properly looked, and it *was* a beautiful thing, tiny and delicate and such a lovely green. Normally I would've just brushed it away without looking. She hasn't compartmentalised things into "good" or "bad", everything's just filed under "interesting".

'When she gives me a hug, or when I go into her room in the morning and she's standing in her cot in her little pyjamas with this great big grin on her face just because I'm there. And those fat cheeks when she's grinning up at you. It's the purest love in the world.' Laura was starting to look as if she might believe him. I just wanted to get him in the bedroom and shag him senseless.

'Also,' he continued, 'I look after myself more now, I'm aware of my own health because I know how much she depends on me. It's a huge responsibility, but it's a reason to exist too. You know your place in the scheme of things.'

Laura said, 'You don't happen to have a brother, do you?'

Michael laughed. 'I do, but I don't think you'd swap Dan for him. Does Dan know where you are, by the way?'

Laura made a face. 'Not exactly. He could probably guess. Anyway, give him a chance to find out what it's like being stuck at home with the baby. He gets back from work and he thinks all I've been doing is watching daytime TV. Which I have, of course, because what else are you supposed to fill the day with when you're changing nappies and warming up bottles every half an hour?'

'Oh, God, I remember those days,' Michael said. 'Mind you, my mum got the worst of it because I was at work too, so I only had to do it in the evenings and at weekends. But, really, it passes quicker than you can possibly imagine now. By Christmas it'll be such a different story. He'll be sitting up, maybe even trying to crawl, eating solid food, and sleeping through, if he's as good as Lily.'

'Christmas? I'll be dead by Christmas!' Laura shrieked.

'No, you won't.' He laughed. 'You'll get through. Anyway, I

have a suggestion. It sounds like you and Dan need a break, so Anna and I will babysit for you.'

She pounced on this. 'When?'

'Tonight, if you like,' he said. 'As long as you can bring – what's the baby's name?'

'Seth.'

'Seth? Like in *Cold Comfort Farm*?' I said.

'No, after Nicolas Cage's character in *City of Angels*.' Named after an angel. That was more like it.

'Well, if you can bring Seth round to my place, we'll look after him there. That all right with you, Anna?' I nodded, astonished at how quickly everything seemed to have reverted to normal between Michael and me. 'Okay, so go and give Dan a ring and see what he thinks.'

Laura went to use the phone in my bedroom, which took a bit of time. Time that Michael and I filled with some intensive hand-holding and gazing into each other's eyes. When Laura came back into the room she said, 'We'll bring him round at about six, then, if you give me the address.' She sat down and finished off her wine. 'I'm sorry for being so self absorbed,' she said. 'Thank you for the pep talk and the wine and everything. So, what's going on with you two?' she asked. 'Are you getting married, or what?'

Michael and I just looked at each other for a couple of seconds, and he said, 'Are we?'

And I surprised myself by saying, 'Yes, I reckon we are.'

In fact, I was certain.

47

It amused me that when Dan and Laura dropped off the baby, while Laura and I discussed the film they were about to see, Dan was advising Michael about changing Seth's nappy. 'Make sure his willy is pointing downwards,' Dan said, 'otherwise, when he pees it squirts straight over the waistband of the nappy.'

Michael saw the sense of this. 'I wouldn't have thought of it,' he admitted. 'It's not something you have to worry about with girls.' Modern men: don't you just love them?

Dan and Laura went off happily enough, after checking about seventeen times that we had the number of Dan's mobile, plus the number of the cinema and the midwife and the doctor and the coastguard, etc.

Seth didn't seem to do much. He slept, mainly, cried a bit, and Michael changed his nappy, warmed up a bottle and fed him, then burped him by sitting him up, holding him under the chin and rolling him around like one of those toys with a weight in the bottom. It squashed Seth's face up so he looked like a little Buddha. He issued a loud belch (along with a small amount of milk across the back of Michael's hand) and then dozed off happily in Michael's arms.

'You should really try this,' Michael said. He looked unbelievably sweet, holding the little sleeping baby. 'Do you want to hold him?'

'Erm, no, it's all right. He looks happy where he is.'

'You'll have to get used to it, if we're going to have kids.'

What? Oh, help! This wasn't something I'd thought of – getting to grips with Lily was going to be enough of a challenge for one lifetime, surely.

But again I proved to be a constant revelation to myself. 'Pass him over, then.'

He was gorgeous. So tiny, but surprisingly heavy as well, a solid little warm bundle. His hedgehog-like face was constantly moving in his sleep, anemone lips pursing, smiling, then pursing again, faint trace of eyebrows moving up and down. Don't even mention the tiny curled-up fists.

My throat and eyes started to fill with tears. I couldn't believe that my hormones had taken control of my rational, civilised self in such a blatant way.

Later, after Laura and Dan had taken Seth home, when Michael and I had finished off a bottle of wine, made love and Michael had drifted off to sleep, I lay awake for what felt like hours. All I could think of was the baby's little face. Every time I closed my eyes there he was, looking up at me with his little almond eyes.

I glared at my hormones metaphorically in much the same way I fancy Captain Bligh gazed upon Fletcher Christian. But when I looked at Michael's sleeping face, I was full of love, and everything made sense.

48

'Anna, I hope this is the right number – you know what Nic's memory is like. All that Ecstasy, probably. I warned him about these designer drugs – you know where you are with a nice bit of blow and the occasional tab of acid, but try telling that to young people, these days. It's Marlene, sweetheart.' I'd guessed. 'I'm up in London at the weekend and I was wondering if you might be free at some point. I've got the strongest feeling that I need to talk to you. You're emitting some very potent psychic energy. I couldn't feel it when you were in my house because, let's face it, there was a lot going on and I was still getting used to Steve being on the other side. But he's settled in there now, you'll be glad to hear, and I know he wants me to have a word with you too. Do give me a call on my mobile, or I'll ring you.'

49

I walked from the tube station to the hotel where Marlene was staying. It was an appallingly hot day, so hot you could almost see solid objects shrinking from dehydration. Sunshine seared blindingly off the passing cars and the white- and cream-painted Georgian town houses, which were almost all converted into hotels. The people I passed looked affluent and purposeful, and matched the buildings in tailored cream and white. Women pushed children along the pavement towards Holland Park in trendy, expensive-looking conveyances with three little all-terrain wheels and bright canopies, like tiny rickshaws.

By contrast, the air-conditioning made the hotel almost too cool. I asked for Marlene at the desk and was directed to the basement. The smell of incense prickled my nose as soon as I descended the stairs: Marlene was making herself at home. I knocked at the door, and she flung it open, blinking in the dingy light from the hallway; the room behind her was almost completely dark except for a dim lamp. She was wearing the same white dress she'd worn for Steve's memorial gathering, accessorised with chunky, contemporary amber jewellery.

We hugged, and she felt thin and frail; her hands were cold. She indicated a chair next to the little lamp, and sat next to me. There was a table in front of us with tarot cards laid out. I was slightly alarmed to see that one of them was Death, a horrible image of a helmeted skull, like a Hell's Angels tattoo.

'Care for an Aqua Libra?' she asked. 'It might help you relax. You look a little stressed.'

I said no, thanks, but accepted a glass of plain water. I can't be doing with these herbal drinks: they all taste like tin. I pointed at the Death card. 'That's a bit ominous,' I said, laughing nervously.

'Oh, no, dear, a lot of people make that mistake. No, he's a good sign, is Mr Death. The card of new beginnings and the end of something whose time has passed. It's an important lesson to learn, one that the tarot is good at demonstrating. The circle of life.'

'Like Disney's *The Lion King*?'

'I haven't read him, dear, but I'm sure you're right. Now, to the reason why I asked you to meet me today – it's lovely to see you, of course. Did I mention that? Now, you know I don't normally give people unsolicited advice . . .' she went on. This was not, in fact, my experience of Marlene: in the short time that her son and I had been a couple I had been the recipient of quite a lot of advice, albeit mainly along such lines as I really ought to use eyeliner and how just walking through the door of McDonald's was practically terminal for my karma. However, I said nothing. She carried on, 'It's just that, like I said, I've been getting the strongest feelings about you. Your face just keeps coming back again and again whenever I'm opening myself to the spirits.'

I was wishing I hadn't come. What was she going to say? It occurred to me that, just possibly, she did actually possess some kind of psychic power. She must have sussed that something had gone on between Peter and me. Help.

She closed her eyes and clasped her fingers loosely under her chin. 'You're a Scorpio, aren't you, sweetheart?' She frowned. 'Not that it matters too much, but I like to know what I'm dealing with, planetarily speaking. Now, I've been having the strongest feeling linking you to a child and, of course, now that Peter has appeared it all makes sense.'

'It does?' Oh, my God.

'Of course it does. Your relationship with Peter is as clear as crystal.'

Oh, my God. 'How do you know?' I asked.

She opened her eyes and flung back her hair, slightly crossly. 'I *am* a clairvoyant, you know, sweetheart. Anyway, please try not to interrupt. My spirit guides are finding you a bit offputting as it is. Unenlightened Scorpios are always a bit chaotic on an astral level.

'As I was saying, I'm experiencing you as a maternal figure, which I was finding initially confusing.' I opened my mouth to say something, but a look from Marlene silenced me. 'When I say that, of course, I don't mean "maternal" in the biological sense, as I'm sure you're intelligent enough to realise on your own. What I mean, and what the spirits are trying to tell you, is this.' She closed her eyes again for dramatic effect, and lowered her voice to a pretty spooky near-baritone. 'You and my son are meant to be together. In fact, a marriage has already taken place on a cosmic level. You and Nic have been married in a former life. This is why you and Peter get on so well – don't think I haven't noticed, dear, there's not much you can conceal from me. He has inherited some of my psychic abilities, and I can tell that he already thinks of you as a mother. It's as inevitable as the changing of the seasons. You and Nic and Peter are a family.' Marlene opened her eyes to look at me. 'This is no laughing matter,' she said.

'I'm sorry.' I was laughing as much with relief as genuine amusement. 'I don't want to sound rude, Marlene, but that's just . . . rubbish.'

'You're not doing well for someone who didn't want to sound rude.'

'I really am sorry,' I said, 'but there's no chance at all of me and Nic getting back together. We're not even compatible.'

She reached towards me for a small wooden box, which contained a selection of hand-rolled cigarettes with twisty little ends. 'Care for a spliff?' I shook my head, and she lit one for herself. The aromatic blue smoke drifted towards the ceiling and hung languidly in mid-air. Marlene renewed her attempt. 'I really feel you should think about this, Anna. I can only advise you based on my enhanced understanding, and you, of course, have the free will to ignore my advice. But I have to tell you, Nic is heartbroken.'

'About Steve?'

'Well, yes, of course. My talent as a clairvoyant seems to have skipped a generation there, and poor Nic seems genuinely to believe that once a person is dead, that's it.' So Nic wasn't as daft as he seemed, then. 'But it's you he's heartbroken about.'

I was getting cross now. 'I've had enough of this, Marlene. Nic and I were finished a long time ago, and if he's not over it yet, which I doubt, then it really isn't my problem. It was obviously a mistake for me to come to Steve's memorial thing, but Peter asked me so—'

'Well, there you are, then. You cannot resist being the mother figure to Peter. You're simply treading the path that was mapped out for you a long time ago.'

This woman was off her chops. It was time to leave. As I got up to go I had one last try. 'If it makes things any clearer, I'm engaged to someone else,' I said.

She took a long draw on her joint and held in the smoke for as long as she could without turning blue, then blew it out with a sigh. She looked tired, and for the first time since I'd met her, I thought she looked old. 'Okay, I'll come clean with you,' she said. 'Steve . . . Well, it's made me realise a few things about the way we brought Nic up. We were being true to ourselves, and the spirit of the times, and we thought it was for the best. He had an unstructured, free childhood. But now I look at him, and I see a lost soul. We gave him so much freedom but we didn't give him a proper path to follow. He's just confused and all over the place. And I think he needs some stability. Frankly, you're the nearest thing to stability he's ever had. He was happy when he was with you. And you get on so well with Peter.' She dabbed the remains of the joint into an ashtray and sat back, regarding me. She must have seen that her words were having no effect on me, because her tone hardened again and she said, 'It's up to you, of course. I've pointed out the path you should be taking, and if you choose to ignore my advice you're free to do so. But you're making a big mistake.'

I left the room, and the building, feeling as if I'd just been threatened. I was shivering slightly, but the hot sunshine on my shoulders warmed me instantly, and as I walked towards Holland Park I felt pity for Marlene more than anything else. The poor woman had been more affected by Steve's death than she'd let on.

<h1 style="text-align:center">50</h1>

Sadie phoned for an update.

'I've decided to marry Michael,' I said.

'Oh, God,' she said, 'Another one bites the dust.' There was a pause. 'Sorry. Just had to light a fag. Do go on.'

'Well, that's it, really. He came round a few days after I saw you, and we got, you know, pretty passionate, until Laura arrived, and then in the evening we babysat for Cameron—'

'Who's Cameron?' she asked.

'Laura and Dan's baby.'

'I thought it was Seth?'

'He was, but now he's Cameron after Nicolas Cage's character in *Con Air*.'

'They're going to have to settle on a name soon, or he's going to grow up with a dreadful identity problem. Look at me.'

'Why?'

'Darling, my full name, would you believe, and don't ever tell anyone, is Sadie Julia Michelle Prudence Rita. My parents were, and are, huge Beatles fans, and since I was practically a menopause baby and they reckoned – wrongly as the arrival of my younger brother proved – that I would be their one and only, they had to use all their favourite Beatles song names up on me. You may well laugh, but it's a burden I've had to bear. Thank God that at least it gave me a choice: I couldn't have coped with Prudence as my first name.'

'What's your brother called, then? Mean Mr Mustard?'

171

'Stuart. After Stuart Sutcliffe, the tragic fifth Beatle. But, anyway, to continue the Fab Four theme, you're all set to become Mrs Taxman?' I nodded happily and then realised she couldn't see me nodding, and said that I was. 'Darling,' she said, 'are you sure you're not making a hideous mistake?' Oh, not another person telling me I was making a mistake! 'Shouldn't you at least pop over to Sweden—'

'Denmark.'

'Quite. And give little Sven a proper go, just to be sure?'

'Sadie,' I said, 'I'm as sure as sure can be. I love Michael, absolutely and totally, from the ends of his hair to his toenails.'

'Ugh.'

'And we've talked about Lily. He knows it's going to be difficult for me, and he's okay about it. It feels sorted, I'm happy.'

She sighed. 'I'm going to have to meet this paragon before long, because I just don't believe anyone can be that good. But I'm truly glad you're happy. Even though I do think marriage is a bit of a barking mad thing to do, if it's what you want, then fine. And don't take me too seriously about the little Dane. I'm only jealous. I haven't had a decent shag in weeks. I'm beginning to think my hymen might heal over at this rate.'

51

My mum was disappointed that we weren't going to get married in Yorkshire. 'But we've got such pretty churches! I'd always pictured you getting married at St Thomas's – mind, I never pictured you being well into your thirties by the time you did it, but—'

'I'm only just into my thirties,' I corrected her.

'Well, you're not in the first flush, put it that way. Just an idea, why don't I ring Reverend Thorowgood and see if you can pop down and discuss arrangements?'

'I don't think—'

'Can you just take these sandwiches through to your dad and Michael? Will Lily have some, or should I do something else? They're egg and tomato.'

'She'll be all right with these,' I said, through clenched teeth, hefting up the huge plate. Dad and Michael were sitting on deck chairs in the garden, and Lily was playing on the lawn. She toddled over to inspect the food, selected a sandwich, expertly threw the tomato on to the grass and crammed the rest into her mouth, then wandered away again to resume her game.

'Mum thinks we should get married at St Thomas's,' I said, giving Michael a meaningful look.

Dad said, 'I thought you didn't want a church wedding?'

'We don't,' I said, looking to Michael for back-up. 'The only time I ever go to church is when one of the clients at work dies.'

'I used to be a choirboy,' Michael said casually.

I squealed in delight, and my dad said drily, 'It's marvellous to be at that stage when you're learning summat new about each other every day, in't it?'

I ignored him and enjoyed the mental picture I'd formed of Michael in one of those white robes with a ruffled collar, maybe holding a little candle. Then I thought of something else. 'Plus we're going to get married in London,' I said. 'It makes more sense: Michael's family are there, and all our friends. That way, there's only the two of you travelling. If we had it up here, we'd have to hire a coach.'

'Aye, it does make sense. It's not traditional, though, is it? In our day the wedding always took place in the bride's parish.'

'It will be,' Michael pointed out. 'In the parish where the bride lives now.'

Dad eased himself up out of the deck chair and picked up another sandwich to take to Lily. 'You're right,' he said. 'I'll have a word with her.'

The Reverend Thorowgood was thus spared a visit from us, but as a conciliatory gesture I asked Mum if she would come shopping with me in Leeds for my wedding outfit.

It always sounds a bit batty to be going shopping for clothes in Leeds when I live in London and have the entire resources of the West End and, theoretically, Knightsbridge at my disposal. But the drawback with London is, it's just so big. Far too much choice. The shopping area of Leeds is nice and concentrated. And they have a Harvey Nicks, so don't get snobby about it.

However, maybe bringing my mum hadn't been such a good idea.

'Right, then, first stop Beaux Brides in Armitage Street.'

'Shouldn't it be Belles Brides?'

'I don't know, Anna. You're the one with the French O level. It's this way.' She gripped my elbow and steered me firmly down a side street. She had obviously planned her route in advance, with the military precision of one of my own Christmas shopping runs. I must have inherited her shopping gene.

Beaux Brides was as frightful as its name implied. The window featured three fifties-style mannequins decked out in the sort of enormous lace-and-flounces creations that you just know cost the eyesight of scores of women in Bangladeshi sweatshops. Early retreat was impossible: for one thing I was still being gripped firmly by my mother, and opening the door caused a bell to ding somewhere at the back of the shop whence a small, permed woman emerged. She was the sort of person people describe as 'middle-aged', which I don't think we have in London. She spoke broad Yorkshire trying to be posh, as in: 'It's a reet popular line, is this, Modom.'

To be polite, I tried on a couple of what Mum and the saleslady (who were bonding like nobody's business) called 'frocks'. The first, and Mum's favourite, was a high-necked, Princess Anne/Captain Mark Phillips thing, with a heavily boned bodice and yards of superfluous material hanging off the back. 'Leg-o'-mutton sleeves,' Mum murmured, approvingly. It took both her and Mrs Slocombe several minutes to get the hundreds of tiny pearl fastenings done up at the back, and when they were finished I wanted to scream at them to get me out again. I've never been in anything as itchy and uncomfortable in my life. It was more claustrophobic than one of those total-body rubber fetish suits with matching gas mask. Not that I've ever worn one, but I read the Sunday supplements, and I have had occasion to traverse the backstreets of Soho – merely as a shortcut between Oxford Street and Charing Cross Road, you understand.

Once we'd put Beaux Brides behind us, I steered Mum firmly in the direction of Harvey Nichols, using as an incentive the excuse of a sit-down and a nice cup of tea in their café.

Mum was aghast at most of the clothes I looked at. 'Bottle green? What kind of a bride wears bottle green?' and 'Don't even think about that one, Anna. It's a wedding, not a ruddy funeral. Is that what you want to see every time you open your wedding album?'

As the day wore on and we were no nearer making a purchase, she started lobbying to revisit Beaux Brides. 'That Princess Anne one was really elegant,' she said wistfully. 'And your Michael would look so dashing in a topper and tails. Don't look at me like that, Anna. Young people these days have no concept of romance, I'm sure they don't.'

52

I had to admit, even to myself, that I was growing really fond of Lily. At twenty months, she was talking away, lots of words and even little sentences, and her personality was really showing through. This surprised me, because I'd never credited her with one before. She was very loving, giving Michael, his parents and even me affectionate hugs whenever she felt like it. It was so spontaneous and sweet it could turn your day round: standing in the bathroom cleaning my teeth, cross because I was late and I'd just laddered my tights, Lily would dash in and throw her arms exuberantly round my leg and say, 'Aaah.' Some mornings I was slowed down considerably as I had to make my way from bedroom to bathroom to kitchen with a small child attached to me. I was surprised to find I didn't mind.

It was making me realise what Michael meant when he said having Lily around made life better. It was like having my childhood back: I was amazed that she was learning the same songs and nursery rhymes I'd known, and amazed that I could still remember them to sing to her. And she was the one person in the world, bar none, who listened to me sing with apparent enthusiasm.

The thing I liked best was reading to her, particularly at bed-time when she was freshly bathed and in her snuggly pyjamas. She would sit on my lap while I read her *The Cat in the Hat* or *Madeline*, and when she'd heard a story a couple of times she could join in with the words. One story had a tiny picture of a spider on one page, and when we got to it we always had to stop and do 'Incy Wincy Spider'. If I forgot, Lily would jump up and down on my lap, kicking her little heels against my shins, and say, 'Do it! Do Incy Wincy! Do it!' If anyone in a story got a big hug, I got one too, and I loved the feel of her soft cheek against mine.

I was spending more and more time at Michael's house, to the point where we'd been talking about me giving up my flat and moving in, and Michael had a key cut for me. Sometimes after a hard day at work I thought fondly of my quiet, child-free flat, but increasingly I was happier with Michael and Lily. Their house felt more like home, and I'd even got the hang of incorporating child-safety measures into everyday life: Michael had now stopped following me around closing the bathroom door, relatching the baby gate at the foot of the stairs and shoving sharp knives and corkscrews to the back of the kitchen worktops.

The week after we got back from Yorkshire was mayhem at work. Having slimmed down to a size considered acceptable by his partner, Colin had departed for his fortnight in Tenerife. Apart from Christmas, this was one of our busiest times of the year and we had to find people to cover for all those taking planned or unplanned leave now that the weather was good. With Colin away the rest of us were working full stretch.

By Friday afternoon of the first week I was shattered. I was looking forward to spending the weekend with Michael, doing nothing more strenuous than sitting in the garden making sure Lily didn't impale herself on something. I got the bus to Crouch End.

It was packed and, as it turned out, it would have been quicker to walk, but you never know that when you get on a bus. The traffic was horrendous, and the bus nudged its way painfully slowly through the traffic, passing the same pedestrians over and over again. The only air coming in through the open windows was as hot as a hairdryer and had the furnace smell of diesel exhaust and dust. I closed my eyes, and pictured myself stretching out my legs on the cool, shaded grass in the garden, drinking a glass of wine, reading a book maybe, or just talking to Michael about how our day had been; simple pleasures. All this after Lily was safely put to bed, of course. It still irritated me sometimes that so much of our life had to revolve around her, and that real relaxation was only possible when she was asleep, but I was getting used to it.

After what seemed like a decade the bus got to my stop, and I barged and elbowed my way off between a solid mass of people in a way that would have horrified my Yorkshire relatives but was something you had to do in London. Otherwise you might end up in a bus depot somewhere hideously remote and never find your way back. I was sweaty, tired and had developed a powerful headache.

Michael's house was in a street on such a switchback of a hill it made me think of San Francisco. It was a horrible slog up that hill at the best of times, but today it was a hideous ordeal. I could feel sweat in my hair and my shirt was clinging to my back. As I got nearer to the house, I became aware that someone was standing outside. Just my luck – a Jehovah's Witness or a Mormon to get rid of before I could even get my shoes off. At closer inspection, this was an uncommonly pretty Jehovah's Witness – I ruled out Mormon because they're always men in suits. This was a woman of about my age or slightly younger, with expensive-looking clothes and expensively streaked blonde hair. She had a face you couldn't help but describe as cute: one of those snub-nose Meg Ryan jobs. I wanted to slap her for looking so cool and poised when I felt like I'd been squirted from the hot bowels of hell.

She smiled at me when it became clear I was aiming for the door she was standing outside.

'Oh, hello,' she said, blinking at me with baby-blue eyes. 'I think I must be at the wrong house. I'm looking for Michael Taylor. Does he still live here?'

'Yes, he does,' I said.

'Well, I don't think he's at home,' she said.

'Does he – is he expecting you?'

'Not exactly,' she said. 'I thought I'd surprise him.'

This was too much. 'And you are—?'

'Fiona,' she said.

I suppose everybody else would have seen that coming from a mile back. Just when everything's looking rosy, and wedding outfits are being contemplated, the skeleton is bound to jump out of the closet. Happens every time, but I was still unprepared for it. I attempted to gain the upper hand by introducing myself as Michael's fiancée. I was pleased to see that this rattled her cage ever so slightly, but she reasserted what I assumed to be her professional poise in a flash, and congratulated me in that socially elegant way I've never quite mastered.

'Do you mind if I come in and wait for him?' she asked. 'It's such a hike all the way out here.' As if Crouch End was deepest Botswana, or somewhere. If she'd walked, maybe, but I would put money on it that she'd taken a cab.

'Where are you staying?' I asked, as I unlocked the door, hoping that my voice implied *anywhere but here*.

'At the Dorchester,' she said smoothly. Forget slapping her – punching her would be so much more satisfying. But I'm a civilised person so instead of offering her handbags at dawn on Hampstead Heath, I offered her a Coke. I expected her to turn it down and whip out a bottle of Evian, or at least demand Diet, in the way of Americans who find caffeine and sugar just too damn risky. Instead she said. 'It's not Diet, is it?' When I said no, it was proper, fat Coke, she accepted, and we went out into the garden, where the sun was still fairly hot.

Fiona selected a shady spot and sat down on the grass. She flicked open her can and took a long drink. I can't stand people who can drink Coke that fast without burping. 'The thing with Diet Coke, or Diet Anything,' she said, 'is the artificial sweetener. Total poison. I mean, sugar is bad enough, heaven only knows, but at least it's natural.'

'Michael told me you work on TV news.'

'He told you about me?'

'Of course he did,' I said defensively, thinking, Why wouldn't he? 'All about Lily, and everything,' I added. She considered this for a moment. The thought flickered through me, What if he hasn't told me *every*thing? But I dismissed it.

'So you get on with . . . Lily?' she asked, stretching out legs that looked as if they were no strangers to the Stairmaster.

'Yes, I do,' I said, hating her sitting there with her legs and her hair, barely remembering Lily's name but being more part of her than I ever would be.

Right on cue, I heard Lily and Michael's voices inside the house, then Lily appeared in the doorway, wearing orange dungaree shorts and a bright yellow sunhat. She stopped short on seeing that I wasn't alone and just stared at Fiona without moving. I'd been on the receiving end of Lily's deadly stare a few times myself, and by now I was used to it. It was just her way of sizing someone up. Fiona, however, seemed quite freaked out by it. When Michael appeared behind his daughter, he just stared at Fiona too, and she stared back. It reminded me of the scene at the end of *Face/Off* where everyone is pointing a gun at someone else. It seemed to be up to me to break the ice.

'Fiona's here,' I said, unnecessarily I know but I had to say something. The ice, however, remained resolutely intact. Fiona tried a chirpy 'Hi!' which only had the effect of making Lily hide her face against Michael's leg. Oh, well done, Lily, I thought. I was watching Michael's face for a reaction: the one I was worried about would be the pleased one but, to my relief, there was no sign of it.

Things didn't get much better. Although Michael had always said that Fiona might have to be part of Lily's life, now that she had actually appeared he didn't seem best pleased. As for Fiona, Michael's presence seemed to make her pose a bit more, go all flirtatious. I tried to reassure myself that some women are like that in the presence of any man. For heaven's sake, even Laura's a bit like that when Michael's around. It certainly didn't seem to me that Fiona had been driven back to London by an overwhelming urge to see her child. I don't think she spoke a direct word to Lily the whole time: in fact, she reacted much as I had when I'd first known Lily myself, a sort of politely suppressed horror.

She visibly relaxed when Michael said he ought to be getting Lily to bed. He picked up his daughter, and said, 'Aren't you coming, Anna?'

'Sorry?'

'Aren't you coming to read Lily her story?' he said pointedly, and added in Fiona's direction, 'She can never get to sleep until Anna reads her a story.' Complete lies: generally at bedtime only Daddy would do, and I was more than happy to have an hour to myself for reading and general pottering while they got on with it. But I dutifully followed Michael into the house. When we were well out of earshot he said, 'What's she doing here?'

'As if I have any clue,' I said.

'Daddy bath,' Lily added. Michael reassured her that it would indeed be Daddy doing the bathing, but that he needed to talk to Anna first.

'Daddy bath!' Lily insisted. 'Anna not.'

'Okay, okay,' he said to her, and started to run the bath. I perched on the loo seat and watched him undressing her.

'Did you know she was coming?' I said. I felt I had to ask, even though Fiona had said that she was going to surprise him.

'No,' he said, loading Lily's toothbrush with the disgusting-looking bright red toothpaste she favoured. 'And I really wish she hadn't.'

'She's very attractive.'

'I suppose she is, in a groomed sort of way.' He turned away from the tooth-cleaning to look at me. 'Anna Anderson! You're jealous!'

'Well, there's no need to look so bloody smug about it. Of course I'm jealous! She's gorgeous and successful and probably loaded. She told me she's staying at the Dorchester; famous people stay there! Plus she's your ex-lover. Of course I'm jealous.'

'But I'm marrying *you*,' Michael said reasonably, and I had to concede that I was ahead on points there.

'The worst part of it is, she's Lily's mother,' I said, 'so there'll always be that connection, for the whole of Lily's life.'

'Which is why it's important for you not to get jealous. You know that anything between me and Fiona was over when Lily was born – not long after she was conceived, actually.'

'That's the bit I don't want to think about, thanks.'

'Anna, stop it. There's as much point in you being jealous about me and Fiona as there is in me being jealous about you and Nic. And you see him a lot more than I'm ever likely to see her.'

'But he's Nic,' I objected.

'And she's Fiona,' he said. 'And they're both history. You've got to trust me, like I trust you, and we'll be fine.'

When we went back downstairs I noticed straight away that Fiona had been retouching her already perfect makeup. This was a modification so subtle that Sherlock Holmes himself might not have noticed it, but to eyes sharpened by a serious case of insecurity it was as plain as the Meg Ryan nose on her face. Out of politeness Michael asked her to stay for dinner and, annoyingly, she accepted. I thought these showbiz people always had lots of exciting premières and stuff to go to, but apparently she'd kept this evening free. Gosh, thanks.

Actually, dinner wasn't as bad as it might have been. Michael, bless him, made frequent references to our impending marriage, and when the conversation strayed to people and events they had in common he tactfully steered it back to something more neutral.

'Still working for that news network?' he asked her.

'Mmn, no,' Fiona said, chewing a mouthful of pasta and taking a sip of wine before continuing. 'I got head-hunted by another company. It's really exciting because I'm presenting the whole show rather than just segments.'

'What's the show?'

She waved her hand self-effacingly. 'Oh, you wouldn't have heard of it over here. What about you?' she asked me. 'You said you do some kind of social work?' She said this as if I'd just come hot-foot from a leper colony – although, according to Dan, it's not politically correct to call it 'leprosy'. It's Hansen's Disease. She paid about as much attention to my reply as I pay to party political broadcasts on TV.

Mercifully, Fiona asked Michael to call her a cab as soon as dinner was over. 'Busy schedule tomorrow,' she said, pronouncing it 'sked-yule,' in the American way. 'Meetings with sponsors and so on. Yawningly dull, but it's all part of the job, unfortunately. Look, I'm here for another couple of days and I would like to see you all again before I go, if that's okay.' At this my heart sank. I had hoped this would be the last time I would ever have to see her in my life.

'Of course you can,' Michael said, rather stiffly. 'Give us a call and we'll sort something out.' The cab arrived, and she air-kissed both of us on both cheeks, though it seemed to me that there was less air between her and Michael than there might have been.

As the taxi tore off down the hill, Michael looked at me. 'Well, what was I supposed to say?'

'I don't know. You could have said we were going away for the weekend.'

'You could have said that yourself if you'd thought of it.' We went through the house to the garden. It was dark now, but the air was still warm; there was a slight breeze and a scent of honeysuckle. We sat on the kitchen step.

'Is she going to be popping up all the time now?' I wanted to know. 'Will she be wanting to see Lily, and take her out places and play mother?'

'I don't know,' he said. 'I hope not. Things were perfect the way they were, and I wish I knew why she's suddenly decided to appear.'

'Apparently she wanted to see you and Lily.'

'See Lily, maybe. Not me. And if she wants to see Lily more often, I don't suppose we can stop her. *I* don't want to stop her. She is Lily's mum, after all.' I suddenly felt very pissed off indeed, resentful and jealous. I think it's because it was the first time I'd ever heard Michael use the word 'mum' when he was talking about Fiona; he'd always said 'mother' before. There was something familiar about 'mum', something cosy and comforting that made me think of tomato soup and freshly laundered clothes, and of someone who'll cry when you're an angel in the school nativity play.

I didn't want Fiona to be Lily's mum.

*

True to her word, Fiona popped up again over the weekend. But the more I saw of her – and this isn't just jealousy speaking, though of course that hadn't gone away despite the pep talk from Michael – the less I trusted her. I had the feeling she was after something and, of course, the 'something' had to be Michael.

The second time she came she brought someone with her, a small, chubby, bearded man with greying hair, dressed head to toe in faded denim, with a huge camera bag strapped to his chest. He looked like an overfed war correspondent.

She introduced him as 'Fabrizio', and added that he was a 'terribly brilliant' photographer, and she'd brought him to take some souvenir portraits of Lily.

Lily loved having her picture taken, so Michael dutifully changed her into her prettiest dress, as requested by Fiona, and brought her down to the garden where Fabrizio had set up his equipment. For the best part of an hour Lily was coaxed into various poses, some on her own but most of them with Fiona. Finally, Michael was persuaded to join them for a couple of shots. Happy bloody families.

'Okay, that should do it,' Fiona said.

'What about a couple with Anna?' Michael suggested. Fiona and Fabrizio exchanged a barely perceptible look, but enough to set my feminine-intuition-radar beeping. It was clear enough to me that she still wasn't particularly interested in Lily. On the other hand, she didn't seem that interested in Michael, either, but I guessed she was probably trying to be cool and let her media-babe persona and their shared history do the rest. I watched Fabrizio load his camera with yet another reel of film, and wondered what Fiona had told him about his day's assignment. Getting cosy shots of the soon-to-be-family Taylor apparently hadn't been part of the brief.

Well, to hell with that. I took up a proprietary position next to Michael on the lawn, and Lily, bless her heart, demanded that I hold her. The three of us smiled brightly into the camera lens.

Before they left, Fiona promised to send us copies of the best pictures.

A professional photographer? I just presumed that's what media people did for souvenir snaps when the rest of us would get out our little Kodak snappy or pop into a Photo Me booth.

53

'Anna,' Veronica's voice buzzed in my ear with the pleasant timbre of a dentist's drill, 'it's Nic for you. Putting you through!'

I hadn't heard from Nic since I'd left Somerset, and it was rare for him to phone me at work, but this time it was indeed him, rather than Mick, the purveyor of pens.

'Hi, Anna. It's me, Nic. How's it going?' I braced myself for the inevitable whinge, followed by the equally inevitable 'Anna-I-need-your-help.' Worse again, I wouldn't have had the heart to refuse, given that he was recently bereaved, and I'm basically a soft touch.

But to my total shock: 'I rang to see how you are,' he said, his voice all concern.

I was deeply suspicious. 'Erm, I'm fine, thanks. Absolutely fine.'

'Things going okay with Mike?'

'Michael. Yes, things are going very well indeed. In fact I've got some news. We're getting married in September.' This was greeted by silence, then, 'Are you sure?'

'What do you mean, am I sure? Of course I'm sure. You're invited, naturally.' Which he hadn't been, until that moment, but it seemed discourteous not to ask him. I just had to hope that Michael would be understanding.

'Well, I hope you know what you're doing,' he said,

sounding more like the sulky Nic I was used to. 'I'm not sure he's the right guy for you, Anna.'

'How do you know? You've only seen him for about five seconds on Hungerford Bridge!'

'I know, I know. But I can't help thinking that you didn't give *us* much of a chance.'

'Pardon?'

'We were good together, Anna.'

'Oh, please,' I said. 'You sound like you're in a bad soap opera. And we weren't good. We were crap. That's why there is no "us" any more.'

'I thought we really connected,' he persisted.

'We were crap.'

'*We* weren't crap,' he said. 'I was crap.' He was taking the crap part on board at least, I noted thankfully. 'I just wasn't any good at relationships; I wasn't very good at life. But a lot has changed in the last couple of weeks. Meeting Peter has changed a lot.' His voice sounded more animated than usual. 'Isn't he great?' he said, and I had to admit that he was. 'He's so . . . capable,' he went on, and I couldn't argue with that either. 'It's made me do a lot of thinking about life in general, and relationships, and . . . well, I've been wondering if we should give it another go.'

I couldn't believe this. 'Pardon? Nic, do you never listen to a word I say? I'm with Michael now. I love him. We're getting married.' Another silence, during which I hoped he was allowing what I'd said to sink in.

'Well, can I meet you after work?'

'Is there any point? And I've got to get home to Michael anyway. We're living together now.'

'Okay, I get what you're saying.' Hallelujah. 'But can we meet anyway? I'd just really like to see you, just, you know, to talk.'

'I have to go. I'm busy,' I muttered, through clenched teeth. A cosy chat with Nic was the last thing I wanted to do after work.

But, in typical Nic fashion, he whinged on and on until I gave in. Finally he clinched it by playing the emotional blackmail card.

'I've got no one else I can talk to about Steve, and everything.'

'All right!' I snapped. 'I'll see you in the Flag about five thirty, okay?' and plonked the phone down.

Veronica had come into the room with a pile of timesheets: she was looking most interested in the conversation.

'Was that Michael?' she wanted to know.

'No. You know it wasn't Michael – you put the call through, for heaven's sake.'

'You could have rung out after that – I don't listen on the line, you know.'

'Only because Clare might catch you.'

'Don't be like that, Anna. I'm just concerned, that's all. I thought maybe you two had had a spat.'

'A "spat"? I don't know what that means. What's a "spat"?'

'You know,' she said, irritatingly. 'A tiff.'

'No. We haven't had a tiff. Or a spat. Or a set-to. We're bliss personified, thank you.'

'There's no need to get sarky. I'm only concerned.' She fiddled with the point of her blouse collar for a second, and said, 'Dennis and I had a bit of a spat at the weekend, but we made it up.' She leant towards me confidingly. 'It's amazing what you can do with low lighting and baby oil.' She turned and left the room. Which was just as well, because I thought I was going to be sick.

I wasn't looking forward to seeing Nic if he was going to be all clingy. Then I had a brilliant idea: what I needed was the presence of a third party to defuse any possible tension. Michael was out, for fairly obvious reasons, and so was Laura; always supposing I could part her from her beloved offspring at such short notice, she would rather, as Sadie would say, chew her leg off than sit in a pub with Nic.

Sadie! The very person.

I called her and arranged to meet her just ahead of when I'd said I'd see Nic.

'I just can't believe the cheek of him, saying he's ready to give it another go!' I told Sadie, filling her in quickly before Nic appeared. 'And you know I told you about his mother, the other week? It's unbearable. They're both mad as fruit pies.'

Sadie laughed her smoky laugh. 'Oh, to have all these men falling at one's feet, darling. My sex life is about to be declared a national emergency at any moment. Things have come to such a pass that George Preston has been making cow-eyes at me over his bit of carpet-covered partition wall, and I'm almost thinking of giving him the nod.' She glanced around the pub, and her eyes widened slightly, then narrowed like a stalking cat. 'But actually, sod that. If, as they say, there are plenty of fish in the sea, Catch of the Day has just appeared.' She inclined her head ever so slightly towards a tall, striking-looking man dressed in jumble-sale chic who had just come in. He had incredible grey eyes. Interesting.

'Sadie,' I said, 'meet Nic.'

Nic was not best pleased to find that I'd brought a chaperone, and said as much when Sadie went to the bar.

'What did you expect?' I hissed. 'That I'm going to be sitting here waiting for you to come in and get all silly? You're lucky I didn't bring Michael.'

'But you didn't, did you?' he said, in the tone of voice people normally reserve to say, 'Aha!' or 'Touché!'

I was too tired for this. 'What's this all about, Nic? You didn't say anything about it while I was staying at Marlene's.'

'Would it have made a difference if I had?'

'No.' It would have been incredibly embarrassing, though. 'So why have you now decided you want to get back together with me? It's not like you haven't been out with other people since we split up. There was that Peggy-Sue person, for one.'

He tried to take my hand. I pulled it away, and looked

anxiously over to see if Sadie was going to be long. She was still waiting to be served, but she glanced back at me, then at Nic, and gave me a meaningful look.

'Marlene thinks we should be together,' Nic said petulantly.

I might have known. 'Since when did you believe any of what Marlene says?'

He ignored this. 'She says a marriage has already taken place, cosmically speaking.'

'I know.'

'You know?'

'She told me,' I said. 'And I told her that was crap.'

'But it isn't crap,' he said, in that 'Aha!' tone again. 'Just look at the way Peter's so comfortable with you. It all makes sense.'

Mad as a balloon. Grief, or years of drug abuse, had clearly unhinged him.

Mercifully, Sadie returned with the drinks, and turned her attention immediately to Nic. 'I hear you're suffering from unrequited love,' she said to him, with an impressive lack of tact that made me slightly nervous about whether she would mention Peter. I wondered if it had been such good idea, after all, to invite her along.

'And is it any of your business?' he retorted.

Sadie was undeterred. 'You can just forget it. She's mad about this Michael,' she said. Leaning towards Nic she whispered dramatically, 'He's a tax inspector, you know.'

'So?'

'So he is nothing less than Her Majesty's instrument of revenue collection.'

'Inspection,' I said. 'Collection are a different lot altogether.'

'Whatever, his powers are granted by the Queen herself, and our friend here loves him terribly and is deeply in his thrall.'

'In his what?' Nic looked at me. 'Your friend,' he said, 'is mad.' Which was rich.

'I'm just mad north by north-west,' Sadie purred. 'I'm not the one chasing wild geese and barking up wrong trees.'

Nic blinked at her. 'So what are you chasing, then?' he said. Ooh, he was such a flirt, considering he was supposed to be here to persuade me to have him back; but he was matched by Sadie who, now that she had his attention, was ignoring him and asking me something about work.

Poor Nic was floundering; he was ill-prepared for Sadie. But I could see that he was intrigued. I had to admire Sadie's technique: he wouldn't be able to hold out for long at this rate. Fairly soon he was doing that metaphorical tugging-on-her-sleeve, but accompanying it with huge dollops of that sexy thing I used to find so irresistible till I knew him better. My main concern now was, had I warned Sadie enough of what a liability he could be? I didn't just want to offload him and let him become someone else's problem. Well, I did, but not someone I knew and liked, for heaven's sake.

What the hell? Good luck to them. There would be plenty of time to warn her later.

I was keen to get back to Michael, and it wasn't long before I was able to make my excuses and leave, but before I did, I pulled Sadie aside and said, 'Do not, under any circumstances, mention his son.'

'Darling,' she said, 'I do not plan to spend the evening with family chitchat. Trust me, I know what I'm doing.'

And she most clearly did. Nic was powerless to resist.

54

I have to hand it to Sadie: she's a well-mannered girl. The next day she rang me to say a polite thank-you for passing my unwanted ex-boyfriend on to her. 'Darling, don't change your mind whatever you do, but what on earth were you thinking of, rejecting that lovely man in favour of a tax inspector?'

'You really ought to meet Michael one of these days,' I laughed. 'So things went well with Nic, then?'

'To be honest, darling, it all turned into a bit of a haze, though I have an odd but pleasurable recollection of him singing "Subterranean Homesick Blues" in bed at one point.' The old singing in bed: I remembered it well.

'So are you seeing him again?'

'Oh, definitely.' Her voice was more animated than I'd ever heard it: she usually sounded languid to the point of comatose. 'He's a total darling. However, not tonight,' she added.

'Why not?' I asked.

Sadie tutted. 'It's easy to tell you've been in a jolly monogamous relationship for some months,' she said. 'You've forgotten how important it is to keep the buggers wanting more. I've told him I'm going to a party and he isn't invited.'

'And what are you doing really?'

'I'm going to a party!' she said. 'Do keep up. And he isn't invited. You are.'

The idea of a party was a tempting one, but what with Fiona sniffing around and everything I wondered whether it would be more sensible to stay at home. Sadie was having none of that. 'I'm not asking you to run off and join the Foreign Legion,' she said. 'It's only someone at work having a house-warming party. I'll have you home and tucked up with Mr Revenue by midnight.'

'But—'

'Come on, Anna,' she pleaded. 'One teensy party isn't going to kill you.'

I might still have said no, but it was the best offer I'd had since the previous weekend when Laura had called.

'I just rang to ask you if you and Michael and Lily wanted to come over on Saturday night,' she'd said. 'It's the Eurovision Song Contest on television and we're going to make a night of it, get some wine and nibbles in. Dan's even run off some scorecards on the office photocopier so we can all vote. Royaume-Uni *douze points* and all that.'

I mentioned this to Sadie.

'Oh, good Lord,' she said. 'They're going to be asking for one of those heated footwarmer things for Christmas next.' I didn't tell her that it had actually been good fun; it would only have confirmed her view that all us (practically) marrieds-with-children were beyond the pale.

Michael came into the room as I was putting the phone down.

'I've put Lily down for her nap,' he said. 'I think she's getting a bit of a cold.' Oh, lovely. When Lily had a cold she produced unfeasible amounts of mucus and got even more clingy and attention-seeking than usual, which was as good a reason as any to go out. And, of course, being Michael and being generally rather lovely, when he heard I'd been invited to a party he insisted I should go.

55

'You didn't tell me it was in South London,' I grumbled to Sadie, as we waited at London Bridge station for a train to somewhere obscure. Since I've lived in London I've realised that people are tribal in terms of whether they favour north or south of the river. It seems to depend on where you pitch your tent when you first arrive, and since I've always lived towards the northern reaches of the Piccadilly Line, South London is another country. I can cope if I'm within striking distance of a tube station, but we were heading for one of those places that can only be reached by an unreliable little train running to an incomprehensible timetable.

'Apparently house prices are much cheaper down there,' Sadie said. 'Olga and Billy got a four-bedroom end-of-terrace for what you'd pay for a bedsit where I live. Still,' she said, wafting her hand around to indicate all points south of the Thames, 'what a trade-off, eh? I'd rather live in a damp tea chest in Islington than have to do this journey every day.'

If the journey had been horrendous, the party, when we finally reached it, didn't look too promising either. Olga and Billy had apparently forgotten the golden rule of housewarming parties, which is: have the party before you've installed the shag pile and the Lawrence Llewellyn-Bowen wallpaper. The presence of said domestic beautifications meant that Olga and Billy were taking turns standing guard at the front door asking guests to remove their shoes. There was already a scale model of the Matterhorn in abandoned footwear in the hallway by the time we arrived. I wondered what the people next door were thinking about their new neighbours as we stepped into a room full of people attempting to hold a conversation against a thundering musical backdrop of some of the naffest hits of the eighties.

'Good God,' Sadie roared into my ear. 'I had no idea Olga and Billy were into post-modern-ironic. We need to get pissed very quickly.'

I had to agree with her; it was clearly going to be the sort of party that's best viewed through the bottom of a glass. The hosts were so tense about their furnishings that they spent the whole evening rushing around with J-cloths, blotting at real or imagined stains and grease-spots and shooing smokers into the garden. 'Just like being at work,' Sadie reflected. So we drank a lot, and bitched about the other guests, and Sadie flirted outrageously with various men, only to desert them as soon as she had their full attention.

'I'm missing Nic,' she confided to me, 'and I never thought I'd hear myself say that about a man. He is just so adorable.' She slurped at her wine.

I was missing Michael, too. 'Maybe we should go home?' I suggested hopefully, expecting a sarcastic comment about my failure to make the grade as a party animal, but to my surprise she agreed.

'Just need the loo,' she said, and wove off in the direction of one of the staircases. It didn't matter whether it was the up one or the down one: there were bathrooms all over the place.

I sat down to wait for her, squeezing myself into a corner where I wouldn't get elbowed by people who were attempting to do the zombie dance routine to Michael Jackson's 'Thriller'. I'd drunk far too much too quickly, and thought I'd be paying for it in the morning, so I decided to get a drink of water to stave off dehydration. Olga and Billy were in the kitchen: he was washing up, wearing yellow Marigold gloves, and she was scraping guacamole off plates into a pedal bin. Why do people bother with parties? I wondered. Olga and Billy would have had a far better time on their own with a glass of wine and a video, which is exactly what I wished I'd done. I drank my water as quickly as I could and put the glass into Billy's outstretched Marigold, then left them to it, and went to find Sadie.

'They've got a full array of matching electric toothbrushes up there,' she informed me.

'I've never used an electric toothbrush,' I said. 'I don't like the idea of something vibrating in my mouth.'

Sadie gave me an arch look, and we dissolved into giggles. 'I got one as a Christmas present but I've never dared use it,' she said, as we went to find our coats. 'My bathroom window is right opposite my lecherous neighbour's bedroom, and I would hate him to misconstrue that noise and think I was having to resort to a vibrator. A girl has her reputation to consider.'

On our way past the kitchen, Sadie spotted several unopened bottles of wine on the floor under the table. Olga and Billy had finished the washing-up, and had presumably gone to stand guard over their soft furnishings; the kitchen was empty. Without a word, Sadie grabbed a couple of the bottles.

'May as well get something out of it,' she said, and stuffed them into the two large 'shoplifting' pockets on the inside of her coat.

'We shouldn't,' I said. 'It's for the party.'

'And the party's crap, so we're going to finish it elsewhere,' she said.

'You're pissed,' I said, but I underestimated how pissed she was. After thanking Billy for a lovely party – there was no sign of Olga who'd last been spotted clutching a Fortnum and Mason's carrier bag which she was filling with empty beer cans – we stepped out into the warm evening air.

'Do you think they have taxis down here?' I wondered.

'Everyone has to pay taxes,' Sadie drawled. 'Would have thought your Michael would have told you that.' We walked towards the main road, with me supporting Sadie who was weaving slightly across the pavement. The main road was fairly deserted; it was about midnight, but there didn't seem to be many cars around and certainly no taxis. Another thing I've noticed about living in London is that I'm all cocky and confident in the areas that I know, at whatever time of day or night, but as soon as I'm in an unfamiliar neighbourhood I anticipate muggers round every corner. Standing on a deserted pavement next to a row of metal-shuttered shops with only a drunken female for back-up was not the most comfortable feeling I've ever had.

Suddenly Sadie spotted a black cab coming towards us. 'Taxi!' she screeched, flinging her arm in the air. At first it looked as though he wasn't going to stop, but he pulled into the side of the road fifty yards ahead of us. We broke into that upright jog that unfit people do when they need to move quickly, and that's when Sadie tripped and fell heavily to the ground. There was a crashing sound as the bottles in her coat pockets smashed, and red wine started to ooze across the pavement.

The taxi driver had got out of his cab to find out what had happened. 'Fuckin' hell,' he said, when he saw the stain spreading around Sadie. 'Is that blood?'

I crouched beside Sadie, who was getting up from a totally

prone position on to her knees. 'I seem to have impaled myself,' she said, with as much dignity as she could muster.

The taxi driver wanted to call an ambulance, but decided it would be quicker to take us to the hospital himself, which he did with a heroic disregard for the state of his upholstery.

We were all convinced that Sadie was about to die at any moment, particularly Sadie who was being terribly brave and issuing me with instructions about her funeral. 'No hymns. I want Nancy Sinatra singing "These Boots Are Made For Walking". And lots of orchids. Masses of them,' she said in a tragic half-whisper.

However, once we got her into the A and E department, a no-nonsense nurse had a quick look at the injuries, decided they were fairly superficial – amazingly – and told us to wait in the queue with all the other Saturday-night drunks.

'Oh, this is so humiliating,' Sadie moaned. 'And I've ruined this dress. It's full of holes.' She looked like she'd been in a bomb blast, her dress and coat soaked in red wine and ripped by the glass.

'You smell like a wino,' I said, adding insult to injury. It was now almost one o'clock, and I'd told Michael I wouldn't be late. I went to find a payphone to ring him.

I dialled his number, but there was no reply. I listened to the ringing tone, waiting to hear his voice, sleepy or cross or amused, but the ringing continued, and the answering-machine was apparently turned off. I hung up and returned to Sadie, feeling anxious. Where was he? Why wasn't he answering? I tried to dismiss any thoughts of Fiona, and decided he must have turned off the ringer so Lily wouldn't be disturbed.

If you're going to have an accident, don't do it on a Saturday night: it's peak-time in Casualty. We ended up in the hospital for the entire night while Sadie was examined, X-rayed and all the little slivers of glass picked out of her and the larger cuts stitched up.

In the meantime I was sitting in a waiting room that looked like the reception centre to hell, with fights breaking out around me and people snivelling and puking and grumbling. As the effects of my own alcohol consumption wore off, I wished I was wearing magic shoes so I could just click my heels and be back in Crouch End. I pictured Michael's sleeping face. When you talk about two people 'sleeping together', it usually means sex, but the operative word is really 'sleeping'. After all, the sex-to-sleeping ratio declines steeply as the relationship goes on, but even when you're at it like knives in the heady early days you're still going to spend at least seventy per cent of bedroom time asleep. So you have to ask yourself, not 'Who's the bloke who makes me want to clutch the sheets and bite the pillow?' but 'Who can I face waking up next to every morning when his breath smells like hamster shit and he's possibly dribbled on my pillowcase?' Though I must point out that Michael's breath and lack of dribbling made him an exemplary sleeping partner. I wished I was tucked up with him.

56

After dropping Sadie off in Islington, the taxi got me back to Crouch End at about six o'clock in the morning. I was hungover, tired and aching after a night spent sitting on a plastic hospital waiting-room chair. I thought I'd have a quick bath then maybe get a little snuggle with Michael before Lily got him up.

As soon as I opened the door I realised this was not going to happen. I could hear Lily crying at full throttle from her bedroom, and the sound of Michael's voice attempting to calm her down. Maybe I could just sneak up the stairs and get into the bathroom anyway, just to make myself presentable before I said good morning.

That wasn't going to be possible either, as I heard footsteps coming down the stairs. Then Fiona appeared. 'Oh!' she said, surprised to see me, but not as surprised and horrified as I was to see her: it was that *Face/Off* thing again. I noticed that Fiona was looking as ropy as I felt: she looked like she hadn't had much sleep either. I was going to have to kill her.

'Good party?' she asked, with that unnerving professional smile.

'What's going on?' I asked.

'I am totally shattered.' She flopped down on the sofa and yawned.

'Why?' Did I want to know why?

'We've been awake all night.' I didn't know whether to kill her, cry, run upstairs and kill Michael, kill myself or just sit down and laugh myself to death.

Upstairs, Lily had stopped crying, and I heard Michael coming down the stairs.

Fiona stood up and stretched. 'I'd best leave you both to it,' she said, as Michael came into the room. 'I'll call you later.' She kissed his cheek.

'Thanks, Fiona,' he said, as she left the room. A few seconds later I heard the front door shut.

Michael gazed at me: like Fiona, he was looking fairly rough. 'Where've you been?' he said. 'I've been going out of my head here.'

'Has she been here all night?'

'Who? Fiona?'

'Of course bloody Fiona!' I yelled at him.

He made a shushing noise. 'You'll wake Lily.'

'As if that's the most important thing right now.'

'She's been ill,' he said. 'Lily. She was really ill. I thought it was meningitis or something horrible like that. She had a temperature of almost forty degrees'

'Is that bad?'

He looked exasperated. 'Anna! It's very bad.' He sat down. 'I was really frightened,' he said. 'She's normally so healthy, and I didn't know what it was, and I didn't know how to get hold of you.' I sat next to him and put my arm around him. For a moment I forgot all about Fiona; all I could think about was Lily, and it felt like the biggest betrayal in the world that I hadn't been here when she and Michael needed me.

'Is she all right now?' I asked.

'The doctor came, at some point in the middle of the night. He said it's probably just an ear infection. I felt a bit stupid for overreacting, but if you'd heard her – she wouldn't stop screaming.'

'You were right to call the doctor,' I said. 'Can I go up and see her?'

'I suppose so,' he said. 'Just try not to wake her up. She's out cold on Calpol.'

I tiptoed upstairs to Lily's room, pushing back the door that still had the picture of Little Miss Sunshine on it. The curtains were drawn, and in the gloom Lily's breathing sounded like Darth Vader. She was lying on her back in her cot with no covers and just wearing a vest and nappy, her arms thrown above her head; she looked so little and vulnerable.

I remembered one time when I'd gone with her and Michael to the baby clinic for one of her immunisations. We were sitting in the waiting room, Michael holding his daughter and me holding the little envelope with her medical notes in it. Everybody had one of those envelopes; the receptionist got them from a carousel thing behind her desk and most of them were pretty thick and bulging with papers. Lily's was practically empty: she'd never been ill, she'd hardly had time to have any illnesses. I turned the envelope over, for want of something more entertaining to read, and noticed at the bottom there was a space to enter date and time of death. Even then, when I hadn't bonded with Lily at all and would cheerfully have sent her to a finishing school in Switzerland until she was eighteen, if such places accepted one-year-olds, I couldn't bear the idea that someone was already making provision for the end of such a little life. I made sure Michael didn't see the envelope.

Looking at Lily now, I realised how much she meant to me.

I went back downstairs. Now I'd reassured myself that Lily was all right, I wanted to know why Fiona had been there.

Michael told me that she'd just called round unexpectedly and, finding him in a bit of a state, had stayed. 'She was pretty good,' he said. 'Making cups of tea and everything.' As if I needed to feel worse, I'd managed to give Fiona her opportunity to do her devoted mother number. As if it wasn't bad enough that she was attractive and successful and sniffing around Michael and Lily all the time, now I'd let her get her foot properly in the door.

I expected Michael to be angry that I'd stayed out all night, but when I told him all about Sadie's accident his only comment was, 'Just a bad night all round, then.'

57

Lily was still fairly rough all day Sunday, so Michael decided to take Monday off to look after her. As I was leaving for work he was still wandering around groggily in his dressing-gown, half-heartedly entertaining Lily. By then the antibiotics were starting to work and she was almost as full of beans as ever.

I had offered to stay at home myself but Michael insisted that I went to work.

Colin was back from his holiday, and he was already at his desk when I arrived. On my desk was a large straw donkey. 'For me? You shouldn't have.' I laughed.

'Too right I shouldn't. We spent half an hour in Customs while they took that thing apart looking for drugs.'

'Did they find any?'

'Oh, pu-lease. You know I'm not that sort of boy. All drugs were consumed *in situ*, thank you very much. Anyway, take care of old Pablo, and watch out, 'cos he's held together with vicious little nail things. Definitely not for little Lily to play with.'

I tucked Pablo under my desk, and Colin proceeded to fill me in on his holiday. Their hotel had been full of what Colin called 'rampaging homophobic Club 18–30 types'. Luckily he and Daniel had met a lesbian couple in the airport on the way out, and they had mainly appeared in public as a foursome. The ruse had been so successful that Colin and Daniel had been invited to visit a straight strip club 'with the lads'.

'So I said to this huge, hairy bloke, in my best macho voice,' he essayed a butch growl, '"No thanks, dear, I can get that any time at home."'

'You called him "dear"?'

Colin rolled his eyes. 'I know. As soon as I'd said it I realised it was possibly a *faux pas*. But this guy was so pissed he didn't notice. So luckily we managed to avoid that little treat. Honestly, we spent the entire time reminiscing fondly about Old Compton Street. Where I can't wait to go and show off my tan, by the way.

'So what's the latest with you?' he wanted to know. I told him about Fiona's appearance. 'Oh, my God!' he said. 'I certainly wouldn't be letting an ex of Daniel's hang about all the time. I'd be showing them the front door in no uncertain terms.'

'I don't really have any moral high ground about it, though. She's Lily's mother and she just wanted to spend some time with her. Or that's what she said, anyway.'

'You didn't believe her?'

'I'm not sure,' I said, sighing. 'I'm just jealous, I know, but she just doesn't seem that bothered about Lily when they're together.'

'So you think she's after Michael?'

'I don't know,' I said. 'Partly I'm so obsessed with him I think everyone's after him. Partly I'm wondering why she should be hankering after an old flame when presumably she's got the pick of all these American celebrities and media people. She's absolutely gorgeous, by the way, which doesn't help.'

'You don't have a lot to worry about, I reckon. And look at you, anyway, girl, you're gorgeous yourself. She'd be no competition at all, even if she looked like Meg Ryan.'

Thanks, Colin.

58

After work I'd promised to call in on Laura and Cameron; Dan was still at the office.

'You look a bit happier,' I said to Laura, when she answered the door with a sleeping baby over her shoulder.

'Michael was right,' she said, in a whisper, leading the way into the house. 'It does get easier. I don't panic now when Dan goes out – I feel I can cope. He only ever wants one of three things, anyway.'

'Dan?'

'No, Dan wants one of four things. Cameron only ever wants food, or a clean nappy, or a sleep.' I tried to dismiss the picture of Dan wearing a nappy that had popped into my head.

Perhaps sensing even in his sleep that he no longer had his mother's undivided attention, Cameron woke up and wailed, a thin, animal sound that was nothing like Lily's full-throated roar. Laura produced a bottle of formula milk from the fridge, plonked it in the microwave and two minutes later Cameron was slurping away happily.

I told Laura about Lily being ill, and Fiona just happening to be in the right place at the right time.

'So is this Fiona still hanging around, then?'

'No,' I said, realising how relieved I was. 'She's had to resume her jetsetting lifestyle, thank God.'

'So she's back in America?'

'Not quite so glamorous,' I said. 'Manchester. Something to do with her job, I wasn't really listening when she was explaining it, just mentally punching the air at the thought that she would soon be out of my face. She's flying back to New York after that, so with luck we'll never see her again.'

'You don't sound convinced,' Laura pointed out. I wasn't. When Michael had first told me about Fiona, she was a faraway, unreal figure: he'd seemed so sure that she wouldn't ever want to have anything to do with Lily's life. Occasionally I would wonder about this person who would always have a link with us, even if we never set eyes on her. When I was feeling particularly insecure or pre-menstrual I would sometimes imagine that Michael could recognise Fiona in Lily and might miss her, and that as Lily got older she would surely be interested in meeting her real mother, but most of the time I managed to put those thoughts out of my mind.

'Honestly, Laura, if you'd seen Fiona – she's absolutely gorgeous. I'm willing to bet she doesn't even have any cellulite.'

'You're jealous, huh?' Cameron had finished his bottle, and Laura threw a cloth over her shoulder then hoisted him up to wind him, patting his back with hearty slaps.

'Jealous? I'm a mass of insecurity! He's been all reassuring as usual, of course, but I don't trust that woman, and I'm just glad she's out of the way . . .'

'There you are, then,' Laura said, jiggling the baby. 'She's gone, and you're still here, and you and Michael are getting married next month. Panic over.'

Cameron emitted a long, wet burp.

When Dan came back from work he had some news. 'Sadie was off work today. She rang to say she'd been stabbed on Saturday night.'

'Oh, my God,' Laura said. 'Is she okay?' And then, to me, 'I don't think it's anything to laugh about, Anna.' I told them exactly how Sadie had managed to get herself 'stabbed'.

'She's such a drama queen,' Dan said. 'Wait till I see her. And another thing she told me is that she's in love.'

'Again?' Laura laughed.

'Apparently it's the real thing this time. And the funniest thing about it is . . .' I could guess what was coming '. . . she's in love with Nic the Pric!'

Laura stared at me. I pulled a face. 'Sorry,' I said. 'I think that was my fault. I introduced them.'

'Oh, God,' Laura said. 'Now we're going to have to go through that whole thing again. How wonderful he is, how handsome and sexy and intelligent and all that bollocks, followed in a few weeks, or at best months, by the discovery that he's a paranoid, insecure dopehead with a heap of irritating habits, followed swiftly by, "He's completely unbearable and if he phones, pretend I'm out all day."' This was a pretty accurate summary of my relationship with Nic, but maybe Sadie's would be different.

'She'll eat him for breakfast,' was Dan's assessment.

59

When I went home I had visions of a lovingly prepared meal, a bottle of wine, our favourite music and an evening of unfettered shagging with my adorable fiancé. I repeated that word over in my mind: 'fiancé'. It had an acceptable ring to it, I decided.

I found Michael in the sitting room, with all the windows closed even though the room was stiflingly hot; Lily was asleep on the sofa beside him, her arms thrown above her head. I was surprised: he didn't usually let her fall asleep in the late afternoon, because then she wouldn't go to sleep till long after her usual bedtime and we'd all suffer. Obviously something was up. He greeted me distractedly. I sat down on the floor beside him so I didn't disturb Lily, my stomach in knots.

'What's the matter?' I asked, my heart pounding. Was this to do with Fiona?

He stroked my cheek with his finger like he did to Lily when she was upset. 'Nothing,' he said, leaning forward to kiss me. 'I suppose I'm still a bit groggy from not getting much sleep over the weekend.' I stood up and opened the window, letting in some cool air and terrifying a blackbird in the garden into a noisy retreat.

At this, Lily woke up and started whingeing. One side of her face was red and her fine blonde hair was sticking to her hot cheek; she rubbed her eyes fiercely with her fists. Michael picked her up and attempted to give her a hug, but she was turning rapidly from a baby to an independent, often cussed toddler, and feeling ill hadn't improved her mood: today she wasn't having hugs. She wriggled free and on to the floor.

'Bath,' she demanded.

'I'll bath her, if you like,' I volunteered.

'No, it's okay, I'll do it,' he said. 'You could start on the dinner if you like. Come on, babes.' He picked up Lily's blanket, which went everywhere with her, took her hand and they walked towards the stairs.

I trudged to the kitchen as sullenly as possible, and took out my irritation on a defenceless lettuce.

60

Later, while we were eating, Michael told me he had been thinking about going to visit his brother for a few days.

'That's a good idea,' I said. 'We could go next weekend.' I

still hadn't met Chris, who was in the RAF and lived in Lincolnshire. For the first time since I'd known him, I thought Michael looked slightly shifty.

'I thought I might go tomorrow,' he said.

'But I can't take tomorrow off,' I said. 'I need to give Clare a bit of notice.'

Suddenly the mayonnaise jar seemed to have acquired an irresistible allure: Michael was staring at it fixedly. 'I thought I'd just go on my own,' he said. 'With Lily, of course.' He looked up at me. 'Give you a bit of a break.'

'But I don't want a break.'

Michael sighed. 'To be honest,' he said, 'I think Chris wants to have a pre-wedding man-to-man talk.'

Well, that was a first. I hadn't got the impression that Michael and his brother were that close. I picked up the empty plates and put them into the sink slightly more noisily than necessary. 'Maybe you'll come back in a better mood,' I muttered.

'Maybe I will,' he said. I heard him pushing his chair back to stand up, then he was behind me, with his arms wrapped round me. 'Don't worry,' he said. 'We'll be back before you know it.'

61

The next day, Michael packed a small bag of clothes for him and a larger one for Lily, plus toys, nappies, travel cot – Lily seemed to require more luggage than Madonna in *Evita* – and loaded the car.

He put his arms round me and kissed me. 'We'll miss you,' he said, 'but we won't be gone long. Two or three days at the most. Here's Chris's number.' He handed me a piece of paper ripped from one of Lily's *Noddy* comics.

I waved sadly at them as they drove away, and Lily waved back enthusiastically from her little seat in the back, before picking up her blue toy steering wheel and proceeding to drive. Michael's hand waved at me out of the open window as the car disappeared down the hill.

I went inside, and rang Laura. Even though it was only eight thirty in the morning, it was a safe bet, now she had the baby, that she would have been up for hours. 'Michael's gone away,' I moaned, 'to see his brother. And I wasn't invited.'

Since he'd given her that pep talk after the birth of Cameron, Laura thought Michael was wonderful and would take his side against anyone. 'Well, he's getting all his duty visits out of the way before the wedding, that's all,' she said. 'I bet you weren't that keen to visit Biggles, were you?'

'I wouldn't have minded,' I said. 'He's going to be family, after all.'

'Take it from me,' Laura said. 'Just make the most of your last in-law-free weeks because your husband's family are not just for the wedding, they're for life. More's the pity.' I guessed from this that Dan was not in the room; the subject of Dan's ghastly relatives was something to be discussed only behind his back.

'But Michael was acting really strangely yesterday,' I said. 'Sort of distracted. I can't help feeling he's missing That Woman.'

Laura was not in the mood to indulge my paranoia. 'You're reading too much into it. It's plain for all to see that he adores you like crazy. You're so lucky.' She sighed. 'I wish I'd met Michael before I'd met Dan.'

'Laura! You don't mean that!' I said, secretly thinking, Of course she means it, any red-blooded woman would mean it.

'No, I don't mean it. Poor Dan might have his faults, but I've got him trained now. I wouldn't swap.' How that would have gladdened Dan's heart, had he heard it! 'Anyway, what you need is a spot of retail therapy. Any chance the Saintly Clare might let you have a long lunch?'

'I guess so,' I said. 'If I spend the morning being ultra-nice to Colin I'm sure he'd cover for me a bit, then I can work late tonight. I've got nothing to come home to, after all.' Laura groaned, briskly informed me of a meeting place and time, then went off to let Dan know that he would be in charge of Cameron for the afternoon.

62

'Have you ever noticed,' Laura ranted, when I met her in Oxford Street just after midday, 'that when women look after their children it's just called looking after their children and when the child's father does it it's called "babysitting". Like they're only-and-ever-will-be amateurs. It's pathetic.'

'Michael doesn't call looking after Lily "babysitting".'

'Well, there you are, then. Exactly.'

Laura decided that she was ready for some new clothes that didn't look like parachutes. Her belly was starting to subside ('The midwife gave me this leaflet of exercises to get my body back in shape, but these people can never have had a baby themselves. You're far too knackered for exercise'), and her boobs no longer strained at their moorings like over-inflated balloons. Her maternity clothes were hanging shapelessly on her, and of course her pre-pregnancy gear was all over nine months old and therefore beyond the pale.

We spent a glorious hour giving our credit cards the beating they so richly deserved.

I bought a couple of things to wear on our honeymoon, wherever that was going to be. We hadn't booked anything yet, planning to get a last-minute bargain to anywhere that could offer sunshine, a beach and a room with a big, big bed. I shopped accordingly, mainly swimsuits and lingerie that had

Laura gagging with envy. She made up for it by going mad in her favourite clothes shops, delighted to be a normal size again.

But we had the most fun buying children's clothes. Laura got loads of stuff for Cameron; I bought a couple of dresses and the most adorable little hat for Lily, and I couldn't resist one of those little pyjama suits with feet for Laura's baby. So much for the child-hating Anna Anderson, I thought. Baby, look at you now: word-perfect in the lyrics of 'The Wheels On The Bus Go Round and Round' and totally at home in Baby Gap. Just holding the tiny garment was making me feel borderline maternal, which was too weird to contemplate, so as soon as we got out of the shop I insisted we get right away from the world of child and steered the way to a trendy bar.

As we were walking into the glossy, air-conditioned, beech-and-chrome bar, Laura started complaining about pain in her pelvis when she walked a long way, due, she said, to the pelvic bones not having returned to normal yet after the birth. I tried not to pay too much attention because I found her endless stream of details about the horrors of childbirth too ghastly to contemplate. So while she found a seat near a window and subsided into it heavily, shored up by our bags, I fled to the bar, and decided that what we needed to complete our lunchtime decadence was cocktails. The barman determined that the only choice on this summery day was strawberry daiquiris. I agreed happily with his choice and he scuttled off to get creative with fruit. I was not in any hurry to get back to Laura until her train of thought had moved on from matters obstetric, so I picked up a magazine that was lying on the bar.

It was one of those American tabloid trash magazines, full of bogus gossip about soap 'stars' no one here has heard of, accounts of alien abductions and photographic 'evidence' of UFO sightings. The barman returned and started filling the cocktail shaker with ice.

Suddenly I felt like he had poured the ice down my back. 'I don't believe this,' I muttered.

'What's that, love?' the barman said, and glanced at the magazine. '"Cat Saved by Ghost of Elvis".' He laughed. 'I don't think you're really meant to believe that.'

I carried the magazine over to Laura, and plonked it down in front of her.

'What's up?' she asked, seeing the expression on my face. The barman came over with our drinks. Laura was looking at the photograph on the bottom of the open page.

'It's Michael,' she said. I nodded. 'And Lily. So who's this . . .?'

'Look what it says underneath.'

'"24/7 News's Fiona Edgar reunited at last with the family she left behind."' Laura looked at me in disbelief.

The article described how a recent 'romantic' visit to London had reunited the 'hot British anchorwoman' with 'the man she had never stopped loving and the child she desperately missed'. The photograph was one of the batch that had been taken in Michael's back garden.

'"Fiona is so happy now she's back with Michael," revealed a close pal of the stunning blonde anchor of cable channel 24/7 News's prime-time show. "He's the only guy she's ever really loved." The couple have a daughter, Lily, 2, and are reported to be looking for a house on Long Island."'

63

So I hadn't been imagining things: Michael had definitely been in a funny mood since Fiona left, and now I knew why. What an idiot I'd been, spending all that time anguishing about Peter, and for what? Only to have Michael get back with his ex and move to New York.

'You can't believe what you read in these things,' Laura said, trying unsuccessfully to calm me down. 'They just make them up.'

I flicked through the pages, fighting back tears of rage and pain. This celebrity couple had broken up. That celebrity had a drugs problem. This one was seriously considering having her breast implants removed. This talk show host was on a cranberries-only diet. It all looked fairly plausible to me.

Laura was getting cross with me now. 'You have to talk to him,' she said. 'He probably doesn't know anything about this. You know Michael – you can trust him absolutely.'

'I thought I could,' I said, and wondered what had really happened the night I was at the party with Sadie. I felt so betrayed. Laura was right: Michael always seemed like the last person who would mess anyone around, and he'd given me all these assurances that Fiona was nothing to him and that he loved me.

But I wasn't surprised – I'm always waiting to be kicked in the teeth. Sometimes I think that's the only reason I bother smiling, to give those boots something to aim at.

Michael must have realised that I was never going to be proper parent material for Lily. And he was right. However much I'd grown to love Lily over the past nine months, I was obviously not the kind of stuff a mother is made of. So he was going back to the child's mother, who also happened to be beautiful, clever and rich.

The barman returned to our table to collect our empty glasses. I don't think either of us had tasted his lovingly made strawberry daiquiris, and he was looking slightly miffed. He glanced down at the magazine, which was lying open with the offending photograph visible. 'Mm . . . Cute!' he said.

'She won't look so cute when I've finished with her,' I muttered.

'Oh, no, I meant him,' he said, stabbing his finger at the picture of Michael.

'That's her fiancé,' Laura informed him, indicating me. The

barman sat down on the seat that wasn't covered in our shopping, and skimmed through the article.

'Oh, my God. You're kidding?' A glance at my face convinced him we weren't. Without another word he got up and went back behind the bar, to reappear a minute later with two tall glasses. 'G and T,' he said. 'On the house, since it's an emergency. And there I was, farting about with strawberries.' Another minute later he brought us each a thick slice of chocolate cake, again on the house. That barman was a prince among men, but it was going to take more than chocolate cake to make me feel better.

'It just isn't like Michael,' Laura said, still persisting in her belief that he was Mr Wonderful. 'He wouldn't do this to you.' I sniffed into the large tissue provided by the barman. 'What are you going to do?' she asked.

The barman offered his unsolicited opinion. 'If I was you, I'd go round to his house and torch his underwear,' he said. Well, that would do for starters.

'No,' Laura said firmly. 'This is what you'll do. I'll ring work for you and tell them you're not well, and you'll go home and ring him at his brother's, and give him the chance to explain.'

But did I want to hear his explanation?

64

I can hardly remember the journey home, except that I was clutching all those parcels full of stuff for Lily, and clothes that I'd got for our honeymoon and feeling about as wretched as you could get. A vestige of faith in Michael was trying to reassert itself, but it was having a hard time against the bout of low self-esteem, which wouldn't let me dare hope that I could seriously compete with everything Fiona had to offer.

I hadn't tidied up before going to work that morning, and the kitchen and living room were still strewn with Lily's toys and breakfast leftovers. I tried to remember where I'd put Chris's phone number. I searched my pockets first, then all exposed surfaces, then the drawers and other concealed places. I tried retracing my steps when I came back in from waving Michael and Lily off, but the scrap of *Noddy* comic had disappeared.

I sat down at the kitchen table and dialled Michael's parents' number. It rang for what seemed like ages before an answering-machine clicked on. 'Erm, it's Anna. I've lost Chris's number so could one of you call me, please?'

My stomach was in knots. I had the American magazine in front of me on the table, and Michael was smiling up at me from the page. My gorgeous, kind, wonderful man. My Michael with his amazing smile and cute bottom, who loved Danny Kaye, David Bowie, autumn and red wine. He had one arm casually around the shoulder of his apparently not-so-ex, who was holding their beautiful daughter in her gymnasium-toned arms. I felt like my heart would break.

Then a thought occurred to me, and I jumped up from the table. Fiona had left a business card with her contact numbers on it. I remembered seeing Michael tucking it carefully on to the shelf in the kitchen where he put bills and so on before they were paid. If I couldn't speak to Michael, maybe I could talk to Fiona; she might be back in New York by now.

I was shaking when I sat down to dial Fiona's number.

This time the phone was answered almost immediately.

'Good morning!' the voice said, with that sincere mock-enthusiasm that only Americans can manage.

'Fiona?'

'I'm sorry, Fiona's away right now. I'm her personal assistant, Monica. May I be of any assistance?'

'I hope so, Monica,' I said, trying to keep my voice from shaking. 'I'm trying to get hold of Michael Taylor.'

'Ah,' Monica said, and there was a tiny pause. 'May I ask who's calling?'

'My name's Anna. I'm a friend of Michael's,' I said. I didn't need the humiliation of Monica knowing the full extent of my tragedy.

'He isn't here right now,' she said, and my heart started beating again. And then she said, 'But if there's a message, I'll make sure he gets it as soon as I see him.'

I slammed down the phone, threw the magazine across the room with so much force that the kitchen clock fell off the wall, laid my head on the table and sobbed.

Eventually I calmed down enough to ring Laura, and Dan came round half an hour later and picked me up: I didn't want to be in that house a second longer.

65

I was hardly in a mood to go to work the next day, but Laura persuaded me that it would be better than hanging around at her place feeling miserable. I'm not sure her motives were entirely altruistic: in between attending to Cameron she'd also spent much of the previous evening and night holding my hand, passing me tissues and listening to me going over and over what a bastard Michael was and what I was going to do to him if I ever saw him again, and how much I loved him and desperately wanted to see him again no matter what.

The morning passed in a blur. Colin took one look at my face and sensibly decided to leave me more or less alone, and on the few occasions when Veronica showed her face at our door he ushered her out before she could speak.

Then, at lunchtime, I had a visitor. Jean, Michael's mother.

Colin discreetly discovered something he had to do elsewhere, and left Jean and me alone in the office.

'Where've you been?' was her first question. 'I got your

message, and I've tried to ring you a hundred times. Is anything wrong?' For a moment or two I couldn't speak: as always, she reminded me so much of Michael. Eventually I said, 'I stayed with a friend last night.'

'Is something wrong?'

'You could say that,' I said, and tried hard not to start crying right there in the office.

'Do you get a lunchbreak?' Jean asked. After my extended lunch and non-reappearance of the previous day, I didn't think Clare would be too keen to let me out of the building, but a visit from my – as she thought – future mother-in-law was apparently an exceptional case.

We went to McDonald's. It was noisy and busy enough for us to have a private conversation, and this was clearly what Jean had in mind.

I told her about Fiona, and the photograph in the magazine, and about Michael being in New York. She listened to me rant, and then said, 'Hang on, I'm a bit confused here. How can Michael be in New York when I spoke to him only this morning at Chris's?'

'He's at Chris's?' I asked, stupidly.

'Of course,' she said. 'I talked to him myself, and to Lily too. He was quite worried when I told him I couldn't contact you. He tried to ring you at work himself yesterday afternoon, but they told him you were unwell and that you'd gone home. Then he couldn't reach you there either. That's why I came to look for you.' By now I was confused, and I could see from Jean's face that she was, too. The food we'd bought lay uneaten on the table.

'I can't work this out,' I said. 'I tried to ring him in New York, and Fiona's secretary said he was there.'

'I can assure you he is most definitely in Lincolnshire,' Jean insisted.

'But he's been acting so strangely,' I said. 'He hasn't been himself at all. There's something on his mind, and whatever it is he wasn't talking to me about it.'

Jean tucked a strand of her glossy hair behind her ear. I noticed that her hair had recently been cut and probably coloured; she was looking really good.

'I think I know why he might have been acting strangely,' she said. I held my breath. 'Don't worry!' Jean said quickly, reaching across the table to pat my hand. 'I'm not sure what this business is about the magazine article, or why this secretary believes he's in New York, but I know my son and I know he adores you.'

I hardly dared to believe what she was saying, and waited for her to continue.

'The reason he's been upset is that his father and I are separating.' I opened my mouth to say something, but the correct response eluded me. 'David is terribly upset and is threatening all sorts of things, including striking me out of his will, which I don't care about, and not coming to your wedding, which I do care about. To be honest he's so upset we're not sure what he might do. He shot off up to Chris's in a vile temper, and Michael has gone up to see if he can calm him down a bit. Hopefully a bit of time with his sons and his grandaughter will calm him down a little.'

'I'm sorry,' I said. 'I didn't know.'

'Michael's only known for a few days.'

'But why didn't he tell me?'

'I suppose he was trying to protect you from all this family mess, so soon before your wedding and everything. But instead he's obviously just managed to upset you.'

We ate in silence for a couple of minutes. I was just picking at my fries: I wasn't very hungry. Jean was the sort of person who could even eat a Big Mac delicately, her lipstick remaining perfectly in place. Glancing about, I noticed that most of the people around us had small children with them, and that looking respectable wasn't their number-one priority: ketchup, chicken nuggets and fries were being strewn everywhere, and uncomplainingly mopped up by the hard-working staff. Say what you like about McDonald's, they're certainly child-friendly. Except that when I was a child, the thought of Ronald McDonald's leering, scarlet-haired clownface would have had me waking up screaming in the middle of the night. Luckily at that time the golden arches had still to make their presence felt in our part of Yorkshire.

Seeing all those little kids made me miss Lily. It was incredible how she'd become part of my life. When I was out with her, I quite enjoyed it when people assumed I was her mother: it gave me a warm, proud feeling. My granny used to have a little dog called Scampy. He was so cute that he practically had his own fan club. You couldn't walk through the park with him without being stopped at least five times by people who wanted to pet him or talk about him. Being out with Lily was a bit like that: people just couldn't stop themselves smiling at her, and they always commented on her big blue eyes. Once, the three of us had been sitting in another fast-food place, and a woman wiping the tables had said to us, 'I normally can't stand kids, but that one has such lovely eyes. She should be on the telly.'

My thoughts returned to the present situation. I asked Jean why she and David had split up.

She smiled in a radiant way that was reminiscent of Michael when he was talking about Lily. 'I fell in love with someone else,' she said, which threw me. 'His name's Julian. The Christmas before last, I was out shopping, buying books for David, and I got chatting with the man who was serving me. It turned out that he was the co-owner of the bookshop, which specialises in arty books. I'd never seen him there before, though I used to go in quite often. I gave him my phone number because I'd ordered some books and he rang me, about the books officially, and then we went out for lunch, and so on and so forth.' She was enjoying telling me about all this, and in a way I felt sorry for her: one of the joys of falling in love is telling everyone about it, and until now she hadn't been able to.

'We went to the opera, which David can't stand. *Albert Herring*.' I had no idea who or what *Albert Herring* might be. She continued. 'After that we went out together quite regularly, to galleries and so on. Things were just platonic for months,' she went on, glancing at me to see if I was about to be shocked. 'After all, I was – I am – a married woman, and he's quite a bit younger than me. But the attraction was there, and eventually I realised I was in love with him. It took longer to grasp that I wasn't in love with David, if you know what I mean.'

'Not really.'

'Well, after being married to him for so long, the thought of not being with him was like cutting off a limb. I simply couldn't imagine it. It wasn't even as though he'd done anything wrong. He's never been less than my best friend since the day I met him. I just hadn't realised that he'd become nothing more.' She was quiet for a few moments. 'There was also Lily to consider.'

'Lily?'

'I so much wanted her to have a stable life. She didn't have a mother, after all, and I thought she needed two happily married grandparents, to give her that stability – a role model, if you like. So, in a way, you've made it a bit easier for me to leave.'

I wasn't sure what I thought about being a factor in Michael's parents' break-up, but I had to admit that Jean looked happier than I'd ever seen her before.

'In fact,' she continued, 'it had been getting to the point where I didn't think I would ever leave, but when you're in that situation I think someone has to force the issue somehow. I found myself deliberately picking stupid fights with David about things we wouldn't normally even discuss, *Albert Herring* for one. You can't be married to someone for thirty years and get away with that for long. He soon twigged.'

'What happened?'

'He just asked me straight out one morning if I was seeing somebody else. There wasn't anything to say except admit it.' Her memory of that morning filled her face with sadness. 'The last thing I wanted to do was hurt my family,' she said. 'David and Chris are practically disowning me. Only Michael seems to understand but, then, we've always been close.' She sighed. 'I never imagined I would get to my ripe old age and go off the rails.' I made a rapid calculation: Jean must be in her mid-fifties. Her second Saturn Return had come early. 'I only hope David can learn to live with it in time, because we certainly can't go back to how things were before.'

'So what are your plans?'

'Well, for now I'm going to live in Julian's flat in Clapham. So I'll only be down the other end of the Northern Line – hideous thought. But I'm aware that you both rely on me to look after Lily while you're working, and I would really love to continue. I couldn't stand the thought of not seeing that little girl nearly every day.'

Soon after that Jean had to leave, and I went back to work, feeling only a little happier than I had during the morning. Although Michael wasn't in New York, and despite his mother's reassurances that he wasn't about to leave me in favour of Fiona, she hadn't been able to explain the magazine article or Fiona's PA apparently expecting to bump into Michael at any minute.

Back at the office, Colin, Veronica and Clare were ready to form a fan club for Jean.

'You didn't tell me your future mother-in-law was so glam!' Colin said admiringly. 'She has a look of Dame Judi Dench about her. Better haircut, though.'

66

Jean had given me Chris's number. All afternoon, every time I had the office to myself, I kept picking up the phone to ring Michael, but I really wanted to wait until I had some proper privacy. I couldn't shake the idea that Po-faced Vo might listen in. On the way home I rehearsed what I was going to say if he was really there in Lincolnshire, and what I was going to do if he wasn't.

But when I walked in at the door, I was greeted by gorgeous cooking smells. I went into the kitchen, and Michael was standing at the cooker tasting whatever he was cooking from a wooden spoon. Lily was sitting on the floor playing with her dolls' house (in which lived an assortment of not-to-scale dolls, farm animals, a plastic eagle and a wooden snowman, which had been a Christmas tree decoration she'd refused to let Michael put away). She dashed over to me as soon as she saw me, throwing her arms exuberantly around my knees. I bent down to kiss the soft hair on the top of her head. Michael wiped his hands on a tea-towel and gave me a kiss.

'You're back,' I said, maybe unnecessarily.

He went back to the cooker for a second, turned down the heat, then took my hand and led me to the table. We sat down. 'I was worried about you,' he said. 'I rang you, here and at work, and couldn't get hold of you. So I decided to come home.'

'Why didn't you tell me about your parents splitting up?'

'Mum told you, then. I don't know,' he sighed. 'I just didn't want you to be worried.'

'Michael,' I said, 'I'm really fond of your parents, but it's hardly something I wouldn't be able to cope with, if you can.'

He looked down at his hands. 'I know,' he said, 'And, to be honest, that wasn't the only reason.'

Oh, now we were getting to it. 'You mean Fiona?' I said.

He looked puzzled. 'No,' he said. 'Why do you say that?' I walked across the room to where I'd left the American magazine on a stack of newspapers. I shoved it in front of him on the table. His eyes glanced over it without taking anything in, and he looked at me questioningly. I pointed at the picture. 'What? That's Lily . . . and me.' Hearing her name, Lily came over to have a look.

'Daddy!' she confirmed, adding, ''Ily.' Gratifyingly for me, the other person in the picture didn't seem to interest her at all, and she wandered off again.

Michael was reading the article, and his face was thunderous. 'She had no right,' he said. 'No right at all. This is . . . I've got a good mind to ring up this rag and give them a really juicy story.' Something on the stove started to bubble over with a hiss of steam, and he jumped up to turn the heat off.

'What really juicy story would that be?' I asked.

He turned to face me. 'Do you mean you believed this rubbish?' I didn't say anything. Lily was having trouble getting the front of her dolls' house closed, probably because a doll's leg was trapped in it. She pushed and pushed, making exaggerated straining noises before giving up with a nerve-jarring, defeated wail. Michael knelt down to help her, then sat back and looked at me, waiting for me to say something.

Eventually I said, 'So none of it's true?' and waited for him to laugh and say, 'Of course not, I would never leave you.' But instead he did the pouting thing he always did when he was trying to find the right words. Lily was wailing once more because the dolls' house door wouldn't shut again, a persistent, reedy noise that was getting on my nerves. It was also getting on my nerves that Michael patiently closed it for her again: even now, Lily was always the first in the queue for his attention. And, of course, he would put her first when choosing between her natural mother and me.

'No wonder you couldn't wait to get away.'

'That was because of my parents, you know that,' he said. 'It takes so little for you to stop trusting me.'

'This isn't little!' I said. 'It's there in black and white! This magazine is going all over the world, with this picture of my so-called fiancé playing Happy Families with the golden girl of American TV. I just feel humiliated. In fact, I feel so bad I can't even describe how bad I feel.'

Whenever we had the slightest disagreement, or even an

animated debate about a film we'd seen, or something in the news, Lily always got agitated, and tried to distract us. I could never work out whether this was because she was worried about us arguing, or whether it was just because for a couple of minutes she hadn't been the centre of attention, but now I started to be aware that she was persistently trying to draw our attention to herself. She was leaning against Michael's leg, waving the wooden snowman at him and chanting, 'Daddydaddydaddy.'

'Oh, shut up!' I snapped.

Lily didn't notice, but Michael looked at me as if I'd slapped her. His voice was like ice. 'Don't ever take your bad mood out on my daughter,' he said.

Bad mood? I was furious, but I made a big effort to keep my voice as quiet and calm as possible. 'That's just the problem, isn't it? She's *your* daughter, not mine. And I'm only ever going to be second best, because I'm not her mother.'

'That's not true.'

'So try telling me what's going on.'

He took hold of both of my hands in his. 'You seriously think I'd rather have Fiona than you, just because she's Lily's natural mother?'

'And the rest,' I muttered. 'Media babe and her New York lifestyle.'

'Oh, you're so wrong,' he said, squeezing my hands and looking at me earnestly. 'I never for one minute thought you were second best to Fiona, and I'm sure Lily doesn't, either. I don't know how much Fiona is going to be involved in Lily's life – as little as possible, when I find out what's been going on – but you and I will be here every day. It'll be us watching her grow up. We're a family, you, me and Lily.'

He picked Lily up and sat her on his lap, and as if they'd rehearsed it, Lily pointed a chubby forefinger at each of us in turn and said, 'Daddy . . . Anna . . . 'Ily.'

I felt like someone had opened a window in me and a thousand butterflies had flown out.

'Dipsy . . . LaLa . . . Po!' she added.

67

I carefully folded up a T-shirt and placed it in the top of the bag. After a moment's thought, I added a couple more, and a towel, and a pair of socks. Then I had to sit down and calm myself for a second. Well, I told myself, there's no backing out now.

When Laura and I were students, she had decorated the walls of the flat we shared with a selection of those posters that were popular in the eighties, featuring a perky photograph of an animal or small child, and an improving or philosophical caption in a nasty typeface. The one that came me now was: 'The only way out is through.' I seem to remember it being attributed to Beethoven, but I might be making that up. It was illustrated by some kind of acrobatic rodent. Anyway, it seemed alarmingly apt to my current circumstance.

The phone rang, and at first I didn't know if I wanted the distraction; I just wanted to sit here in the quiet, savouring a few moments on my own. I tried hard not to answer but, conditioned by my years at Caring Concern, I found myself walking over to the bedside table and picking up the receiver.

I was glad I had: it was Peter.

'I just thought I'd call to see how you're feeling,' he said.

'Terrified,' I admitted.

'I know,' he said, 'but it's going to be all right, you know it is. And you won't be on your own.'

He had such a soothing voice, with his soft Danish accent. There was a little pause.

'Isn't it strange how things change in a short space of time?' I said eventually. 'It's almost exactly two years ago today since I first met Michael.' God, I was so madly in love with him after

223

just one proper meeting. 'And it was two years ago when Nic told me he had a son.'

'And I turned up at Heathrow Airport expecting to meet my long-lost father, and instead met this incredible, beautiful woman.'

I smiled tearfully. 'You have no idea how much that gives my confidence a boost, hearing you say that in my present state. But I'm also feeling somewhat vulnerable and liable to burst into tears for the slightest reason. Let's change the subject, okay? So . . . have you heard from Nic recently?'

'Yes, he sends postcards, and e-mails me when he can. They're having a really good time. Sounds like hard work, though: they're building long-drop latrines, apparently.'

'Ugh. What are *they*? On second thoughts, I don't want to know. It's weird, though. I could never have imagined Sadie doing voluntary work,' I said.

'I think she took a bit of persuading, but now they're there, Dad says Nepal is their spiritual home.' Now why didn't that surprise me? 'And they don't ever want to leave. I'd like to try and visit them if I can raise the money somehow. I don't want to lose touch with my dad so soon after I found him.'

'And what about Marlene?' I felt duty-bound to ask.

'I'm surprised you're interested, after what she did,' he said, 'but, yeah, she is okay. She came to stay with my mom and Anke a while ago, and they got on quite well. Gran thinks they're in harmony with the earth goddess. They think she's a bit crazy, but they like her okay.' He paused. 'She is sorry for what she did to you and Michael,' he said. I didn't trust myself to say anything. 'But, you know, she thought she was doing it for good reasons. She wanted you and Dad to be together.'

'So she decided to give Fate a helping hand by getting Michael reunited with his ex-girlfriend? By employing blackmail?'

'It wasn't quite blackmail.'

'Well, I don't know if I'll ever be able to forgive her.'

'Harbouring ill feelings is very bad for your karma,' he advised.

'Oh, don't you start with that hippie crap!' I said. A silence. Then: 'I'm all ready for the big day, anyway. Bag's packed,' I said, endeavouring to sound practical and organised.

'That's good,' he replied, and suggested, 'You should be relaxing. It might be the last chance you get for a while.'

'Tomorrow's a big day for both of us, isn't it?'

'That's true,' he agreed.

'What about you? All packed?'

'Just about,' he said. 'There's such a lot to organise before I leave, I'm sure I'm going to forget something. Still, Berlin is not so far away. If I forget something important I can always come back.'

'What time's your train?'

'Eleven thirty in the morning.'

'I'll be thinking about you,' I said.

'No, you won't,' he laughed.

68

Thank goodness for Peter, I thought, not for the first time. Because it was Peter who finally straightened things out.

He had phoned Marlene one day, just for a chat, and for some reason my name had been mentioned.

'You're very fond of Anna, aren't you?' she'd said. He'd replied that he was. 'And your father is fond of her too.' Peter had also agreed with this. 'It's just a matter of time before those two are together again,' had been Marlene's opinion.

'I don't think so,' Peter said. 'Anna is getting married to Michael, and Dad has a new girlfriend.'

'Well, I don't think we need to worry about the new

girlfriend,' Marlene had said dismissively. 'And as for this Michael, well, let's just say he's taken care of.'

'What do you mean?' he'd asked, and after a bit of persistence got Marlene to admit that she'd been in touch with a journalist in New York whom she'd known through Steve, suggesting that it might be an idea to delve a little into the background of the British newsreader who was making a name for herself. The journalist pretty soon found out about Lily and Michael, and rang Fiona for her angle on the story before it went to print.

Fiona's angle was that the cable station she was working for had a very pro-family boss. She knew that she could kiss her job goodbye if that sort of publicity got out.

So she thought fast and that's when she turned up on our doorstep in Crouch End, hoping that by getting a few photographs of herself with Michael and Lily she could pretend that she had a happy family back in Britain. That's when the article I'd seen in the tabloid came out: she'd hoped that that would be enough for the press and that they'd lose interest in her after that. As a precaution, Fiona's friends and her PA, Monica, were told to be cautious in dealing with anyone who might ring them asking about her long-lost British sweetheart.

As soon as Peter heard all this, he rang me straight away.

'You won't believe what I just heard,' was his opening remark, and he repeated what Marlene had told him. I was amazed, and my first impulse was to get the first train to Somerset and do some serious harm to that interfering hippie witch. 'But, don't you see?' he said. 'It means Fiona didn't really want Lily. Or Michael.'

'That's not the point,' I said. 'The point is, did he want her?'

'Well, did he?'

'He says not,' I said, 'but I've always got this niggling worry that he might have been tempted.'

I heard Peter sigh in an exasperated sort of way. 'So what if he was? What is so unnatural about being tempted? Haven't we all been tempted at some time?'

'I suppose so . . .' Peter, of all people, knew that I had.

'The important thing is, it's you he wants.'

I explained to Peter that I still had the problem of not being Lily's natural mother, and not knowing if I would ever be good enough for her and Michael.

'That's silly,' he said. 'Look at me, I've got two mothers, and even though Karen is my birth mother, I couldn't really say I love Anke any less. They both love me, they both helped to feed me and teach me, and hugged me if I was hurt or upset. They both listened to me. And now I've got this father as well, and somehow I love him, too, never mind what you think of him. A child can't have too many people to love them. All you have to do is love her, and the rest comes naturally. And I can't think of anything better for Lily than to have a mother like you.'

69

I'm walking out of the door to the house I finally think of as mine as well as Michael's. The bag that's taken me a week to pack, even though there's not much in it, feels heavy, but not as heavy as I do: gravitationally challenged, as they might say in Social Services if forced to come up with a term. When I was a kid, if I had to go somewhere I didn't want to, like the dentist, my legs used to feel as though they were on back to front, and I had to do battle with my reversed limbs just to keep moving forwards. I feel like that now, and it's not helped by the fact that I've had nothing to eat for hours, and I feel light-headed and slightly sick. I insist on carrying my bag myself – I need something to hold on to.

This is the most exciting day of my life. Out of all the days I have ever lived, this is the one that is going to make the most difference. By tonight, nothing will ever be the same. No wonder I'm terrified.

It's a cold, sunny, cobalt blue October morning. Exactly the same weather as the day two years ago when I had lunch with Nic in that Buddhist café. My thoughts fly back to that day: how I'd been walking in the park feeling so sad because I'd just met this beautiful tax inspector and felt like I was turned inside out with love, and I thought I wouldn't see him again. In a space of just a couple of days, my life had been turned completely around.

'Anna?'

My thoughts snap back to the present. It really is a lovely day: the air is cold and clean-smelling, even here in London. I take a deep breath.

In the car, I struggle to fasten the seat-belt around myself. I pull the lapstrap out and down really low under the bump, and the baby, possibly disturbed from a dream, kicks hard at me. I pat at the bump, and the baby seems to respond and calm down.

'Not long now,' I tell it, and feel a little bit sad that the baby's gentle, floating existence will soon be at an end and she will have the grimy, noisy, dangerous reality of London as her home. Sometimes I have a feeling bordering on panic that this world isn't fit for such a tiny life. She certainly won't have an Enid Blyton lemonade-and-adventures childhood, or even a *Blue Peter* here's-one-I-made-earlier one. But her life is going to be as good and as much fun as we can make it: I've been promising her that since she was the size of a strawberry.

'Ready?'

I'm ready.

'I'll be glad to let you take a turn carrying this for a change,' I say. Michael smiles. 'No, I mean it,' I say. 'I'm going to get them to surgically attach one of those sling things to you while we're at the hospital, and you'll have to carry her around till she starts school. Then watch me laugh when you're complaining about backache and haemorrhoids.'

'I never laughed,' he objects, being more than usually careful while pulling out of the end of our road, which is narrow and not very visible to oncoming traffic. And of course he never did. 'Anyway, I won't mind carrying her. I'll be happy to carry her. She ain't heavy, she's my daughter.'

'Oh, please don't start singing! And she is bloody heavy, believe me.'

Our daughter is going to be born in less than two hours from now. Things haven't been quite straightforward, and as I should perhaps have expected from any offspring of mine, she has resolutely decided she will not be coming out in the conventional manner. A Caesarean has been scheduled.

Lily is staying with Jean and Julian in Clapham; they're taking her to a circus on the common tonight, and tomorrow Jean will bring her up to meet her baby sister for the first time. Lily is so excited at the idea of having a sister: she's been practising feeding, burping and changing nappies on her dolls and teddies for months, and isn't afraid to show them what Oprah calls 'tough love' when they're naughty. Which is something we're going to have to keep a close eye on.

Michael will be with me during the operation, and he reckons it'll be a doddle compared to Lily's birth, because this time he gets to keep my head company while all the gory stuff goes on at the far side of a green sheet. I'm told I won't be in any pain (at the time: afterwards is another story, according to the midwife, but Laura, both grannies and, of course, Michael are poised to take care of my every post-partum need). I'll just feel an odd, rummaging sensation in my insides for a minute or two, like I'm the bargain knickers bin at a Marks & Spencer's sale. Then our baby will be lifted up in the air, slimy and screaming.

And from my own, admittedly limited, experience and what I've heard from every parent I've ever met, including my own, the screaming doesn't really stop. Nor do the worrying and the sleepless nights. Not with her first tooth, first birthday, first day at school, first boyfriend, first mortgage. So we'd better get used to it.

I glance over at Michael, who turns briefly to me before looking back at the road, giving me that smile, which I still think is as beautiful as it was the first time I saw him.

'Baby,' I tell the bump, giving it a little pat so she knows she's being spoken to, 'do you know what the best thing about being born is going to be? You're going to get to see your daddy's smile. Lucky little baby.'